Praise for

"A crash course in unma[...] [...] [...]
can society that make all strangers into potential enemies."
Asante Addae, Independent Black Film Association

"At Issue in the Public Eye is Edrea Davis, with the fall release
of SNITCHCRAFT, a 'newsmaker' with the movers and
shakers for exposing the money, power, and corruption behind
the use of informants. Snitching on the snitches. Why Edrea,
you crafty devil you!"
Sharon J. Hill, "NEWSMAKERS" Journal

"SNITCHCRAFT is a must-read book for a look at how the
system can cause you to lose control of your own life. Kudos to
the Powell family for empowering themselves through faith and
prayer."
Cathy Harris,
Author of "How To Take Control Of Your Own Life"

"SNITCHCRAFT perfectly depicts the consistent yet incon-
sistent struggle of all black men to reclaim their identity in
society. It's refreshing to read a book that fashions an African
American male character with such remarkable dexterity."
Kirk Clay, Common Cause

"Edrea Davis artfully weaves together a moving story of love,
family, faith, and betrayal, while providing a birds eye view of
the corrupt environment created by the use of snitches."
Melanie L. Campbell, NCBCP

SNITCHCRAFT
A Dogon Village Novel
Paperback

ISBN 10: 0-9786974-0-5
ISBN 13: 978-0-9786974-0-2

Cover Photo by: Colin Anderson courtesy of Brand X Pictures
Book Design: Jamila Jones

For information on bulk discounts contact Dogon Village Books at (818) 613-9521 email: production@dogonvillage.com www.dogonvillage.com

PRINTED IN THE USA

To

my father
LEE O. DAVIS
who taught me that 2+2=4

And

my late mother
BARBARA JEAN HOBSON DAVIS
who taught me the power of faith and perseverance

"If you see a turtle on top of a fence post, you know he didn't get there by himself."
Southern Aphorism

Acknowledgments

All praise to my Creator. Without Her, I would not be.

The older I get, the more I understand how that turtle made it up on that post. Through this process, I realized that the book in all of us starts on our birthday. I've learned how each and every person we encounter in life – good, bad, or indifferent – has an impact on our thoughts, actions, and, what we become. I'm still climbing, but I'm getting closer to the top of the fence. There are so many people that I would like to thank for lending a hand to lift me. A few gave me a push, some lifted me with their hands, and others allowed me to stand on their shoulders until I was able to balance myself. There's just not enough room to mention everyone.

I send much love and a heartfelt thank-you:

to my resilient **ancestors** who made the road a lot easier for my travels and taught me to strive for excellence.

to my father, **Lee Davis**, you're my hero. Your words of wisdom are peppered throughout this book. Thanks for my appreciation of history, jazz, and sports.

to my wonderful sons **Kwamhe** and **Kemauhl**, who helped make me, "me." Through you, I learned the true meaning of unconditional love. To my daughter-in-laws, **Christy** and **Danielle**, and all my brilliant grandchildren, you're a blessing in my life.

to my sister, **Felicia Davis**, a distinguished leader and skillful political strategist. Your knowledge and feedback is invaluable. And, thanks for dragging me along for a ride all over the world.

to my brother, **Omar Davis**, my promotions superstar. Thanks for your insight. And, **Angela Gavin**, thanks for all you do.

to my sista' friends. To borrow from Maya Angelo, I am blessed to have "chosen sisters." **Janice Williams**, we traveled three continents together as children, and took a spiritual journey together as adults. Thanks for your divine guidance and friendship. **Makeda Smith**, my mentor and mentee. A true Hollywood Diva. There are not enough pages in this book to express my thanks to you. You're my ambassador of Quan!

to my longtime friend, Dennis Bryant, you're truly special.

to my friend, Dr. Zeddie Scott, thanks for being so understanding.

to the next generation who continue to strive for excellence: Kemauhl, Kwamhe, Tamara, Dejai, Tysheim, Diarran, Anayah, Rasheed, Dakwam, Tashonie, Illai, Malik, Jasmine, Asha, Llana, Jonathan, Johnny, Takenya, Khaliq, Hakeem, Shaquna, Jarques. I'm afraid the world is not ready for all of your strong personalities!

to my extended family: Ronald Davis, for honing my business skills; Matthew and Maurice Hobson for being there when I needed you most; and my personal nurse, Mrs. Winnie Farrar, for seeing me through difficult times. Much love to: Michelle McCloud West, Julieta Hobson, Matthew Gilmore, Felecia and Takemi Howell, Romaine and Tia Wall, Eddie Harley, Robyn Lander, Denise Davis, Jerome and Nona Kenney, Carmen and Gladys Acosta, Frenchola McCall, Tanky and Karen Bell, Keisha Gaskin, Becky Parker, Dean Wilson, and Audrey, Eleanor, Tanya, Dwight, and Bobby Hobson,

to all of my friends old and new: Andrea Mitchell, Wendy Zupa, Laura Anderson, Ruby Pulliam, Janice Clarke Smith, Supreme, John Edwards, Agnes Bradley, Charles Cato, Duke Duplechien, Lloyd Williams, Dennis Bowie, Billy Davis, Annella Banks, Jeannie Perry, Linda Alfred, Vicki Farrar, and Cecil Fuller.

to a few of the leaders working in their own way to keep the movement moving, I applaud you: Dr. Yvonne Scruggs-Leftwich, Rev. E. Randel Osburn, Melanie Campbell, Kirk Clay, Helen Butler, Lazone Grays, Nancy Harvin, Arndrea Waters, Melvin Morris, Faye Anderson, Brenda Davenport, Brad and Deya Starks.

to all of the people who endured my chaos working on this book, thanks for your patience. Christrine Traxler, Tai Lynne, Carlton Cooper, Jamila Jones, Robert Denson, and my friend and marketing guru, Nnena Nchege.

Finally, I would like to thank all of the newspapers, book clubs, and libraries who help to breathe life into SnitchCraft. And, to all of the men and women doing time as a result of a dishonest snitch, keep the faith!

Stay Blessed,

SnitchCraft

Edrea Davis

A Dogon Village Novel

Prologue

"Dumb ass," JC grumbled, as the angry young driver leaped out of his pimped out Cadillac Coupe DeVille, headed toward the drop top Mercedes he had just skidded into. From a window above, JC watched as a trail of drivers rear–ended each other, at least eight cars deep.

How could one person cause so much drama? JC mused.

After an irate exchange among car horns, a string of indignant commuters jumped out of their vehicles waving fisted hands and pointing fingers at the cornrowed youngster. The crowd backed down when the gangsta' wanna-be raised his spotted arm, aimed his index finger at the rowdy bunch, and curled it like he was pulling the trigger of a gun.

The driver of the Benz tossed her cell phone into the passenger seat and looked straight ahead. Her top was down and the back seat was full of packages.

She could easily become a victim of road rage, or, even worse, any one of the mob of people rushing about could reach into her vehicle and snatch her Prada bags from the back seat, JC thought.

One would believe this was a New York City street, but the sunshine and seventy-five degree December weather indicated otherwise. It was lunch hour in the "City of Angels."

John "JC" Powell gazed down at the melee from a window of a large government building on the corner of Temple and Spring Street. He struggled to decipher the throbbing base that resonated to the second floor. *Snoop Dogg's "The Game is to be Sold, Not Told,"* he surmised. Being the Cadillac connoisseur that he was, JC reckoned the one below was made in 1972—a popular model among those who embraced the "thug life."

JC observed the approaching lights from a police car. The voice inside of him wanted to yell out the window to let everyone know, *things are not as they appear. The young thug is innocent; the fly girl in the Benz is the dumb-ass.* Instead, he stood paralyzed, staring blankly at the chaos below like a child yearning for the outdoors on a rainy day.

For nearly an hour, he remained propped like a statue, his hands behind his back, studying the enticing social disorder in the distance. After a time it was as though he could see right through the roof of the burgundy Cadillac and make out every minute detail—the original wood grain finishes, authentic Gucci floor mats, and an ostrich steering wheel cover. JC figured the Caddy belonged to a Blood, the spots were tattoos, and, most importantly, the decorated arm could get twenty-five grand for the restored vehicle.

As JC slipped deeper into thought, he wondered, *Why are these kids paying so much money to look like thugs? Don't they realize that old-school hustlers hustled, NOT by choice, but by circumstance? Don't they understand that the point was to escape the thug life, not embrace it? What happened to values? Respect? Loyalty? Where did black men go wrong? How the hell did we let this shit happen?*

Suddenly, a low but stern voice announced, "Mr. Powell, it's time to go."

JC turned and crept slowly to the door. His gait lacked the soulful bop that had taken years to perfect, and childlike optimism no longer radiated from his seductive green eyes. However, the burdens of the day had not affected JC's sense of style—he always took a lot of pride in his appearance. Six feet tall with a six-pack to match, confident and quick-witted, JC was able to sport flashy ensembles with a sophisticated flair. The selection for that day had been thought out meticulously. It was deliberately subdued. A gray pin-striped suit with a blue silk lining that would only matter the true fashion aficionado; a white shirt, blue and gray silk tie, and matching blue and gray alligator shoes made the look complete. Despite the stressful expression on his boyishly handsome face, JC looked a decade younger than forty with his flawless ruby-brown complexion.

The distant voice belonged to a man garbed in a brown sheriff's uniform. He clenched JC's upper arm and escorted him down a long hallway that ended at the double doors to JC's future.

As the size nine gators dragged along the drab gray corridor toward the unknown, JC replayed highlights of his life in his head, wondering where his surefire plan went awry. Oblivious to his surroundings, he never noticed the people crammed on wooden benches that lined the walls, nor did he hear the children passing time playing games around him. His mind was somewhere else.

What jolted JC from his fog were five black-and-white portraits hanging five feet apart from one end of the hallway to the other. They all had the same pose, a side profile of the upper body, stiff and lifeless. All of them were white men in black robes. *The system*, he thought.

As they slowed down to allow people to pass in an intersecting hallway, a disheveled man in a wrinkled suit ran up to join them. In his awkward movements, he almost dropped his briefcase. It was JC's court-appointed public defender, Harry Smart. JC paused, gazed down at Mr. Smart with contempt, and then proceeded toward the end of the hallway.

Now more attentive and focused, JC realized he had lost all concept of time; the double doors appeared no closer than when he started. Beyond the busy intersection, more portraits were perched on the wall on the opposite side of the hallway. They had the same rigid pose. All of them looked to be in their fifties or sixties, white and male. All but one. Second from the end was a lone black man. JC initially thought it was Justice Thurgood Marshall. It was actually Judge David Williams, the first black federal judge west of the Mississippi. In 1969 President Richard "Watergate" Nixon appointed him to the bench in California.

The deputy squeezed JC's arm slightly, bringing him to another stop directly in front of the double doors. JC took a minute to gather his composure. He lowered his head, closed his eyes, and mumbled a few words under his breath. With renewed fortitude,

JC opened his eyes and glanced over his shoulder, examining the hallway he had traversed. That time he saw everything. Entire families restlessly waiting to support their loved ones. Innocent children playing, unaware of their bleak surroundings. And, the paintings of the ten wise men—District Court Judges. JC wondered, *How much loot does the brother make to hang with the big boys?*

The officer tightened his grip on JC's arm and led him through the doors into a packed courtroom. The muffled chatter abruptly stopped. All eyes were fixed on JC as he shuffled straight up the center isle to his seat. He managed a forced smile when he saw his family and friends, who filled up the first four rows behind the defense table.

The courtroom acoustics amplified the clanking of the deputy removing the tightly clamped silver bracelets from JC's wrists, and the tense silence caused the inappropriate joke the arrogant federal prosecutor whispered to his assistant to reverberate throughout the room. The deputy placed his hand on JC's shoulder and steered him downward into his seat. The incompetent esquire plopped in the chair next to him. After his performance over the three-day trial, JC could think of many adjectives to describe Harry Smart, "smart," however, wasn't in the ballpark.

Beads of sweat accumulated on JC's forehead with each excruciating tick of the clock. Seconds became hours. His heart throbbed like a djembe drum. Ten minutes passed before the bailiff instructed the courtroom to stand for the Honorable Judge Smith's arrival. His robed majesty entered the courtroom and seated himself. The gallery followed. More waiting. With his hands tightly clenched together above the table, JC stared into the air, as if in a catatonic state. After five minutes, the Judge summoned him out of his trance; instructing JC to stand. JC stood with his lawyer at his side.

The balding, sixty-something Judge addressed JC without ever looking up from the stack of papers he was scouring. Sounding much like a recording, he said, "Mr. Powell, you have been convicted of a very serious crime. Before I enter a sentence, is there anything that you would like to say?"

JC gasped for air. He caught his breath, snapped to attention, and stared directly at the top of Judge Smith's head, which was still buried in his reading material. Speaking in a slow, confident tone, and careful to enunciate each word as clearly as possible, JC announced, "I'd just like to say that I am not guilty of these charges. All I did was try to take care of my family. If it takes a lifetime, I will prove my innocence."

Judge Smith's head swung toward JC. With raised eyebrows he said, "Well, for now, Mr. Powell, a jury of your peers found you guilty of a very serious crime. In accordance with the mandatory minimum sentencing guidelines, I am obligated to sentence you to fifteen years and eight months in a federal penitentiary."

Although JC knew his fate before entering the courtroom, hearing the official announcement hit him like a fifty-foot tidal wave. His knees became weak. He leaned forward and placed his hands flat on the table in front of him desperately trying to keep his balance. The sound of a woman sobbing prompted him to glance over his shoulder to see his best friend, Candace Banks, slouched over in tears. JC's older brother, Paul, was consoling her. His mother, Ester Powell, stood next to Paul with her eyes closed, immersed in prayer.

Chapter 1

A few years back, the summer of '94 to be precise, as Luther Vandross crooned "Endless Love," about twenty loud, smack–talking men were packed around a table in a smoky after–hours joint on 145th and Saint Nick.

"Pass, make that number... I bet he nine to five before he seven eleven," the men yelled on the sidelines.

Four twenties dropped on top of the bright green table followed by two red dice swiftly rolling across the felt, stopping on two fives. As a large black hand snatched the dice from the table, the voices escalated. "Ten top house...flowers."

Five men, ranging in age from thirty to forty-five, except an old-timer who was close to sixty, played a game of poker next to the men shooting crap. Large wads of cash lined the tables. The way the men were dressed, each adorned with high-priced clothes and jewelry, anyone could tell these were not round-the-way gamblers; they were definitely big time ballers.

Beyond the small group of ghetto elite stood a makeshift bar covered with pricey liquor bottles. The bar was tended by the cigar-smoking owner, Paul, who was propped on a stool reading the newspaper.

A former semi-pro boxer, thirty-nine-year-old Paul was super-buff and well dressed, but in a militant, medallion-wearing way. Aside from a meticulously groomed jet-black mustache, Paul was clean-shaven, including his head, with silky smooth, copper-toned skin. He was clad in his usual all-black—a black silk shirt, black linen pants and black and bone-colored alligator boots. His daily accessories included a diamond-trimmed Rolex watch, one diamond stud earring, a diamond-filled star-and-crescent medallion around his neck, and two diamond rings. Of course, one was a pinky ring—the sign of a true hustler.

Paul had assimilated into the Harlem landscape. There was nothing Southern about him; from his speech to his attitude, Paul was strictly New York. He had gained an appreciation for jazz, the arts, African history, and literature. Before the thugs took over, he spent countless hours standing on street corners discussing politics and exchanging conspiracy theories with his neighbors—the Harlem elite. Paul had become a true New Yorker.

A knock at the door caught everyone's attention. The men watched as a large bouncer put his eye to the peephole, then started unlocking the three bolt locks that protected the men from outside forces.

Paul yelled to the bouncer, "Hold up. Who the hell is it?"

"It's your brother," the bouncer replied and continued to open the door.

The gamblers went back to business, their voices escalated. "I take twenty to ten... Bet.... Dice don't make six or eight... Ten on six and ten on the eight."

JC, Paul's enterprising younger brother, tipped in, done up in a flamboyant, pimp-style suit. His neatly coiffured, shoulder-length Jheri curls were tucked under a fedora carefully hovering between eleven and five o'clock. Both hands were smothered with bulky diamond rings, from pinky to index finger. You could immediately see in everything about JC, from his perfectly manicured nails to the lean and dip in his gait, that he was a real ladies man. He had corrected the broken English dialect he spoke with when he landed in the city, and the lingering twang worked wonders with the ladies. JC was well liked by all—a good old country boy.

Although JC loved games, he didn't gamble or drink—a promise he made to his mother as a teen. The only reason for his frequent drop-ins to the club was to chat with his big brother; the two were thick as thieves since they fled to New York to escape their poverty in Georgia. A glimpse of the rocks the two flossed you could see the pact with mom did not extend to making money off gambling or bootlegging liquor, but rather, the use of it.

With the exception of his periodic non-stop orations on life, JC was a man of very few words, an observer. However, over the past few weeks, he had been on his soapbox, pleading with his brother to get out of the game. JC felt their reign as top hustlers was over; it was time to pass the torch.

Back in the day, black hustlers made big money in Harlem operating bars and after-hours joints, places where people could go any time of day or night to dance, drink, or pick up a few bucks shooting crap. Most proprietors ran numbers out of their establishment to make a little extra cash. Drug dealing and the pimp game flourished, but were left to those with more of a criminal element. Running numbers was only a minor transgression to most residents in the black community. Quite often, you would see mothers and Bible-carrying grandmothers running numbers to make ends meet. There were even a few churches known for giving out the winning number during their Sunday morning sermon.

Up until the eighties, hustlers, patrons and the community peacefully coexisted in this underground world. Of course, where there's liquor and gambling, isolated incidents occurred, but random violence was not tolerated. These were merely businessmen and women making money to take care of their families. Many of them were war veterans who made it out of the service without mental illness or drug addiction. Others were early graduates of Historically Black Colleges who, after struggling to secure a college degree, understood they were not welcome in corporate America and turned to the underground economy to make a living.

Things began to change after the government discovered the money in the numbers racket and took over the business. What was once illegal became a legal industry run by the state. The lottery changed everything in the streets. Drugs became the number one product and, as a result, the violence escalated and began to permeate every aspect of the black community.

Drug-crazed "stick-up kids" were robbing black-owned stores and after-hours clubs. The police were the last people to help the club owners. In fact, although several of New York City's finest were paid under the table by club owners to ignore their illegal activity, the cops also picked up a few dollars tipping off the stick-up kids on the location of the clubs. The entrepreneurs under siege were eventually forced to take matters into their own hands. They began arming themselves, bought intricate security systems, and hired ruthless ex-cons to stand guard for their empires.

Paul ran a small private after-hours joint that catered to top-dollar hustlers. Bets were large and only those with deep pockets knew about the club. It kept out the riffraff.

When JC entered the room, the gamblers welcomed him like he was a minister stepping to the podium for an Easter Sunday sermon. He offered silent nods and a few high-fives and headed toward Paul, throwing him a sign indicating he needed to talk with him. Paul kept his eyes locked on his paper and continued to read, avoiding eye contact with JC.

"What you been up to, JC?" One of the gamblers asked.

"Just tryin' to get paid," JC replied as he took a seat on a stool by the bar.

Everyone was amused. They all idolized JC because he had all the loot in the 'hood. Paul was the man when he rented a brownstone on 138th and Seventh Ave, better known as "Strivers Row," but JC topped Paul when he purchased a posh condo across the bridge in ritzy Englewood Cliffs, New Jersey.

The gambler replied, "It's all gone, JC. Ain't no more. YOU got all the money."

The roar of laughter was interrupted by another knock at the door. The bouncer peeked out to see Goldie, a small time pimp from the block. He was sporting long black hair pulled back into a ponytail, a large rimmed hat, and a country, old-fashioned, bright green suit.

"Who is it?" Paul yelled.

"Goldie," the bouncer said.

"Don't let him in, I heard he's a rat," JC said. If he had his druthers, half of the men already in the room would not have gotten in. Aside from his brother, JC trusted no one.

Even though the brothers were consummate hustlers and respected most others in the game, no matter what their commerce, the two had disdain for low class street pimps and block ballers. After the death of their father, JC and Paul were left with four sisters, a great aunt, and their mother. They always respected women and distanced themselves from men who mistreated them. They had no problem with big baller pimps who were businessmen with sense enough to treat their women well—the ones who catered to wealthy execs and provided a much needed service at fights or super-bowl games—but they stayed away from the bottom feeders.

Goldie was persistent; he knocked again. One of the gamblers decided to advocate for Goldie and shouted to Paul, "He's a'ight. Let him in. Let me smell some of that ho' money."

There was more laughter. Paul gave the bouncer a nod of approval and the guard unlocked the door to let Goldie inside. The gamblers resumed. The dice took off across the green halting at seven and the crew got loud again. "Crap, give up the money."

Goldie sauntered into the club. Before the bouncer could close the door, four hooded boys, armed with high caliber pistols bum-rushed the place from behind him. The thugs, who looked no older than sixteen, ordered everyone against the wall. The gamblers raised their arms and placed their palms against the wall where framed pictures of Malcolm X, Angela Davis, and Marcus Garvey joined other crusaders directly above.

One teen stood guard as another collected the money and jewelry off the table and from the people in the room. JC stared coldly into the eyes of the hood assigned to his side of the room as he reluctantly removed each of his diamond rings, necklaces, and Rolex watch, then tossed them into the bag the thug was holding.

While everyone's attention was on one resistant gambler who got whacked on the head with the butt of a gun, Paul slowly reached under the bar where he kept his forty-five in a hidden slot. The teen standing guard pointed a pistol to his head. Paul halted. As Paul and the hood exchanged menacing glares, JC moved his foot to the side, stepping on a button on the floor.

After collecting all the valuables in sight, the obvious leader of the pack yelled, "We gotta go, hurry up, we gotta git outta here." The other two hoods continued to ransack the place as if they were desperately searching for something. This was a small apartment doubling as a club. There was a kitchen area behind the bar, and at the end of a long hallway was a bedroom next to a small bathroom. One of the kids started toward the back of the apartment.

"Come on," the ringleader ordered as he exited the apartment. His accomplices obeyed and ran out behind him.

Paul grabbed his gun from the slot beneath the bar and the angry gamblers followed the teens down the stairs to a small lobby where two huge men with shotguns were waiting. It only took a quick second for the teens to realize they were surrounded. They quietly lined up against the wall to allow everyone to reclaim their belongings.

JC convinced the men not to beat the teens down. Instead, he lectured them on how hard they all hustled to get what they had.

Paul disagreed with JC. He said, "Man you might as well be speaking Chinese to them thugs. They don't understand nothing but an ass whooping. JC I'm telling you, Harlem ain't the place for your humanitarian efforts. You always trying to save somebody. It will be just the ones you try to help that stab you in the back."

JC was positive that he got through to at least one of the juvenile delinquents. He believed the aborted robbery must have been a sign from above. *If nothing else*, he thought, *the thugs had perfect timing.*

Chapter 2

Later that night, JC and Paul strolled through Paul's neighborhood having one of their many life–planning sessions. From the signs reading "Carriage Parking," to the brownstone Malcolm X once called home, "Strivers Row" was a constant reminder of Harlem's rich history.

It was around two AM The streets were busy and crowded. It looked more like five in the evening any other place in America. On a hot summer night, the streets of Harlem were like an outdoor flea market. All you needed was a sign, a table, and something to sell – flowers, peanuts, or grandma's sweet potato pie – it didn't matter. If you came up with a good sales pitch, you were in business in Harlem.

A local politician, a magistrate judge, and a professional boxer were among the crowd of neighbors gathered around to enjoy the sounds of a sax player blowing a smooth jazz tune. The two stopped to mingle and get the latest update on current events – with a militant spin of course. After a few minutes, JC tossed a ten into the open Sax case on the ground beside the talented horn player, and the duo continued perusing the sale items for the night.

Compared to JC, Paul was low-key on the jewelry but the diamond-lined cane he carried at all times had enough ice to ornament twenty gaudy pimps. Clearly, the cane was what the crooks were frantically in search of. Paul was a couple of inches taller than JC—about 6' 3—and two-hundred and ten pounds of pure muscle. Plus, people in the streets knew Paul was always packing a gun and would use it, so the brothers walked though Harlem without fear.

As they approached a bookstore displaying a poster of Akbar Jones, a popular civil rights activist known for being assaulted and jailed several times with the late Martin Luther King, Jr., there was an uproar of applause. In the background, they heard a minister-like voice from inside the bookstore proclaim, "Where do you think the drugs and guns came from? We don't have planes or the money it takes to get drugs in the country."

Paul stopped to light a cigar as he listened to Akbar accuse the government of flooding black neighborhoods with drugs. Paul knew that his brother suggested this little stroll so he could continue preaching his "stop hustling now gospel." He waved his hand at him. "JC, I'm telling you, I'm not in the mood for your 'get out the game' sermon tonight. Not tonight." He swung his cane forward, leaned a tad to the right, and resumed his revered, Harlem strut.

JC, who was slightly ahead of Paul, turned to him and responded, "This time I have a plan." He paused. "The only thing is that we have to leave New York."

"Leave New York? There you go talking crazy again. Where are we going? Back to Georgia?"

JC hesitated before he responded. "Los Angeles. Let's move to Hollywood where the real money is."

"You got to be out of your mind. Now I know you're crazy. We don't have no connections in Los Angeles and they are wild as hell out there. Even the people who live there call it the devil's playground."

"There's money to be made out there. We need to invest our cash, make some real loot," JC said.

"Yeah you done lost it. If I didn't know better I'd think you were smoking that stuff. There's more money in New York than anywhere in the world. Anyway, what can we do in Hollywood? Please tell me you're just messing with me tonight."

Paul mumbled a few expletives under his breath and kept walking. JC said, "There you go. Talk to me. You always got to say things under your breath; talk to me. That's irritating as hell."

Paul stopped whining when he noticed a vendor selling books at a table near the bookstore. He went over, still listening to JC, thumbed through a book by Akbar Jones, glanced back at the poster of Akbar, and purchased the book.

JC blurted out, "I bought a club."

Startled, Paul swung around to JC. "A club?"

"Yep, I finally got a nightclub. The club where Candace works was for sale, so I bought it."

"You bought a club?" Paul thought a second. "You bought a club without seeing it?"

"Candace said it needs a little work, but it's a gold mine. The owner is moving out of state so I got a good deal." Candace was JC's ex-girlfriend. She was always bright and had good business sense so JC trusted her judgment. Years ago, at JC's urging, Candace went to school and became a registered nurse. She worked at Harlem hospital until she moved to LA and found out she could make more money bartending.

Paul said, "Oh, JC, you can't be serious. Have you really lost it?"

JC did not respond.

Paul tried hard to be supportive of his baby brother so after running the thought through his mind a bit he said, "A club? Well all right! Are you and Candace getting back together?"

Candace was the one that got away for JC. They were a couple for about ten years, and even had a daughter together, but she up and moved back to her native Los Angeles a few years back. No one knew the full story, but everyone assumed JC's lack of commitment had something to do with her exit.

"You know we're just friends," JC said, and quickly changed the subject. "The family reunion is coming up. We can drive, stop in Atlanta, and head west from there."

"That's in two weeks. We can't move that fast."

"Your wife said she will get things ready and fly out later. Candace already found us a place to stay."

"There you go again. As usual, you just planned around me. Do you realize that I have a mind of my own?" Paul was not really opposed to moving, he often spoke about escaping the violence in New York; he was just resistant to JC constantly trying to run his life.

Disagreement was not foreign to these two. Although the brothers were inseparable, they seldom agreed on anything. JC was an eternal optimist. Paul always stuck with the worst case scenario. With a bit of convincing, JC routinely got his way. Deep down, Paul knew JC was usually on point; he had a sixth sense that warned him when something wasn't right. The story among the family was that when JC's dad died, he knew JC would try to step in his shoes and take care of the family, so, old man Powell sent an angel back to watch over JC.

Their father passed away April 5, 1968, the day after Dr. Martin Luther King Jr. was assassinated and race relations were at an all-time low. Although they were just young teens, JC and Paul immediately went out and found work in the fields in Georgia. They became experts in tobacco, cotton, peanut, and watermelon farming.

The young boys left home each morning by four AM and didn't get home some nights until eleven PM. It was JC, the younger of the two, who always came up with schemes to make a little more money. He would set aside a portion of the harvest and sell the goods to neighbors at a discount. Black folks would wait for JC to come around. He always gave them a good price and they felt they were, in their own way, beating the white man at his own game. Plus, everyone wanted to help JC who was trying so hard to take care of his family.

JC always felt guilty for getting fired for something as simple as skimming peanuts. He didn't feel guilty for the sin of stealing, nor for his mother's embarrassment. JC figured white men had been stealing from them for years; he was just leveling the playing field. His guilt was because, once he lost his job their mother couldn't pay the rent so the family had to be split up. The two sisters right behind JC were sent to Florida to live with family they didn't know, while JC and Paul were put on a bus to stay with their aunt in Atlanta. Their mother kept the two youngest sisters and promised to join them shortly. The plan was good on the surface, but JC and Paul made a detour to the Big Apple instead.

JC gave Paul a minute to calm down then ran to catch up with him. "Paul, you know these young boys ain't jokin'- the crack, guns - it's dangerous. You're constantly saying it's time to get out of here."

Paul stopped and turned to JC, "I'll leave when I'm ready. I won't let some young hoods run me out of town."

"Ain't no money in the streets. Drugs done took over. It ain't no place for your family or Mama - and we got to take care of her and Auntie. They're getting up in age." JC knew the family was his trump card.

"But I don't know nothing about LA," Paul replied, now eye-to-eye with his brother.

JC knew he had him. He put his arm around his brother's shoulder, and, in a low tone said, "Me either, big brother. So, like Mama says, we'll have to step out on faith."

A hot dog vendor on the corner of 140th sent two franks over to the duo. They waved to thank him, turned and walked back toward Paul's house. As they passed the huge poster of Akbar, the preaching voice from inside became audible again. "Some confused souls really believe the movement is over, we have overcome. Pray for them."

Applause erupted from the bookstore. The voice continued, "Back in the sixties, the government didn't hire black agents. They used informants. Stool pigeons were bringing down black folks everywhere. Nowadays, if you get a little something, trust me, they'll be on your tail even worse."

Chapter 3

Akbar Jones' face decked the cover of his recently–released book, "The Politics of Prison: Who's Profiting from the Prison Industrial Complex?" which was safely nestled on the dash of a new red Cadillac parked in front of Paul's five–story brownstone. JC and Paul loaded the last of their suitcases into the car when Paul's plain but pretty wife, Tracy, appeared at the door carrying a cooler. Paul ran over and grabbed the cooler and placed it on the back floor of the car. He put his arm around Tracy and gently kissed her on the cheek while rubbing her pregnant stomach.

"Sweetheart, you know you shouldn't lift anything," Paul said.

Tracy, continuing her nurturing ways with her husband, began to list the contents of the cooler. "There are sodas, water, fruit, fried chicken–"

"Baby, I know you have everything we need. I just want you to make sure you don't lift anything. Don't you do anything. An entire moving crew will be here tomorrow to get everything out. Don't you lift a thing," he said, kissing her on the forehead.

JC stared at them like they were crazy. He eventually realized their loving good-byes could last throughout the day. "Man, we have a long ride ahead of us. We need to get going."

The couple exchanged a few more kisses before Paul got into the car where JC was already comfortably relaxing in the passenger seat. For old time's sake, Paul took Lenox to 145th

Street and headed west—a nostalgic tour straight through their old stomping ground. From The Renaissance Ballroom, Abyssinian Baptist Church, and the Dash Hotel, to the Big Track After Hours Joint, memories abounded. Convent, Saint Nick, Sugar Hill—those few blocks helped transform the two country teenagers into men.

Just as Paul crossed Riverside Drive to go onto the highway, JC asked Paul to pull over by the water. Paul maneuvered into a rest area beside the Hudson River. JC exited the car and stood silent, staring at the New Jersey skyline in front of him. It was a clear day so he could almost see the people inside the towering buildings across the river. Behind him, New York City was as busy as ever. Traffic lined the George Washington Bridge as mobs of people fled the frenzied city to the savor their quiet existence in the suburbs.

JC turned his back to Jersey to take in one last view of the city. Across the highway, he saw a crowd of youth watching a basketball game in a city park while a group of small children played in the playground beside the courts. Scanning the New York skyline, starting uptown, he saw Columbia Presbyterian Hospital where his daughter, Cherie, was born. As he panned right, just beyond the Lincoln Center, he could see signs for the Port Authority Bus station where he set up his first hot dog cart. To his right, on the edge of the water, he could see as far downtown as Pier 83, where he had his first date with the love of his life, Candace Banks. This tiny mass of land, not as big as some of the tobacco farms in South Georgia, had been his home for over twenty years, longer than his time in Georgia.

Wondering if JC might have been having reservations about leaving, Paul hopped out of the car and joined him. They stood still, taking in the sights.

JC ended the silence. "Where's your gun?"

Startled, Paul gave JC a puzzled look.

"The gun man, where's your gun?"

At this point Paul had no idea what JC was up to but he popped the trunk and, after digging beneath the designer suitcases, he emerged with the forty-five caliber pistol he carried with him at all times. JC took the gun, wiped it clean with a rag from the trunk, wrapped the rag around the gun, and put it into a plastic bag. Paul questioned JC about his actions the whole time but he never uttered a word. JC walked over and, before Paul could stop him, he tossed the gun into the Hudson River.

"What the hell are you doing? What did you do that for, JC?" Paul yelled.

Still calm as ever, JC replied, "You said you're gonna change your life right?"

"Change yeah, but not be stupid. We don't know anybody in California. Hell, we don't know where we're going and sure don't know what kind of trouble we might have."

Paul continued to fuss as the two got back into the car, pulled out of the rest stop and merged onto the Hudson River Parkway. They veered right, headed for the top of the George Washington Bridge.

As they sat in traffic midway across the bridge, JC said, "That's our past behind us."

"And neither one of us knows what's ahead of us. Man you messed up, I'mma need my piece. I know I'mma need it."

"This is a new beginning for us."

Paul shot JC a disapproving look but he dared not say a word for fear that it would elicit a sermon from the almighty John Cornelius. Paul always said JC missed his calling; he should have been a preacher, then they would all be paid in full. Paul's silence did not stop JC, who had been on a roll for a few months. About six months prior he had a dream that the whole family was swept away in a typhoon and he was convinced it was a premonition.

JC went on, "You said you're gonna change your life, I'm just helping your ass along. You never had as many problems until you got that damn gun."

"I only pulled it when I needed to."

"You always needed to. Black folks got hold of guns and forgot how to resolve problems. Just want to shoot. No talking, no dukin' it out, just shootin'. All the things you wanted to do. You got some money and a gun and got caught up."

Although JC was shrewd, with street intellect and a penchant for making money that would rival the best Wall Street trader,

Paul was book smart. He was curious and always reading. From science to religion, Socrates to DuBois you name it, Paul had read it. When they first landed in New York, JC supported Paul while he earned his GED and went on to get a Bachelor of Arts Degree in political science from New York University.

"What about your idea for a bookstore?" JC asked.

"That's a lot of work."

"And hustling ain't? Looking over your damn shoulder all the time?" JC knocked on the wooden portion of the glove box and continued, "Luck let us do what we had to do to survive. Keep pushing it we'll end up dead or in jail. I'm telling you, the typhoon is on the way."

A typhoon is more likely to hit LA than Harlem, Paul thought, but wouldn't dare verbalize it since he already knew the next fourteen hours would be a "come to Jesus" ride to Georgia. He slipped a jazz tape into the cassette player, followed the signs for the New Jersey Turnpike, and prepared to hear JC's plan for the reincarnation of the Powell brothers.

Chapter 4

Paul was happy that they had planned their trip for a daytime arrival in McDonough, Georgia. Although they were less than a mile from I–75 and a busy ultra modern shopping district with a brand new Walmart, he could never have maneuvered along the narrow one lane road in the darkness. The small country town may have been only twenty minutes outside of Atlanta, but the city was a world away. It felt more like South Georgia where the family reunion was normally held. Large antebellum homes with wraparound porches sat miles apart. Between them were clusters of tar–paper shacks and shotgun shanty's—an ugly reminder of the severe poverty that still existed in rural Georgia.

"We really are on a March to the Sea," Paul said.

JC just gazed over at him. He knew Paul was headed for one of his rants.

"You know, after General Sherman took out Atlanta, he marched his troops right through this area setting fire to the houses, stores, bridges, farm buildings, anything that would burn. Except anything that was worth something. They stole everything of value. They called it the 'March to Sea.' Claimed their thievery and terrorism was to teach the confederates a lesson. Just like they claimed the civil war was to free the slaves. They didn't give a damn about the slaves. Union, Confederate, Democrat, Republican, they could give a damn about black people. We still haven't seen those 40 acres or the mule."

"Some things are changing," JC said. "Now days it's more

about money than race."

"There you go. Black folks need to think more and stop believing everything they hear. It's about money all right, making sure WE don't keep none. We just go along with anything. Just like we're in Henry County. Named after Patrick Henry. Why honor him? He called slavery an abomination and said he felt horrible that he could not live without HIS stock of slaves. Picture that! Changing? The only thing changing is the way they play the game."

The road led to a square in the center of town where people of all races strolled along the red brick sidewalks that led to a myriad of trendy shops and boutiques. There were large potted plants neatly placed at the curbs alongside old-fashioned lampposts. Everyone smiled and waved at the brothers as if they knew them, or heard they were on their way. In the center of the square was a miniature park with colorful flowers and ethnically diverse neighbors sitting on park benches shooting the breeze. Four wooden benches formed a square around a twenty-foot statue of a confederate soldier. The plaque beneath the sculpture read, "To Our Confederate Dead."

"See what I'm saying? Look at the welcoming committee." Paul pointed over to the monument. "Why do you think they call this Courthouse Square?" Paul asked, peering at a sign while stopped a red light.

JC pointed to a large building. "Maybe that's the courthouse over there." As soon as the words fell off his lips, JC knew he had made a mistake by responding.

"It's people like you that end up caught up. You got to think, JC. They're flaunting their new form of slavery-the courts. I wouldn't be surprised if the next town has a Prison Square. They just traded in their white sheets for black robes. People need to wake up and think."

"You think too much. You need to think about how to get in the right lane to make your turn. We've been around this square three times." JC said.

Less than a mile from the main strip, about twenty adults and children were lined up doing the electric slide in the backyard of a two bedroom bungalow sitting on over an acre of land. On one side of the yard there was a huge stone grill, a long table filled with trays of food, and a patio crammed with lawn tables. Multicolored outdoor lights hung above the patio.

On the other side of the property a group of people were playing volleyball. Volleyball was not a popular game in Georgia. But, after JC's mother saw white people playing it on TV, she ordered a net from the Spiegel Catalog and took it to every reunion.

The Spiegel catalog was a lifeline for the Powell family. The fancy crush velvet sectional sofa that could be seen through the sliding glass doors was a Spiegel special order item. The shiny wood tables and the brown and beige shag carpet were all sale items from Spiegel. And, the poster-sized photos of JC and Paul hanging above the brick fireplace were mounted in Spiegel's best antique gold frames.

Huddled on the side of the house was Junior, JC's very country, gold-tooth wearing cousin. Standing about 5'8, one-hundred and fifteen pounds soaking wet, the busybody construction worker/mechanic/plumber and ex-con, was chatting with his friend, Felix Calhoun. Felix appeared to be in his late twenties and epitomized country cool. He was midnight black, with bright colorful attire and perfectly set finger waves in his hair. Everything matched, down to his sky blue sandals and socks that were coordinated with a similarly colored blue hat cocked sideways.

The Cadillac cruised up the street and maneuvered into a parking space about three houses away from Auntie's house, where the reunion picnic was being held. Suited up—overdressed as usual—the brothers got out of the car and, with no sidewalks in sight, they tipped down the middle of the street toward a group of kids playing kickball in the street. Someone yelled, "New York in the house."

Junior was in such an inconspicuous spot, he startled JC and Paul. They turned toward the voice and Junior appeared from nowhere, hugging JC for dear life. Felix slithered behind Junior, marching with his right leg, and sliding his left leg along for the ride. Excited about the arrival of his big baller cousin JC, fast-talking Junior did the introductions. "Felix, dis my cousins from New York I been tellin' ya 'bout. Big ballers."

Paul didn't like Junior or anyone who would be friends with him, so he ignored Junior and kept walking down the pavement mumbling, "You can find more friends but can't seem to find a damn job."

Junior had often been the subject of disagreements between Paul and JC. Junior's mother died during childbirth. When he was nine, his father, David Powell, died trying to rescue his family during a fire. Junior went to live with their aunt in Atlanta. At twenty-seven, Junior was still living off their Auntie, which, since JC provided for all of the family, translated into JC supporting a grown man. It was a real sore spot for the brother's; one of the few issues Paul refused to give in on. He always warned JC, "all relatives ain't family," and to Paul, Junior wasn't family.

Junior continued, "Cousin JC, dis Felix, he live 'round the corner but he goes back and forth to LA. He can show you the ropes, he got the West Coast on lock down." Junior was more than ten years younger than his cousins so, to show respect, he had to "put a handle on" their names.

Felix had a smooth manner about him; a southern charm. He reached out his hand to JC. "It's an honor to meet you, I've heard a lot about you."

JC smiled and nodded toward Junior, "You can't believe all of what you hear. So you know LA?"

"Yeah, I go out there all the time on business. I'll be back out there in a few weeks. Actually, I've been out there more than Atlanta recently."

"Is that right?" JC said.

"Uh-huh. Here, take my card, if you need anything, call me. I got big time connections for sure."

"Will do. Good to meet you man, let's keep in contact," JC said and proceeded down the long driveway to the backyard where the family was still getting their dance on. He caught up to Paul. "Man you didn't have to be so rude."

Paul never looked JC's way. "That boy looked shady. I don't have no time for Junior or any of his scandalous friends."

"Why you gonna judge the boy like that? You don't know him." JC said.

Paul cut his eyes at JC. "I know he was with Junior. If he's with Junior he must be up to no good. Where did they come from anyway?"

Before the two could get into the yard, they were swarmed by cousins, nieces, and nephews offering hugs and high-fives. Everyone was always thrilled to see the brothers—they were superstars in that neck of the woods. Although he would never admit it, as if everyone couldn't figure it out, the truth was that JC's lucrative numbers business paid for everything. From the house to the ribs sizzling on the grill, all were provided à la JC Powell.

As Paul watched, JC slid into the line and danced until his age caught up with him. Junior and Felix continued on toward the tables. JC jumped out of the line dance and he and Paul made their way over to the lawn tables where Auntie was seated. Paul was now off Junior's case and grumbling about the scent of swine that could be smelled a block away.

Weighing in at two-fifty, Auntie had two gold crowns on her teeth and never bit her tongue. She was the matriarch of the family, their father's older sister. Like their father, Auntie looked and acted more like the Cherokee side of the family. She had high cheekbones and a reddish brown skin tone, which most of the family inherited. Her strong-willed attitude was always attributed to the Indian blood running through her veins.

Although she raised at least six kids belonging to various family members, Auntie and her late husband, Uncle Joe, never had kids. Uncle Joe disappeared more than twenty-five years before when a squall hit while he was deep sea fishing. Although, there were whispers that Uncle Joe really ran off with a younger woman and was alive and well, living in Virginia. None of the younger generation knew the true story, they only knew there was never a funeral. Auntie refused to give up until they found a body.

As they approached the picnic tables they heard her sweet cheerful voice, "Oh Lord! There's my babies! I been waitin' a long time fo' ya'll ta' git ta' Atlanta. Ya'll, these dem nephews that went AWOL twenty some years ago. Ester's kids—where'd she go?" Auntie looked around for JC's mother, Ester Powell.

JC hugged his aunt. "Hey Auntie." He glanced around the

table. Several people were leaning in, laughing at a photo album. "How's everybody doing?"

Still confused about Auntie's remarks, Junior asked, "AWOL? Was you in the service?"

"Nah boy, dey run away," Auntie replied.

"We didn't run away Auntie," JC said.

"What was it if you didn't run away?" A voice from behind asked.

All heads turned to see JC's mother, a petite, proper, God-fearing woman. Although Mama stood only 4'10 and never hit triple digits on a scale, she commanded respect from everyone. She had blue eyes and long straight black hair tightly pulled into a bun at the nape of her neck. She was well into her sixties but had amassed no more than ten strands of gray hair.

Right on Mama's heels was Trevor, JC's nineteen-year-old son dressed in upscale hip-hop attire. Trevor was JC's oldest child by a girl he met when he first landed in New York. She ended up strung-out on drugs and stayed in and out of prison so JC got custody of Trevor when he was only eight months old. Trevor was intelligent, musically talented, but short-tempered. When he started hanging with the wrong crowd and got arrested a few times, JC sent him to stay with Mama. He thought a few years of country living would be good for Trevor, and Mama needed someone around to help her.

JC stood and hugged Mama, who was garbed in a 1994 Powell Reunion T-shirt and had a hearing aid tucked behind her ear. JC mugged the back of Trevor's head and pulled him close to give him a quick hug before sitting down to continue the story. "After papa died, all of us had to be split up. Mama sent me and Paul to Atlanta to stay with Auntie."

"And dey just gettin' here!" Auntie yelled. "Wait." She shuffled through the photo album and pulled out a picture.

Embarrassed, JC glanced at his mother, "Oh Mama, not them pictures! Please tell me you didn't bring those pictures out here!"

Laughing, Paul pulled out a photo of them in fourth generation hand-me-downs, shoes too big and pants too small, and continued JC's story. "It was JC. HE came up with a plan. We met a hustler named Philip from New York at the bus station.

JC asked him how much he made selling watches. That was it. JC started doing the math. He was always figuring out how to make money."

Everyone was gathered around, captivated by the story. After all, JC and Paul were the only celebrities in the family. Mama listened intently as she walked to the food table to prepare plates.

"Wasn't nothing for us to do in Atlanta. We was grown. We took the money Mama gave us and got a ticket to New York," JC said.

"We nothing. That was YOU," Paul said. "Grown? We thought we was grown—fifteen and sixteen—two fools. Thank God for Philip; he showed us the ropes. We sold everything - watches, hot dogs, weed, spirits and—"

JC eyed Paul and cut him off before Mama realized what he was saying. "I wonder whatever happened to Philip, he just disappeared."

"I'm glad he waited until we got the hang of things before he ducked out. We would have been lost souls without Philip."

Still fascinated by the story, Junior stopped gnawing on the rib he had rudely grabbed from a food tray on the table and asked, "Won't ya'll scared, Cousin JC?"

Auntie, who had enough of her pathetic great-nephew said, "Dey ain't scary like you Junior. Look at 'em. My babies on dey way ta' Hollywood. Gonna git one of dem big discos. Tell 'um bout dat."

"I already bought it Auntie. I'mma call it The Empire."

"The Empire. Baby I'm so proud of ya'. From da woods in Georgia, didn't even have no baff-rum."

"Auntie!" JC said.

In her sweet innocent tone, Auntie said, "Well none of us did baby. How many of ya' was in a bed-rum? Six or seven?"

Paul chimed in, "Come on, Auntie."

"Well ya'll outta' be proud. Driving Cadillac's, talkin' proper and openin' a discothèque."

Mama brought two plates of food for JC and Paul. JC's plate was loaded with sweet potatoes, macaroni and cheese, collard greens, potato salad and ribs. The only thing on Paul's plate was tossed salad and barbecue chicken. When Mama bent over to place the plates on the table, she knocked Junior's jacket on the ground. Paul picked up the jacket to put it back on the chair and noticed a crack pipe in the pocket. He never said a word.

Auntie leaned in and checked out Paul's plate. As if they didn't have the same argument every year since Paul stopped eating pork in the seventies, Auntie said, "Ya'll need to put some food on that boy's plate. Give 'em a rib and onea' dem pork chops."

She knew she was going to elicit a rise out of Paul. There was no Powell reunion without a good argument or two. Every year Paul warned Auntie about eating pork. Every year she vowed to eat swine until she's six feet under. Auntie suffered from high blood pressure and heart disease, but she still refused to stop eating her ham hocks, ribs, pork chops and, making things worse, she seasoned everything else she cooked with fatback. JC had cut down considerably on pork, but he still enjoyed a rib or pork chop every now and then.

"But Hollywood, are you sure about this?" Mama asked, determined they'd have to find something else to argue about this year.

"Yes ma'am," said Paul. "I'mma open a bookstore. Spread some knowledge," he added.

"Now that's a wonderful idea." Mama respected education. She was the daughter of sharecroppers and only received a ninth grade formal education but she knew more than the average college graduate. She always said knowledge was the only weapon the black community needed to get ahead.

Mama was quite an entrepreneur as well. After her husband died, she started a laundry service as a side business. She hurried home each day from her work as a maid to supervise her laundry operation. Mary and Lydia, the two older girls, washed the clothes and hung them out to dry. Ruth folded and little Faith alerted the crew when the clothes were dry. JC and Paul delivered the laundry to the customers. It worked out well until the Hampton's, who owned the white laundry across town, complained because they were losing business and Mama was forced to cease her operations.

JC said, "Mama, when we get settled I promise to move all

of you out to California. I'mma get a house big enough for you and all of my women. One big happy family."

"You'd really try some mess like that. Money can't buy everything," Paul said.

Mama added, "You need to stop talking crazy and pray for Candace to take you back."

"You pray enough for all of us," JC said.

"You had better watch your mouth, young man. You are never too old, you know?" Mama was always threatening to spank her kids. No one ever had the nerve to try her to find out if she would actually do it. "Anyway, how do you think you've been getting along all of these years? I've been praying and I am going to keep praying for the Lord to watch over you."

"My babies goin' ta' Los Angeleese wit da' rich folk," exclaimed Auntie.

Chapter 5

"Regulate" by Warren G featuring Nate Dogg, played on the radio as the red Caddy cruised along the ocean into Long Beach. Once Paul saw a sign reading "Long Beach Harbor," a landmark noted in Candace's detailed directions, they began looking for Long Beach Boulevard. Before they knew it they were on a dark winding road; the only light emanated from the ships docked in the Harbor in front of them. Another sign, reading "Queen Mary," was a clear indication the brothers had lost their way.

When the brothers arrived in Los Angeles in the wee hours of the morning, they checked into the Bel Age Hotel right off the Sunset Strip assuming the club was "right outside" LA. The duo thought their trip to Long Beach would be like running over the hill into the San Fernando Valley, only to find out from the hotel doorman that Long Beach was at least thirty miles south of Sunset. Long Beach was so far away, physically and mentally, that everyone they asked offered different directions – the 1, 10, 405, or the 710. Candace could only guide them from inside Long Beach city limits.

The decision to take Sunset to the Pacific Coast Highway-the scenic route-kept Paul's complaining to a minimum. He was too busy soaking up the wealth that surrounded them. Sunset Boulevard provided a quick tour of affluent Beverly Hills, and, when they hit the Pacific Coast Highway, the trip turned heavenly. One side of the highway met with the bottom of the mountain. Directly above were fabulous mansions nestled throughout the steep hills. Several homes hung off the edges of cliffs, waiting for the perfect storm to send them sliding down the mountain into the ocean, which was on the opposite side of the freeway. Condos and fancy restaurants sat feet from the water's edge. There were marinas housing one hundred-foot yachts and parking lots packed with the finest cars money could buy. The brothers boasted on how they had finally arrived.

Dead-ending in the Harbor parking lot, Paul turned around and traveled back up the winding road following the signs for downtown Long Beach. Except for some activity at a hotel, the other unique, official-looking buildings were closed and dark. JC clicked on the inside light so Paul could read Candace's directions to the club. After a couple of wrong turns and an abrupt change in atmosphere, they not only found the street they were looking for, they also discovered the Long Beach ghetto. Bands of thugs slung drugs on corners, low-riders cruised the strip, and store after store was boarded up. It was a far cry from the wealth behind them.

The conditions went downhill the further they drove. Paul frowned at JC a few times, but neither uttered a word. The neighborhood got so bad, both of them were convinced they were lost again.

JC spotted a gas station about a half-mile up the road. "There's a BP, but it can't be the right one, you think? What street is this?"

"They never got street signs in the 'hood."

"Turn here Paul. This must be it."

"Yes'em Miss Daisy," Paul jokingly responded. "Damn, this is worse than the South Bronx."

The car turned onto Long Beach Boulevard and slowed down. It was the shoddiest block they had hit until then. JC said, "This can't be right. Must be a north and south. Stop at the store up ahead and let me ask for directions."

The car pulled over in front of a dilapidated neighborhood grocery store. The passenger door opened and a bright blue gator hit the ground. JC glided out of the car donning a flashy suit and a sky blue "summer" mink coat. He was told that the chilly evenings in LA allowed him to wear fur and leather year round.

JC entered a small grocery store with rows of empty shelves—a sure sign to JC that it doubled as a numbers joint.

A very attractive and cheerful young lady in her late twenties jumped up from a seat behind the counter. Her wide smile was genuine and welcoming. "Good evening sir, may I help you?"

"You sure can. I'm JC and you are?"

"Tamara," the young lady responded as she rubbed on a strange charm hanging from a braided black leather necklace. It looked more like a miniature potato sack than a charm. She wore no other jewelry. No earrings, bracelets, and, most importantly, no rings —a green light for JC to get his flirt on.

"A lovely name for a lovely lady. Well Tamara, I'm new to town and I'd love for you to show me around," he said.

"I know you didn't come in here to hire a tour guide," Tamara replied.

"Uh, I'm sorry. I saw you and totally forgot what I came for," JC said, admiring how Tamara's shoulder length dreadlocks framed her chunky cheeks perfectly. "I'm looking for the Rukus Room."

"The Rukus Room? It's right next-door."

JC glanced out the store window and looked back at Tamara confused and bewildered. Tamara walked from behind the counter and stepped outside. JC followed her. She pointed to a small sign reading " Kus R om" hanging atop a shabby storefront. The front door and windows were boarded up.

"That's it. You enter around back," Tamara said still pointing. Her hand dropped aiming toward an alley on the side of the building. Tamara gave JC a quick look up and down and added, "I really don't think it's your kind of place."

Paul yelled from the car, "I told you JC, I told you. You can't trust other people. You got beat. Let's go! Let's get out of here. This ain't safe."

Still keeping his cool, JC told Paul, "Just park the car and come on." He turned to Tamara. "Young lady, will our car be okay parked here?"

Tamara nodded NO emphatically. Paul parked the car and joined JC. As JC dabbed the sweat oozing down his face with a handkerchief, he noticed a man sitting on the ground in front of an abandoned building a few yards away.

"Excuse me sir," JC yelled to him. "Will you be out here for a while? I'll pay you to watch my car."

"Sure," the man answered as he hopped up from the ground and walked with a slight limp over to them. He struck an official stance in front of the car, as if he were guarding Buckingham Palace.

"I'm JC, he's Paul. You are?"

"Nate. Well, Nathaniel, but they call me Nate."

"Well Nate, here's $10, and if you and the car are still here when I come out, you get $15 more. Deal?"

Nate, who was clean and a little stocky for the average homeless person, leaned against the parking meter beside the car, crossed his arms and said, "I'll be right here when you get back."

"You're wasting your money. He's gonna' go get drunk as soon as we leave," Paul mumbled under his breath.

JC turned to Tamara and asked, "And you, lovely lady, will you come have a drink with me when you get off?"

"In there? No thank you," she snapped. She swirled around and quickly headed back to the store. JC admired her voluptuous shape as she bounced her way inside.

JC teased, "I know where you work. I'll be back."

Paul and JC walked into the alley not giving much thought to the three harmless looking youngsters hanging out a few feet beyond the entrance. At the end of the alley was a huge parking lot packed with a months worth of trash and heaps of empty forty ounce malt liquor bottles. The door to the club was obscured by a dumpster overflowing with old furniture and other household items.

JC entered the club and quickly scanned the room. It was a small, dark, smoky, hole-in-the-wall. The place was filled with old, unmatched furniture and a sloping bar that amazingly supported Dee, a twenty-eight-year-old ghetto fab stripper/porn star dancing on top of the bar—almost nude. Two men were at the bar watching Dee thrust her narrow hips to the beat of a Brian McKnight ballad. A man selected music on a jukebox and another guy was catching a catnap at a table near the bar.

JC's shock turned to euphoria when he spotted Candace working at the bar. She was a natural beauty with lightly–toasted, satin brown skin, high cheekbones, and a smile that could win the devil's heart. It was obvious that she was still hitting the gym at least four times a week; she had a perfect body, thick in all the right places. Her long, wavy, light brown hair was pulled back into her trademark ponytail. Actually, it was her hair that landed her a halfway decent daddy. When she turned three and her wavy hair and hazel eyes didn't change, her mother decided to contact the Puerto Rican guy that worked at the train station to tell him he had a daughter. Lucky for Candace, he accepted her with open arms. The truth is, it would take more than a few DNA tests to tell who her real father was.

JC gazed in delight as Candace chatted with a customer, pulling at her sleeve as she often did to hide the large burn that covered her left arm.

"Mmm, mmm, mmm," JC said, admiring Candace.

"Yeah, look at this shit. What a dive," Paul blurted out.

"You need to stop with the negativity."

Paul drew everyone's attention when he slipped on a loose floorboard and sent a chair hurling across the room. He immediately concluded that beneath that board laid a dead body emitting the horrible stench that engulfed the room.

Candace perked up when she saw the two standing at the entrance. "JC, you made it." She ran and hugged them then turned and announced, "Everybody, this is JC and his brother Paul, the ones from New York I've been telling you about." A few people nodded hello. Candace turned back to JC, "Well, this is it. It needs work but—"

"It's got potential," JC said shaking his head as he checked out the room. It took all he had in him to hide his shock.

"It does. Plus, there are no decent clubs in Long Beach, none. If you promote this place right you can attract a real upscale crowd."

"In this neighborhood?" Paul asked.

"It's not that bad, Paul. They just let this block go," Candace said.

"It seemed like more than a block to me," Paul said.

JC tossed Paul an evil eye. He glanced around the club, then stepped back to eyeball Candace. "It's perfect. I can work with this," he said.

Dee bolted over like a dog in heat. Flirting as usual, she grabbed JC's hand. The oddly shaped earring in her pierced nose brought more attention to the one-inch scar on her cheek. Dee tried very hard to speak proper and often used words out of context. She longed to be important. She wasn't ugly, but she was no striking beauty either. She was tall, 5' 9, and very thin. Aside from her large boobs – a gift from an elderly porn director she 'dated' – nothing about Dee stood out.

In her most seductive tone she said, "Hi, I'm Dee. Now I see where your daughter acquired her incredible attractiveness."

There was an obvious tension between Dee and Candace. JC had been around the block a few times so he recognized the female drama brewing and wouldn't bite. Smooth as silk, JC scoured Candace's body and replied, "My daughter takes after her fine mother. She has Candace's beauty and my smarts."

Tired of Dee's antics, Candace stepped in her way and pulled JC's arm. "Let me show ya'll around."

Paul, a bit puzzled, glanced around the club, his lips mimicking "around?" The place was so small there wasn't much to see.

Candace asked, "So did you find the club OK?"

"It would have been easier if they had some damn street signs," Paul said.

"You think it's a conspiracy?" Candace asked.

"You see that mess in Beverly Hills?"

"Don't get him started Candace, you know how he gets," JC said.

Dee pranced up and pushed her way back in. "JC, I just want you to know, we're glad to have you. If you need anything, anything at all, just let me know. I was born and raised here in Long Beach so I know every nook and cranny. Also, keep me in mind for the new club. I am an expert administerer."

Once again, Candace moved Dee to the side, "I've got this. You just get up there and show them your nooks and crannies."

She pointed to the men at the bar. Candace didn't wear any jewelry on her disfigured arm but on the other arm she wore six thick gold bangles, a diamond tennis bracelet, and three large diamond rings totaling more than six carats—all gifts from JC over the years.

Dee stormed off, pissed.

Paul was shocked at how Candace treated Dee. She always went the extra mile to be nice to people. "A bit salty aren't you?"

"Gold digging thief. She tried to get me fired," Candace said.

"That's wicked," Paul said.

"She's wicked. I'm just waiting for the right time to get her ass back."

"You won't do anything. It's not your nature," JC said.

"Oh, best believe I'll get her. I'm gonna' get her for sure. JC, you watch out because you go for the game too easy and she got plenty of game. Always on the prowl for a man with money."

Paul laughed and said, "I try to tell him, he thinks he's a playa', but he's really getting played."

"You need to find a wife and settle down." Candace said.

"I'm waiting for you."

"Yeah right," Candace replied. "Did you call the contractor? He said he can be here as early as you need him."

JC said, "I'll call him in the morning when we're on our way here. We gotta run now, it's a long ride back and I want to get started early tomorrow."

Paul kissed Candace goodbye. When JC softly pecked Candace on the cheek, he whispered in her ear. She pushed him away playfully. Candace vowed never to take JC seriously.

Chapter 6

All eyes were on the duo as they exited the club and proceeded in silence down the alley back to the car. What was initially a group of three, had grown to more than eight kids who definitely did not belong to the Long Beach welcoming committee. If JC or Paul was nervous, neither let on. To the contrary, their demeanor was inviting; eying the youth as if to say *you really don't want to mess with us.* Paul, who was shrewd enough to leave his cane in the vault at the hotel, kept his hand in his pocket like he was still armed with the protection that now called the bottom of the Hudson River home.

The sigh of relief was almost audible when the brothers hit the front of the building and saw their security officer still stationed beside the Cadillac.

"Ain't that a bitch," JC said.

"I told you I needed my gun," Paul responded, thinking JC was talking about the gang of thugs they had just encountered.

"I'm talking about that place. The club, bar, or whatever it is. What the hell was it? That place is a deathtrap!"

Paul snickered a little and served JC a dose of his own optimism, "It's got potential."

"Yeah, for a damn parking lot."

By then the two brothers were laughing hysterically. Paul said, "Call ourselves moving to Hollywood. This ain't nowhere near Hollywood."

"What was Candace thinking?"

They reached Nate who was proudly guarding the bright red Caddy. He asked, "What's so funny?"

"My brother thought he was a big time player; he bought the Kus Rom," said Paul, who was now nearly in tears.

JC stepped to Nate and pressed a $100.00 bill into his hand. "Thanks man, I appreciate your help."

Nate glanced at the bill, took a double take and then held the bill in the air to make sure he was seeing correctly. He yelled, "Thank you! You a playa' to me."

Paul was still bent over roaring with laughter, talking mess. He said, "Let's go buy some swampland in Florida. Hollywood. Yeah we're in Hollywood all right."

Paul paused long enough to realize JC had walked away. He was on the other side of the street, sitting on the curb directly across from the club. Paul strolled over and sat next to him. They both stared at the dilapidated building and, after a long silence, they busted out laughing again.

JC's amusement was followed by another serious, pensive moment. "What are we gonna to do?" he asked Paul.

"I don't know, but I know this club thing isn't going to work. JC, we can always go back."

"You know me better than that. I'm not going back. I already spent my money and I promised to send for Mama and Auntie." JC was never one to admit defeat, especially so early in the game.

Nate crossed over the four lane street to join them but never took his eyes off a silver low-rider with four teens slouched down in the seats about a block away from them.

Trying to offer a bit of wisdom Nate said, "It really isn't that bad."

Paul chuckled. "What? Will it look better in the daytime?"

"People in Long Beach got to go all the way to LA to party. Fix this place up and you'll make some money." Nate's pitch for Long Beach sounded more like a real estate professional trying to sell property in the city than a fifty-year-old man who made the streets his home.

The mention of money immediately caught JC's attention. He perked up and wanted to hear more. "Is that right?"

"Yep," Nate said. "Plus, people are moving here from LA for affordable housing. Long Beach is on the way up."

JC got quiet again and began to study the buildings. He scrutinized the block closely. Most of the stores were closed down and others displayed "For Sale" signs in the windows, including the corner store. JC thought about the fact that plenty of the most active streets in Harlem had their ups and downs over the time he lived in New York. Everyone knew about the rise and fall of 125th Street. He thought about how the reopening of the Apollo Theatre brought new life and money to an area people thought would never come back alive.

After studying the block for a few minutes, all JC's optimistic eyes could see was the potential to turn the area into a thriving business district. What JC couldn't see was, like New York, over the past few years, young thugs had gained control of Long Beach. Like New York they robbed, stole, and sold drugs for a living. But unlike New York, the violence in that community had grown to include random drive-by shootings fueled by something as simple as wearing the wrong color in the wrong neighborhood. Long Beach was primarily Crip territory and many unknowing outsiders met their fate for merely wearing a Hawks T-shirt in the wrong part of town. The color red was a major sign of disrespect in most hoods in the LBC.

Paul interrupted JC's meditative state. "JC, don't start getting no big ideas."

"Big ideas is what this town needs," Nate said.

"You're pretty smart," JC said.

"I'm homeless, not stupid."

The brothers crossed the street, headed to the car. Nate trailed slightly behind, still eyeing the low-rider down the street. JC asked Nate, "You're alright man. Will you be around tomorrow?"

"Tomorrow?" Paul exclaimed. "Oh here you go, JC. I'm telling you, this ain't gonna work."

Just as they approached the car, Nate ran over, shoving Paul to the passenger side of the car yelling, "Duck, get down, get down."

They stooped beside the car as the low-rider sped by, flooding the area with a barrage of bullets. The gunfire ended as suddenly as it began.

JC shouted, "What the hell is going on?"

"Drive-by," said Nate.

"A drive-by. Who the hell are they after? Somebody trying to kill you?" Paul asked.

Nate looked Paul dead in the eyes as he spoke. "You shouldn't drive that red Cadillac around here. They think you're disrespecting them. Crips rule here. You got to respect people, you know?"

"Respect who?" Paul yelled. "Oh hell no. I'm outta here. I'mma hurt somebody. Oh hell no, this ain't the place for me."

"They weren't aiming for anything, just trying to scare you," Nate said.

JC stood up and dusted off his clothes. Paul continued to fuss as he darted back to the car. "How'd you get those quick reflexes?" JC asked.

"I used to be a cop."

"Is that right? What happened?"

"Couldn't deal with the corruption. You'd be surprised how vicious the crime business can get. You see where I am, don't you? But I'll win in the end."

JC reached out to shake Nate's hand. "I'll see you tomorrow, Nate."

As JC got in the car, Nate yelled, "By the way, I don't drink."

Chapter 7

Day two on the west coast was long, due in part to the time change and partly to JC's eagerness to get started. Before dawn, JC was up, checked out of the hotel in LA, and on his way to the modestly furnished apartment Candace had found them in Long Beach.

It was a small flat on the top floor of an old elevator building on the oceanfront. It was tiny, but quaint. There were two bedrooms that barely accommodated a dresser and a full-sized bed. The Spanish-tiled bathroom and kitchen were standing room only. But, the living room made up for all the apartment's shortcomings. It had character. There were gleaming hardwood floors bordered by antique crown molding, a bay window stretching the width of the room, and a breathtaking view of the beach directly across the street. An antique camel back sofa and a matching chair with lion head arms were on the opposite wall, facing the window.

Paul went back to bed as soon as they reached the apartment. JC started unpacking. Before he finished, Candace arrived to take him to get his first glimpse of the club in the daylight hours.

"Good Morning." Candace said as she whisked past JC, headed straight to the kitchen to put down the bags she was carrying.

"You look mighty cheery this morning," JC responded.

Candace never answered. She clicked on a radio that sat on the kitchen counter, washed her hands, reached into the cabinet beneath the sink, and pulled out a large cast iron frying pan. JC watched in enjoyment as she pulled eggs, beef bacon, fruit, and other items from the bag and prepared breakfast. After gawking at Candace for too long—breakfast was almost ready—JC went into the bedroom to continue unpacking.

"OK JC, come eat so we can get out of here," Candace said.

When JC went to get his plate he was shocked to find that Candace had set up a small table, draped with a lilac tablecloth, in front of the bay window. She had remembered everything when she stocked the apartment. Gold-plated flatware rested to the left of the colorful china holding the artistically arranged eggs, bacon, and grits. To the left of the flatware was a linen napkin neatly tucked inside a gold-plated napkin ring. There was a fancy fruit bowl filled with raspberries, strawberries, and seedless green and red grapes. A sparkling cut crystal goblet housed the freshly squeezed orange juice. And, to add the perfect finishing touch, she placed a small bouquet of lilacs in a tall crystal vase on the edge of the table. JC thought to himself, *I'm going to get that woman back no matter how long it takes.*

"You're not eating?" JC asked.

"You know it's too early for me to eat." Candace took off into the back room while JC dined in bliss. Candace had shrewdly negotiated a corner unit on the thirtieth floor for the price of the condo units on the lower floors. After one look at the astounding view of the beach and the city—like a scene from a movie—JC was completely sold on Long Beach. Candace knew JC would love a place where he could enjoy his favorite pastime—people watching.

From the bay window, he could see miles of beautiful beaches with people tanning, wading in the water, and seated at tables with umbrellas. He saw a pier, a marina, and a collection of ships and boats including the popular Queen Mary. The distinctive skyline had an assortment of oddly shaped buildings. JC later found out that the cobalt blue colored pyramid was California State University, the V-shaped building was a hotel, the tube-shaped building was the Long Beach Convention Center, and the wavy building was the Aquarium of the Pacific. The Sports Arena was the most artistic; it was circular and the exterior was decorated with a mural of sea life.

By the time JC finished his breakfast, he had a well thought out plan for the club. He went back into the bedroom where Candace had finished unpacking his clothes and completely rearranged all the suits he had already put away.

"Ready?" JC asked.

"Let me leave a note for Paul so he knows his plate is in the oven, and I'm good to go."

The ride from the apartment to the club took less than ten minutes, not nearly long enough for JC to savor the closeness Candace's small car allowed. He noticed she had pierced her ears, something she had talked about doing for years. He also confirmed that she still wore the same vanilla-scented perfume she used to send him to the Duty Free Shop at JFK to buy for her at a discount.

Candace drove through the adjacent neighborhood to give JC a tour of the surrounding area. The streets behind the club seemed like a nice working class neighborhood with modest one-story homes and a few small apartment buildings. Candace could tell by JC's upbeat mood he had come up with a plan. She parked in the back lot and headed to unlock the doors to the club.

JC darted to the front of the club to survey the block on foot. The street was deserted. It was too early for the thugs to be hanging out and, with the exception of the corner store, a gas station, and two liquor stores, the rest of the businesses were boarded up. JC peeped down the alley next to the club and there was Nate, sitting on the ground wrapped in a blanket reading the paper.

"JC, you decided to come back," Nate said as he stood.

"Of course. I don't scare easy." JC stepped back and looked Nate up and down. "I have to say, you're the cleanest homeless person I've seen."

"You never heard about the high class homeless people in LA?" Nate said, laughing. "It's not that bad out here. The gas station attendant lets me use the truck stop showers every morning, and the barmaid in the Rukus Room lets me in before she closes up when the weather is bad. Have you met her? She's fine, if—"

"Watch your mouth!" JC joked. He crossed his arms and shot Nate a piercing look.

"Ah, you must be the friend she's been talking about from New York?"

"She told you about me?" JC's smile widened. "About housing, I was wondering if you could help me out. We'll be gutting the place and I'm going to need security for the club to make sure supplies are delivered and no one breaks in while construction is going on. That's big business in New York—robbing construction sites. We can fix up the room in the basement. I'll pay you."

"Of course. I'd be glad to oblige Playa! But, housing is enough. I get a monthly check for a leg injury. I use it for food and other necessities. I just can't afford these expensive apartments."

"I will pay you. Come inside with me now. You and Candace can deal with the details and see what you'll need to start getting the room in the basement together."

"Thatta work for me boss." Nate neatly packed his belongings into a crate and followed JC.

JC went inside and gave the club a once-over. Before Candace could say anything, he was gone. He went next door to the corner grocery store where Tamara was busy working. She greeted JC with a big, innocent smile, appearing delighted to see him.

"Shocked to see me back so soon?" JC said.

"Sure am," Tamara nonchalantly responded.

"I bought the place next door."

"I'm not impressed, that place is bad news." Tamara tried hard to convince people she was a tough girl.

"Watch what I do with it," JC said. "That's why I'm here. Do you own this store?"

"Is that why you were flirting? You thought I was the owner?"

"No, I was flirting because I'm gonna make you my woman. Now, how can I contact the owner?"

Tamara blushed. "He's here. You must know him, he owned the Rukus Room. JC, right?"

"I'm impressed," JC said.

Tamara stepped in a door directly behind her and came out a few seconds later with Mr. Chen, a sixty-eight-year-old, short, hunched-back, Asian gentleman shuffling behind her.

"Mr. Powell, good to meet you," said Mr. Chen.

"The pleasure is mine, Mr. Chen. I thought you were moving to Texas."

"That's my plan, soon as I get rid of this building and two others."

"Well, today may be your lucky day, Mr. Chen." JC pointed at the wall and said, "Can my contractor come over and see if this wall can come down?"

"You want to make club bigger?"

"Yeah, and add a patio."

"Send contractor any time," Mr. Chen said.

"If he can do it, we'll talk business. Now what about your other buildings?"

"Other buildings near beach. Nice area. I give good price for you, Mr. Powell."

"Can we take a look sometime today? My brother needs a spot for a bookstore."

"Yoga studio perfect for bookstore. Perfect. Three o'clock okay for you, Mr. Powell?"

"Three's fine." JC said. He grabbed a pack of gum, pulled a dollar from his pocket and paid Tamara. "Smile, I'll be back for you later."

"You're trying to take my job. Why should I smile?"

"Because you'll be working for me now," JC replied, grinning from ear to ear.

Chapter 8

Construction workers labored day and night for over a month, leaving no reminders of the club's crappy past. The place was completely gutted. The wall between the club and the corner store had been knocked out so it was a huge empty space. Elated at the progress, JC wandered around, smiling as he inspected each task the workers had completed. Brief moments of frustration surfaced through his excitement every time he checked his watch, then glanced at the door. About twenty-five minutes passed before Paul and Candace rushed in with their arms full of bags. JC looked at his watch, eyed Paul, huffed a bit, and continued his inspection.

Paul quickly defended his tardiness, "You know I had to register to vote."

"You need to stop with that mess. Those snakes ain't doing nothing to get black people paid. Listening to all of those Akbar Jones tapes is brainwashing you."

"You need to listen to a few yourself," Paul said.

"For what? Him and his cronies are out there pimping the race card. Yeah we got problems, but it ain't about race, it's about a dollar. Every time you see Akbar Jones on TV, he's marching about something. What the hell is marching going to get you? Why we always got to be victims?"

In an attempt to avert a debate and give Paul an opportunity to unload the rest of the supplies from the car, Candace cut JC off. "Where's Tamara? I thought she would be here helping."

"She had to take her mother to the doctor. She'll be on after that," JC said.

"She's really sweet, taking care of her sick mom. Not your type at all."

He was so upset with Paul, it took a few minutes for the comment to sink in for JC, who was now taking one of the bags Candace was holding. "Why not?" He put the bag on a table by the wall and added, "Anyway, you look out for your mother and you're my type."

"Her mom has Alzheimer's. I drop my mother off at rehab every six months—there's a difference." Candace noticed water on the floor, grabbed a towel, wiped the water up, and hurried over to join JC as he resumed his inspection of the building.

Paul returned with a large box and placed it on the floor near a fancy dartboard and photos in lavish frames that were leaning against the wall. Paul said, "JC, I'm really getting worried. The costs are getting outrageous. I still don't think this was a wise investment; it's just too much work and too much money."

"Do the math. Capacity is about eight hundred. Say we get four hundred people at $15 a head plus fifty VIPs at $30 each. Two nights a week. How much is that?"

"Umm... about fifteen grand."

"Add slow nights, food, and liquor sales. It's more than a million a year at fifty percent of capacity. And we'll get a full house at two bills a head for the Playas Ball."

Paul stopped for a moment. He did the math in his head and cried out, "One hundred grand in one night. I guess you have a point. Yeah, you do have a point, little brother."

The back door swung open so hard it hit the wall. It was Dee making her grand entrance like a tiger in heat. She strutted over to give JC a hug and spoke to everyone except Candace.

"Dee will be working with us," JC told the crew.

Paul replied, "We can't have that mess here."

"She won't be dancing."

In her most sarcastic and condescending tone Candace asked, "Well what else can she do? Me and Tamara will handle the money. I got the bar and your family has the food. What else is there?"

JC smiled at Dee and announced, "She'll be the hostess."

"Hostess? What does a hostess do?" Paul asked.

"I will greet customers and ensure that they are all pleased," Dee said.

"What a perfect position," Candace replied.

The next few weeks turned into months. It was a time JC thought would be the hardest in his life. There were electrical problems, the painter disappeared in the middle of the job, and they were having a hard time getting permits and transferring the liquor license. One dilemma after another.

Everything cost more than estimated, especially licenses and permits. LA ended up being more corrupt than New York. Every city worker that visited needed a kickback to get things done in a "timely" manner.

Nate proved to be a lifesaver with his contacts throughout the city. His people were eager to do him a favor; they liked him and also knew he was a good cop that got a bad rap. Nate claimed the acts of kindness were guilt offerings, since all of them were scared to come forward when he got set-up with a case for supposedly soliciting a prostitute after he naively went to internal affairs to report a crew of rogue cops. The cops were adding black and Latino kids they stopped for traffic violations to gang files even if they weren't gang members. Nate later found out that it was common practice to exaggerate the number of gang members throughout California because there was a bonus paid to officers if they worked in a gang-infested neighborhood. When he discovered that a few bad police officers also instigated the tension between rival gangs, he contacted the State Attorney General's office because internal affairs would not investigate. He was jobless a week later.

JC had tapped out his bank account two months before, and mortgaged the club back when they had to retrofit the wall between the Rukus Room and the corner store. Strapped for cash, he accepted a low offer on his condo in Jersey, but wouldn't be able to close for about two months. He returned to New York to sell his car, furniture, and tie up a few other loose ends. With only three weeks to go until the grand opening, JC returned with enough cash to survive for a few months. He bought a decent car—a Caddy of course—so that Candace or Tamara could drive him, relieving Paul to concentrate on the bookstore, which was picking up business.

Two weeks before the grand opening, the third and last building inspector came to examine the club. That inspector was different. He was a mild-mannered, older man, delighted to be just six months shy of retirement. He and his wife of forty years planned to build a house on some land they inherited in Florida, just over the Georgia border. It was very close to Phillipsburg, the town JC was from. Perhaps his Southern upbringing was why he didn't furtively request kickbacks like the first two inspectors, who were paid under-the-table for passing grades. Like JC, the inspector worked on a farm as a child, so the two strolled through the club exchanging field stories. The inspection lasted until late afternoon, which meant the corner thugs were open for business when the old man was leaving. JC walked the inspector to his car to ensure his safety. As the little old man crept away into the dusk, JC was relieved to see there were some good, down-home folks in Long Beach.

Three days later, JC received the inspector's report, which he immediately took to Paul to examine. In addition to several minor corrections, the entire building had to be rewired. During a conversation with the inspector, JC later found out – in not so many words – he should have contributed to the old man's retirement fund if he expected a favorable report.

Even with his property as collateral, the bank turned JC down for a small business loan due to lack of a credit history. There was only one thing left, short of calling some shady "private bankers" he knew in New York. He was forced to mortgage the bookstore. Determined not to fail, JC borrowed enough to complete construction, order initial supplies, and promote the grand opening of "The Empire."

Chapter 9

"Drive to the front of the building," JC told Candace. He smiled like a kid on Christmas morning as he stared at the Apollo style marquee hovering above the front of the building. Every night at midnight, Nate changed the number of days until the opening on the marquee. The sign read "5 days to grand opening."

The box office sat directly below the marquee. It was less than twenty feet from the street and surrounded by marble and granite terrazzo floors that lead to three sets of double glass doors. Posters announcing the grand opening hung on each side of the doors.

JC hopped out of the car and stood on the opposite side of the street, admiring the sign. Things were finally coming together. The club was opening. Paul was getting enough business at the bookstore to take over the mortgage payment. And, Mama was finally on her way. She would have been there sooner but she refused to leave Georgia until they located a suitable church for her to attend. Her stipulation required Candace to visit churches each Sunday and report on the service to Mama. She also sent Mama audio and videotapes of the services and a list of programs each church had to help people in the community. Once Mama was satisfied that she had found a church home, she agreed to move.

Candace parked in the back and walked around to the front of the building where JC was still proudly standing. Never taking his eyes off the marquee, JC asked for the fifth time, "Did you get the flyers to—"

Candace quickly cut him off. "Yes JC, everything is done. The flyers, the deejay, I will pick up Mama, Trevor, and Auntie in the morning, and you have enough money left in the account to buy food. Stop worrying, everything is taken care of."

As the two entered the club, JC noticed water near the entrance. He looked around to see where it had come from but couldn't tell. The further they got inside, the deeper the water got. JC clicked the lights to find at least three inches of water covering the entire floor. A chunk of the ceiling, the source of the leak, had fallen behind the bar. JC was devastated.

A few hours later, JC sat at the bar, head in hands, waiting for the contractor and plumber to finish reviewing the damage to determine what the repairs would cost. Paul, Nate, Candace and Tamara worked diligently to get the water cleaned up. As usual, Dee the Diva was nowhere to be found. Candace swore Dee was on "ho duty," making a little extra cash when she wasn't around.

When the plumber walked away, the contractor approached JC, shaking his head. "The plumber said it will take two days to replace the pipes. It will take another two days for us to plaster the ceiling and walls. I won't charge you, but the plumbing will cost eight grand and he won't start until he gets half the money."

Candace and Paul heard eight grand and scurried over to join the conversation. Paul said, "That's a little steep. He can't do any better?"

The contractor explained, "The work is extremely complex. To be honest, he really gave you a good price considering the fact that his employees would need to work around the clock to get the job done in time for the grand opening. And they will be pushing it."

JC glanced at the clock, it was five PM. He turned to Candace, who kept the books and managed the checking account. "Candace, write him a check."

Candace didn't budge; she just stared intensely at JC. Both of them knew there wasn't enough money in the account.

"Candace, would you please go write the man a check?"

Candace grabbed Paul's hand and led him to the back office. She unlocked the bottom desk drawer and pulled out the checkbook. "Paul, we don't have that much in the account. JC knows we barely have the money for the food."

"I'd do it but I'm tapped out. I told JC this was a bad idea. We have never been this bad off. I don't know what he's thinking."

JC entered the room, urging Candace to hurry.

"Come on JC, it's time to cut your losses. You can't write that man a bad check, you can go to jail for that. This shit is getting crazy. Come on man."

"Write the check, Candace, and don't worry about it," JC said, as if Paul had never said a word. "Candace I need you to take me somewhere. Paul, can you meet us at Long Beach and Market in an hour?"

"For what? Did you hear anything I said? Do you ever listen to anyone else? JC—"

"Candace, give the man the check, I'll be in the car. Paul, meet us in an hour." JC still never responded to Paul. He just darted out of the room headed toward the back storage area. Candace wrote the check, grabbed her bag and the keys and headed out front where the contractor was waiting.

By the time Candace reached the car, JC was propped in the passenger seat going through a stack of papers. A garment bag was stretched across the back seat. JC handed Candace a street address on Market Street and the two made the three-mile ride in silence.

Candace pulled over and parked on Market Street directly in front of Top Dollar Pawn Shop. JC snatched the garment bag and ran into the store, returning about twenty minutes later without the garment bag, the medallion he wore around his neck or his diamond rings. He pointed and Candace reluctantly pulled off. As instructed, she drove two blocks, made a right turn, and about two car lengths ahead she swung a right into a used car lot.

About an hour later, Paul rode up and down Long Beach Boulevard looking for JC. He was so focused on spotting JC's Caddy, he was oblivious to the two pedestrians standing on the corner of Market Street. He heard his name called in the distance and glanced in his rear view mirror to see it was Candace and JC waving him down. The two ran up and jumped into Paul's car.

Paul asked, "Where's your car?"

The frigid silence told it all. Paul said no more. JC covered the check and then some.

Chapter 10

Mama refused to allow the doors of JC's Empire to open until they prayed and blessed the place. She was long–winded. Mid–way through her thanking the Lord for building their empire, JC leaned over and whispered to Paul, "Where was the Lord when I had to hoc my jewelry?" The two giggled and Mama yanked JC's right hand, letting him know to stop acting up. JC knew that later he'd be getting the usual lecture about how God answered her prayers and sent an angel to watch over him. Mama was convinced that angels kept her little boys safe when they ran off to the mean city. No matter how old he got, he was still her baby.

The Empire officially opened Feb. 9, 1995, six months late. JC was more than satisfied with the contractor's work. The dance floor was large enough to host a band and several hundred people. Brass handrails led to cozy private booths lining one side of the dance floor. A three-foot wall made of glass cinder blocks separated the booths from a game room with two pool tables and a variety of video games.

In the main area of the club, the huge bar was central to the entire club, allowing Candace, the bar manager, to keep her eye on everyone. On one side of the bar was a hallway ending at the door to the conference room. On the other side of the bar were a couple of steps that went up to the VIP area. The backside of the bar opened to a covered patio area with tables, a huge brick barbecue grill, and a birds-eye view of the parking lot.

Opening night was perfect. They had flashing lights, a jamming deejay, and Mama and Auntie were serving free chopped barbecue out on the patio. It was a small gathering, mostly family and friends, but JC was satisfied that, at last, the club was open. He knew it would take some time to promote the club and pack the house, but the closing on the condo was scheduled in a week so he would have enough money to pay the bills for a few months and do some promotions. Life was finally back on track.

Over the next few months, Tamara designed flyers and posters, which Nate and Trevor distributed around town. They held a contest and purchased commercial time on the local radio station offering free entry, thinking they would make money on alcohol sales. Aside from a mysterious fedora-wearing older gentleman who had become a permanent fixture at the bar, the only regulars were the family. The contest promotion drew a few new customers here and there, but nothing clicked enough to attract a real crowd. More people showed up to watch rehearsals Trevor held in the basement of The Empire for a hip-hop group he was trying to manage and produce. After months of trying everything short of sending limos for people, the crew started to believe that perhaps Long Beach just wasn't ready for The Empire.

The word around town was that the gang-bangers were the biggest drawback. This was a valid concern considering the fact that they did congregate less than three feet from the front and back entry of the club, and, Long Beach was constantly featured on the news credited with the fastest growing gang population in Los Angeles County. Drive-bys were a daily occurrence and the list of innocent victims falling prey to the rampant violence escalated rapidly. Parents didn't allow their young children to play outside, and the elderly no longer visited on porches as they had in the past. The gangs were winning; Long Beach was under siege.

Los Angeles was no better. But, people wanting to go out for a nice evening could go into certain areas —West LA, Century City and the like—not worrying about getting caught up in the middle of a gun fight.

As funds ran low, JC called everyone into the office to help come up with a plan. Of course, JC had a few things in mind.

JCsat at the head of a long rectangle lacquer conference table positioned in the middle of the room. Behind him was a sitting area with a black Italian leather couch and matching loveseat and a coffee table. A swanky chessboard boasting authentic ivory pieces was precisely placed on top of the table. On the other side of the office there was an over-sized black lacquer desk, matching file cabinets, and a plush, black leather desk chair. Photos of the family lined the walls. There was an aged photo of a young man standing next to a dartboard hanging on a tree, Paul in Panther attire, and a snapshot of JC, Candace and two children. In the corner was a small refrigerator with a dartboard on the wall above it.

Candace, Nate and Trevor joined JC at the table. Paul and his wife Tracy were there as well. Between the increasing business at the bookstore and his active toddler at home, Paul didn't spend as much time at the club. He attended meetings and stopped in the club regularly, but he wasn't really involved in the day-to-day operations. Dee was too disruptive to allow in business meetings.

Of course, each person in the room offered a different solution, but they all agreed that the thugs outside were the number one problem.

As usual, Paul deemed the situation hopeless. "JC, we been out here almost a year and it's not clicking. It's about time to unload the place. Folk don't want to come around those thugs."

"That's true, but I think we just need a big event," Candace said. "If people see a long line one time, everybody will want to come. Maybe we should think about Trevor's idea for hip-hop nights, JC."

"Who's gonna stand in a long line next to those thugs? Come on, I won't even stand out there with them," Paul said.

They went on for at least an hour exchanging ideas, from hip-hop nights to turning the club into a grocery store. JC never said a word. He was deep in thought.

Finally, JC interrupted the debate. "An event. We'll celebrate our anniversary. We need to make some noise—one good night and we're on. We're gonna let the people know The Empire is here for everyone."

"What's the difference? You still need people to show up. You think they'll come just because you're celebrating your anniversary? What about the gangs?" Paul asked.

"I'll handle that situation. Candace, you and Paul get on the phone and call the boys. Long Beach may not want to show up, so we'll pack the house with Easterners. We gonna do a Playas Ball."

"That's not a bad idea if we could pull it off in short notice. Out of town ballers don't know anything about the gangs," Paul said.

"And if they did, do you think any of them give a damn about a punk with a gun?"

Paul laughed in agreement and started getting excited about the event. "Two hundred a head, no less. I've paid more than three hundred dollars for a Playas Ball. Yeah, two hundred sounds like a plan!"

"I'll call Eddie and see if he will perform. He owes me. Maybe he'll bring his son—that kid is talented. What's his name?"

Trevor blurted out, "Gerald."

"Yeah, he can sang. Candace, I want to have something for the kids in the neighborhood during the day. Can you and Tamara take care of the games?"

"No problem."

"OK, let's have a celebration."

JC jumped up and headed straight out of the front door of the club. When he didn't return for a few minutes, Candace went out front where she saw JC having a conversation with the young hoods standing at the side of the building. One of the kids was engaged in an animated conversation on his cell phone. Candace stood in the door of the club, watching as a black Mercedes pulled up. The passenger door opened and Payback, a triple OG, or third generation "Original Gangster" who ruled the area, stepped out, dressed in a designer suit and high-priced gators.

He approached JC. "You looking for me?"

Candace summoned the crew to the door, worried that

something was about to go down. Trevor and Nate wanted to rush out but Paul stopped them, advising that JC would give some sort of sign if he needed backup. The former hustler knew stepping to an OG man-to-man implied you want to talk. Once your peeps join, that's considered a threat.

JC reached out and shook Payback's hand. "I'm JC Powell, I own The Empire."

Payback stood silent and intense. JC continued, "Your business is hurting my business. I'm here to see if we can come to some sort of agreement."

Payback retorted, "Agreement. Why would I agree on anything with you? I don't need you. I rule Long Beach."

JC drew from his best days as a hustler. He leaned in, suave as ever, and piled on his gracious southern twang. "Respect."

"Respect?" Payback snapped back, crossing his arms.

Payback was still there so JC knew he had him. It was time to work his magic. "That's right, respect. I'm just an old country boy trying to take care of my family. I'm sure you're doing the same. I just ask if you can move your boys down a block, one block, that's it. I'll make sure nobody at the club steps on your toes. A gentlemen's agreement, that means something where I'm from."

Payback took a second to think about JC's proposition. "JC, I like your style." He paused. "A block. I think we can do that." He reached out to shake JC's hand. The youngsters around him expressed a little dissatisfaction with the agreement but had no say in the matter, at least not for the time being.

Chapter 11

The marquee read, "1st Annual Playas Ball featuring Eddie Levert." Limos were lined up in front of the club waiting their turn to drop off old school players and celebrities from across the country. Wanna-be Ballers stood patiently in a line that wrapped around the corner. Each man escorted at least two fly girls; some had three or four on their side. Pimp gear abounded. Big hats, mink coats, and custom made suits. Exotic skin shoes made from a variety of animals like stingrays, alligator, crocodile, lizard, and other reptiles the average person never heard of. The bling-bling was blinding. They had diamonds in the most unusual places—diamond-lined canes, cups, cigarette holders, eyeglasses, teeth, and fingernails. Everyone took pride in being the most gaudy and ostentatious.

None of the Ballers in attendance thought twice about doling out $300 for entry. They would have paid more if JC asked–he had helped more than a few of them when they fell off and needed a little "re-up" money. The Playas spent triple the entry fee by the evening's end, popping bottles of Dom faster than beers at a Super Bowl party.

These were no ordinary street hustlers. They were the emperors of the underground economy. Most of them had not only touched down on every major corner in America, they'd also traveled throughout the world. France, England, Japan and Switzerland were frequent destinations for them. They owned fabulous homes in the states and kept posh condos in exotic places like Thailand, Morocco and Brazil. They hired top-notch lawyers and accountants, became cozy with high-level government officials and politicians, and learned to win at the foreign currency market.

They challenged each other when they were up, and helped one another when they were down—certainly important in a game where assets came and went in the twinkle of an eye. Unlike the thirty and under crew who ratted out friends and family for a deal before cops could snap the cuffs on good, old-school hustlers were loyal. They considered the "Nouveau Hustlers," to be bunch of hoods driven by emotion rather than business sense. True Playas despised the pseudo-hustlers whose violence had drawn attention to those of them who had coasted through life unnoticed by authorities in the past, changing the nature of game forever.

Inside the club was packed and the crowds outside continued to grow as people from around Long Beach came to witness the spectacle. JC, who had abandoned his Jheri curl for a ponytail, stood outside greeting each guest as they exited their limo. Hostesses hired for the evening escorted the visitors to the VIP area next to the bar.

There were over two hundred hood-rich hustlers in the house, decked in their best garbs, and JC was still the talk of the night. He had skillfully teamed a red pin-striped Armani Tindaril suit, with a white shirt and tie, white hat accentuated by a two inch red band, and a white calf-length mink coat. The real buzz was about his custom made ostrich shoes that had genuine diamond chips layered across solid gold buckles.

Once the VIP arrivals began to wane, JC made his way back to the family table on the patio where his mother and sisters barbecued racks of lamb, beef ribettes, salmon, and shrimp kebabs. The parking lot was filled with children's games and the neighborhood kids were still playing in jumpers rented for the anniversary celebration.

Felix Calhoun was in town from Atlanta. He traveled back and forth to Long Beach on business so he had kept in contact with JC after they met at the family reunion. Felix was definitely a smooth-talking hustler wanna-be and slicker than all the eel shoes in the club that night. Dressed in a designer suit and expensive jewelry, Felix snuck up behind JC and whispered in his ear. JC jumped up and hugged him. "Oh man, you made it." JC turned to the people at the table announcing, "This is Felix. We met in Atlanta. Felix, you know Paul, and that's my daughter, Cherie. She's Candace's daughter."

Felix greeted everyone like he had known him or her for years—a real no-no in the Powell family. They were always suspicious of people who got too familiar too quickly. Felix glanced around the club. "I didn't know you was rolling like this. Real nice set-up, man. Real nice."

"Thanks. It's been rough but I think it's finally paying off. Oh, Tamara, come over here and meet Felix."

As JC introduced Tamara, Dee trotted over, pushing her way in next to Felix, who had cashed in his finger waves and was completely bald. "I'm Dee. I spoke to you on the phone a few times. Mmm, you look better than you sound." She kissed him on the ear, flirting as usual. Felix didn't reciprocate. He wasn't that country.

"Dee, can you get Felix a drink? What you drinking man, Remy?" JC said.

"You know it."

Dee yelled over to the bar, ordering Candace to bring Felix a shot of Remy. Candace had hired four extra bartenders to help for the event and the bar was still swamped. She chipped in where she could, but Candace was too clean to work. She was wearing a skin-tight black leather skirt accessorized with a gold Versace belt that highlighted her small waist and perfectly shaped hips. Her black knit sweater trimmed with mink was held together with a lone hook at the breast line, revealing just enough stomach and cleavage to keep JC's attention off the herd of fabulous women on the prowl for a man with deep pockets. Her outfit was topped off with a Louis Feraud mink shawl with a Chinchilla trim. The matching mink hat was cocked just right, almost covering her right eye.

Dee's loud and obnoxious behavior was already getting on JC's nerves. He flagged her away and said, "Go over there and get the drink, Dee. Candace is busy."

Dee huffed off, mumbling under her breath, "I need to hire a real bartender."

Tamara pushed a chair over to Felix so he could sit next to JC and darted back to her post at the door. JC whispered to Felix, "I have to keep at least two women. Dee is the feisty one—always ready for a good argument. Tamara is the sweet one." The two laughed.

Paul, who was sitting on JC's opposite side and overheard him, said, "You need to leave them both alone and find a wife." He always attributed JC's womanizing to his breakup with Candace. Although JC was always honest to women and kept his relationships in the open, Paul wondered how long any good woman would tolerate his meandering. "You're going to end up old and alone," he told JC.

"Don't hate the playa', hate the game." JC said laughing. "Felix, when we gonna meet your wife?"

"She's a homebody."

"Is that right?"

Once the deejay introduced Eddie Levert, everyone's attention went to the stage for the performance, except JC, who grooved to the music while admiring Candace as she directed her bartending staff.

Just as the show was ending, Trevor zipped in, donning low-hanging designer jeans, a FUBU jersey, and neatly styled, crisscrossed cornrows. He pulled his chair to the side of JC and asked, "Dad, did you think about what I asked you?"

JC was so engrossed in the music, he heard him but didn't answer.

Determined to get his way with his dad, Trevor continued to drill him, "Dad did you–"

"What are you talking about?"

"Showcasing my acts here," Trevor said.

"How many times do I have to tell you, I don't want that rap mess in here? I don't need no more problems with them thugs."

"Just because it's rap doesn't mean it's gangsta' music."

"That stuff isn't even music, just a bunch of angry people talking smack to a beat." JC pointed to Levert on stage. "That's real music." He bobbed his head, watching the show for a few seconds. "Plus, half those youngsters are too cheap to buy drinks. They ain't nothing but problems."

Trevor jerked back in his chair and grumbled, "You never listen to me. All I want is Thursday nights. It's a slow night anyway, what can it hurt?"

"You better watch your tone if you want to make it to next Thursday," JC said, staring Trevor in the eyes. "You need to get your ass back in school so you can get out and make some real money. Stop all that crazy talk."

Paul tried to lighten things up. He was the self-appointed peacekeeper between JC and Trevor. "The apple don't fall far from the tree does it? Who do I remember saying have a dream and a plan?"

"Yeah, a plan that makes some damn sense. Not this foolishness he's talking. That mess is a crapshoot," JC said.

Paul laughed. "Crapshoot? And riding a bus to New York without a dime or a place to live, what was that? Escaping New York for the glitz and glamour of Hollywood?"

JC turned his attention back to the show. In his mind he knew his brother was correct; he had taken some crazy chances in his life. So crazy that JC was convinced his mother was right. He imagined that it must have been an angel or something watching over him because it always worked itself out. JC's meditation was cut short when a couple came over and tapped him on the shoulder. He got up to shake their hands and stepped to the side of the table to take a photo with them.

As he sat back down, Paul figured he had cooled off and asked, "Why not give the boy a shot?"

"I hustled all my life for my kids to go to college, have a career, not run around with thugs." JC turned to Felix, pointed at Trevor and said, "He thinks he's a music producer and a manager. I told him he needs to find some real musicians if he wants to be in the music business."

By this point, Trevor was enraged. He huffed, sucked his teeth, and abruptly slid his chair back a few more feet.

Felix said, "I agree that a lot of rap music is junk, but some rap music will make your grandmother do the two-step."

"We rehearse right downstairs and you won't even come down

and listen." Trevor crossed his arms and continued to pout.

Felix said, "You just have to watch who you let in on those nights. I'll help him on promotions. It's what I do. It could be good for business, JC."

Paul looked Felix up and down suspiciously. "Promotions must pay good these days."

"I do okay," Felix said.

"In Atlanta?"

"All over. I do a lot of business in Long Beach so I'm always here. But I have a college degree in marketing." Felix turned to Trevor. "You do need to finish college Trevor. School is very important."

JC slammed his hand on the table. "That's what I'm sayin'." He pointed his finger at Trevor. "You hear that? He went to college. College. He got an education first."

"JC, he can still go to school," Paul said.

JC paused a moment then responded, "Okay. Here's the deal. You know I'm not coming in that nasty basement, so rehearse upstairs tomorrow. If it's not a bunch of cussing and banging, we can try it out."

"That's all I ask." Trevor continued, "Now, about the deejay."

JC said to Felix, "See what I have to deal with? Give 'em an inch," he said, shaking his head. He turned to Trevor and firmly said, "I'm not replacing the deejay. He's in college and I promised his mom he'd have a job as long as he needed one." JC's attention went to Candace walking by in her tight fitting leather skirt. He admired how well the diamond heart necklace he gave her adorned her ample upper body.

Levert came back to the stage with back-up singers to perform "For the Love of Money," JC's favorite song. JC jumped up and grabbed Candace's arm as she passed. "Ooh, there's my song! Let's dance."

Before Candace could officially resist, JC had dragged her to the middle of the crowd. The two were both quick on their feet and quite at home on the dance floor. The crowd backed up to give them room as they broke into the hustle. Every time JC pulled her too close, Candace pulled away, careful to keep a mental and physical distance between them. Holding Candace's hand with all of his might, JC tossed Candace out, twirled her back in, and softly shoved her to the side. Candace and JC had performed this dance hundreds of times in the past and Candace could always count on JC's strength to shield her from the gravitational challenges. That was almost twenty years ago – almost a lifetime. For a brief second she hesitated, but eventually conceded. She crossed her arms and gracefully plunged backward; secure that JC would be there to catch her. The moment her head felt the security of JC's strong arms, their eyes met and for a moment, they both knew the wall was dismantling.

Chapter 12

Trevor was upstairs with his acts rehearsing when JC arrived at the club the next afternoon. Felix was perched on a stool on the sideline, offering directions. JC took a seat at the bar near Candace, who had spent the evening scrutinizing Felix while she set up for the night. He had already rubbed her the wrong way waving his glass at her when he wanted his drink refilled on the night of the Playas Ball. Watching him order Trevor around that evening reinforced her first impression.

Within a few beats of the first song, JC was dancing in his seat enjoying the performance. He was surprised to see how polished the group was, and amazed at Trevor's professional demeanor with the acts.

"See, he's smart and talented. You should stop trying to control him. You have to learn to let go and let God," Candace said. "Let him pursue his dream."

A naughty grin crept on JC's face. With his most charming and provocative southern drawl, he said, "Speaking of dreams, I have a few of my own I'd like to pursue—can you help a brother out?"

Candace anxiously busied herself wiping over the sparkling counter, her chin buried on her chest. She was careful to avoid eye contact with JC when he was focused on becoming more than friends. There was no way she would give in to JC's charm. When she left New York, she had put that episode of her life behind her. As much as she loved JC, she would never again entrust her heart to him.

Trevor and Felix came over to the bar just in time to stop JC from getting his beg on. Trevor was hyped. "Dad, what do ya' think?"

"Excellent! I think you got something there son. Real jazzy. But how do you make money?"

Dee made her usual dramatic entry into the club. With her arms flailing about, she stopped to give Tamara a few orders, whisked past the bar shouting, "JC, I need to speak with you," and then darted into the back room. She was fussing about work that needed to be done and how the dirt kept getting in her purse. The dirt was a daily argument for Dee. She swore Candace was putting dirt in her purse and jacket pockets every night. Candace ignored her, assuming whatever drugs Dee was taking made her paranoid and the dirt was actually tobacco from her nasty cigarettes. As usual, no one paid any attention to Dee's drama.

JC asked Trevor again, "Money. How do you make it?"

Trevor worked hard to gain approval from his dad and was thrilled to have a business conversation with him. "I get a percentage as the manager. I wrote all the songs and own all the publishing so I will get royalties for life once the song is a hit."

"What does it mean in dollars boy? I don't understand that stuff," JC said, still ignoring Dee's summons from the back room.

Extremely animated, Felix peeled off his bar stool, gave Trevor a pound and said, "It means your son is fixin' ta' bubble when these acts get a deal. We're aiming for a six figure advance."

"Is that right?" JC paused for a moment. "You can start next Thursday, but you have to screen the crowd carefully. If we have any problems, you're going to have to stop."

Candace said, "What did I tell you, Trevor? Didn't I say the dollars would get his attention? You should have talked money first. He would have agreed sooner."

"Ain't no shame to my game. If it don't make money, it don't make sense!" JC said as he walked toward the back room. He finally responded to Dee's nagging, "You need to check that damn drama. I'm telling you, I don't keep drama around."

For the next week, Trevor and Felix promoted "Hip-Hop

Thursday's" throughout Long Beach and the surrounding area. They started their last day of promotions around eight Thursday morning, catching the working bunch during rush hour. While Trevor stapled posters to the side of buildings and on trees, smooth-talking Felix convinced store owners to display the posters in their windows and handed out flyers to customers. Felix was at home with promotions. He could have convinced a few senior citizens to hang out that night. He hit parked cars and passed out flyers to work-bound people who were stopped at red lights. Felix was a hustler for sure.

After a few hours of vigorously promoting the first hip-hop night at The Empire, Trevor headed to LAX to drop Felix off so he could catch a plane home to Atlanta.

"We did work this morning. Everybody in town has to know about the event. I sure wish you could be there tonight."

"So do I. But, I gotta get back. It's my wife's birthday. She'd kill me if I wasn't there."

"I feel ya' dog, family first. Which airline?"

"Delta," Felix answered. "I only fly Delta. My wife works for them. Speaking of family, where's your mom?"

"New York. But I always lived with my dad."

"I hear ya'. I'mma be in New York soon. I got a big deal on the table there." He glanced at the signs in front of them. "Departures," he said, pointing. "There it is, pull over right up there, thatta work."

"I'll call and let you know how it turns out tonight. Yo dog, if you give me a call next week, I'll pick you up." He gave Felix a pound. "Thanks again for lookin' out. I couldn't have done it without you."

"No problem. It's what I do."

Later that evening, Trevor's acts were warming up at the club. Tamara was at the bar getting money from Candace to prepare to open. She whispered to Candace, "I broke it off with JC."

Candace dropped half of the ice from the bag she was emptying and turned to Tamara. "What did he do?"

"We had an understanding. If we find someone and get

serious, we move on," Tamara said. "I guess he found someone."

Candace huffed, "Dee? Please. I know JC. She doesn't mean anything to him. She won't be around much longer, believe me."

"She is bothersome." Tamara giggled and leaned in to whisper, "I bought a doll for her."

"A doll?"

"Mmm hmm, cooking wasn't the only thing they were teaching in the back woods of Louisiana! My mother was a Queen."

Candace was speechless. She just stared at Tamara in shock.

Tamara continued, "I hardly see JC anyway. He comes Sunday morning to go to church and leaves in the middle of the night."

"Sunday?" Candace loved telling stories. "A wise old lady once told me." She paused, hunched up and changed her voice like an old lady. "She said, baby, as a rule, people save their best for Sunday. Best shoes, best clothes, best food. So you all right, long as you see your man on Sunday."

The two chuckled. "It's not just Dee." Tamara started to explain, but before she could get it out, Trevor came in, hyped up and anxious about his first night.

"What's up?" Trevor said.

"Not much. You ready for tonight?" Candace asked.

"Yeah. Me and Felix sniped all of Long Beach."

"You know, I saw him in LA a little while ago. He didn't even speak," Tamara said.

"In LA? It wasn't Felix. He left for Atlanta this morning."

"Really? My bad. Well, he must have a twin 'cause it looked just like him," Tamara said as she walked away.

"I'm glad everything is set for tonight, but did you register for school?" Candace asked Trevor.

"There you go. You're about as bad as my dad; sweatin' me on school. I'm trying to get ends. There's a lot of broke brothers with college degrees."

Trevor nodded toward Dee, who was across the room, swinging her arms, giving orders. "I can't stand that witch. I'mma end up goin' off on her."

"You just concentrate on Trevor and leave Dee to me. Trust me, I got that."

Chapter 13

Hip Hop Thursday was a huge success. Every week, more and more people were turned away. Friday and Saturday nights were just as crowded. It had been ten months since the Playas Ball, but people were still talking about the event like it was yesterday. Word of the club traveled and people came from all over Los Angeles County to hang among the "who's-who" at The Empire.

The club drew such large crowds the fire marshals made The Empire a regular stop Thursday thru Saturday nights. Nate kept a careful count at the door so they were never hit with a fine, but the marshals still stopped by, counting heads, hoping one extra body slipped past security. The marshals thought they were harassing JC—he refused to pay any more kickbacks. They didn't realize that, in LA, frequent visits by the marshals established the credibility of the club. They had to be hot.

Jazz Sunday, Monday bid whist tournaments and Wednesday Star Search attracted comfortable crowds as well. Bottom line: the club was making money faster than they could keep track of it. Even at the reduced price of $12 a head, they were bringing in over thirty thousand dollars a week just from the door. The liquor and food netted twice that much. JC had retrieved his bling—plus some. He bought a house in Bixby Knolls, a swanky neighborhood right outside of downtown Long Beach. He also upgraded his Caddy to a Rolls Royce with all the bells and whistles, and employed Nate as his full-time driver. Felix had maneuvered into a position doing promotions, even though Paul thought that there was something seedy about him.

JC was definitely on top. But, he had been in the game long enough to know that with ups come some downs. Although Payback had kept his word and they had no problems from his crew for the past ten months, JC noticed a few new faces among the thugs at the corner and they were inching closer to the club each day. They hadn't quite crossed the line, but JC sensed drama in the making.

Less than three weeks after seeing the new faces on the block, JC and Paul were seated on the patio enjoying a normal Saturday night at The Empire. Candace noticed a couple of thugs selling drugs the parking lot behind the club and went over to ask them to move. Trevor saw Candace headed toward the group and ran behind her.

Candace approached the young men politely. "Excuse me. I thought we agreed that you'd keep your business away from here."

"That agreement got canceled. Havoc's back in town," replied Havoc, a twenty-nine-year-old black Mexican fresh out of prison. His outfit—beige khaki's and a Raiders T-shirt— announced his gang affiliation. He was stout, no taller than 5' 7, and had his shoulder length hair parted down the center with a twisted pigtail on each side.

Trevor ran up. "Take that shit out of here."

"Who the hell you talking to? Do you know who I am?" Havoc stepped closer to Trevor. "If you don't know, ya' betta ask somebody."

Candace blocked Trevor as he lunged toward Havoc pointing his finger in his face. "I don't give a damn who you are, you better move the hell on."

"Trevor, leave it alone," Candace said, pulling him away.

"You betta git ya' mind right partna'. Figure out who I am punk," Trevor said.

Havoc glanced over at the club where the family was seated and saw JC and Paul stand up. He turned to his boys, "Let's be out, I ain't tryin' to get caught up tonight over some bullshit."

Havoc walked around the building with the young thugs following like puppies. Trevor was still hyped and talking mess. He shouted, "That's right, you ain't tryin' at see me, and don't bring your black ass back busta'."

"Trevor, shut up and go inside. Your mouth is going to get you in trouble," Candace said as she pushed him toward the club.

Before Candace could get back to the bar, Dee stormed over to her. "Candace, I've told you over and over, don't leave the bar area. Stop getting in everybody's business and do your job."

As usual, Candace ignored Dee and continued walking. Dee followed, shouting at her from behind. Candace let Dee babble on for a few seconds about other peoples' business. Without ever looking her way, Candace nonchalantly said, "Everybody's business is my job, Dee."

"Why? Because you're JC's baby's Mama? You must still want him."

"Don't get it twisted. I ended it, not him."

"Then you need to recognize, I run this show," Dee said.

Candace faced Dee. "You really have been smoking too much of that mess. Did you ever notice nobody listens to your constant drama? We tolerate you because of JC. But the truth is, you ain't about la-dee-da up in here."

Dee went straight ghetto, stepping toward Candace yelling, "I'm tired of your shit. I'm warning you. I'm not gonna take much more of this mess from you."

Candace turned to her and said, "And?" Dee didn't respond. Candace stepped closer to Dee, eye-to-eye, and very calmly said, "Don't let your mouth write a check your ass can't cash."

JC darted over when he noticed the tension between the bickering duo. "What's going on?"

"Nothing. Dee was just telling me she needs to cover a bad check."

"You need some money, Dee?" JC asked.

Dee gathered her thoughts and made a quick comeback. "I'll attain it when we get home honey." She smirked at Candace and walked away, satisfied that she had just delivered a low blow.

JC's head leaned sideways, checking out Dee's butt as she sauntered off. Her stride was a bit subdued by her tight-fitting flowered bell-bottom pants.

When JC looked up, Candace was still staring at him astonished. "Home?" she said.

"Candace, the girl didn't have anywhere to go. It's just until she finds a place." A big grin rolled across JC's face, "You jealous?"

"Please!" She said, sucking her teeth. "I just hope you know that girl got plenty of game. She don't play well, but it's still game. You better watch your back."

The next day, the family was in the back office having a daily business meeting. The gangs were the focus of the discussion. JC was concerned about Payback's crew reneging on their agreement. He knew one violent incident would send his loyal customers running to the next "hot" club.

"I can't figure out what's up with Payback's boys. I thought we settled our problems," JC said.

Trevor said, "They look up and see a nine in their face they'll learn some respect."

"Trevor stop talking crazy," Paul said. He turned to JC. "JC, you can't run the world. Let them boys have their corner. Hell, let them have the block, long as they don't bring it here."

"We already know the customers won't come around that madness. Candace, call one of them agencies and find a couple of people to help with security."

"I'll get on it right away," Candace said. "Oh, I almost forgot, did ya'll hear about Neicey's mother?"

"Neicey who works with you at the bar?" Paul asked as he maneuvered behind the table to pick up a stack of flyers off the shelf on the wall.

"Yeah she got shot in her front yard, only fifty years old. It's just so sad. Her family is trying to raise money for the funeral. If anybody wants to contribute let me know."

"These youngsters are out of control. Take her $500 from the club. Mmh mmh mmh, just so sad," JC said.

"You got to go sometime," Trevor said.

"You need to check that thug attitude." JC looked around the table. "Anything else?"

"Just one thing." Paul handed each person a stack of flyers. "Akbar will speak at the bookstore next month so I want all of you to give out some flyers. And, I expect to every one of you to be there." He peered over at JC with a raised brow.

"You know I'll definitely be there."

While they all piled out of the room chatting about the gangs and Neicey's mother, JC motioned Candace to wait. "Take the $500 to Neicey, then just go pay for the funeral. Don't worry about the cost. Just make sure they put her away right. And tell them folks at the funeral home this is a private transaction. Know what I mean?"

By the following Thursday, hip-hop night, Candace had hired three extra security guards for the front and back of the club. They were definitely not hired security from an agency. The two in the front were directing an unruly crowd pushing and shoving to enter the club. One of them, Jim, was tall, a bit grumpy, and looked close to sixty years old. The other one, Fat Daddy, stood only four feet six inches, but he was doing an excellent job keeping the line in order.

Havoc, garbed in his usual uniform, was at the front box office with Payback, trying to get into the club. Things got a little heated when Tamara told them she could not let them in because of Havoc's attire. In addition to his gang outfit, several of Havoc's jailhouse tatts were in clear view. A four-inch high tattoo of the number twenty was stamped on the left side of his neck, "HATE" was printed across his knuckles, and two teardrops—boasting his murder count—were painted on his face beneath his left eye.

Nate rushed over to help Tamara who was obviously intimidated by Havoc. "I'm sorry sir. The young lady said you can't get in. Please move on, you're holding up the line."

"I just want to know why we can't get in. I never had a problem before," Payback said.

Nate pointed to the wall slightly behind Payback. There was a poster promoting the Akbar Jones event at the bookstore next to a sign saying "NO GANG ATTIRE OR TATTOOS."

"There is a dress code," Nate said.

Havoc said, "What's up with dat? We just tryin' come in an' have a good time."

Trevor ran up to Havoc with Felix following directly behind. They both took a double look at the feisty little guard effectively handling crowd control. Trevor shouted, "I'm tired of tellin' you the same damn thing. Move the hell on and don't bring your ass back."

Havoc stepped back, opened his jacket with his left hand, and revealed a handgun stuck in the waist of his pants. "You betta' watch how you talk to me busta."

Felix jumped between Havoc and Trevor and tried to calm the two down. "Trevor, Trevor, go inside. Let me handle this. Go inside."

"Betta' tell dat mark whose hood dis is. He gonna get hurt talkin' shit."

"Havoc, we don't want trouble. Please, just move on."

JC, Candace, and Paul went outside to see what the brouhaha was about.

"What's going on? Is there a problem?" JC asked.

Havoc and Felix eyeballed each other for a few long seconds. Payback pulled Havoc by the arm and nodded toward JC. "No problem JC, we out."

"Hold on Payback," JC said. "You don't have to leave. Payback, you're welcome to come to the club anytime, no charge. But you understand, the young man has to follow the dress code. That's all I ask."

Payback acknowledged what JC said and left with Havoc. As the two walked to Payback's car about a block down, Havoc asked, "Why'd you just walk away? We shoulda' busted a cap in they ass."

"Wasn't the time," Payback replied.

"I told you JC is steppin' on your toes, cuz'. I heard he's pushin' a lot of work. Dat's really why he ain't lettin' us near da club. Where you think all dat money comin' from? We outta go take his Rolls, he bought it stealin' yo business. I know you ain't gonna let him do you like dat cuz."

It took a few minutes for Nate and the new security to get the crowd that had assembled in front of the club under control. JC caught Candace's attention. He looked at the newly hired security force and then gave her a probing look. Candace shrugged her shoulders and said, "They needed work."

As everyone headed back into the club, JC pulled Trevor to the side and went completely off on him. "You looking for trouble? You better learn to respect people. You think you tough cause your daddy got some change? Think money makes you a man? A man respects people, you may learn from them. You never know who your Angel is."

Trevor started to walk into the club. JC jerked him back. "You think we was born sittin' on high cotton? No. We was pickin' cotton, all of us. See him?" JC pointed to a homeless man down the street. "There but for the grace of God go US. I'm telling you. YOU better get YOUR mind right, partna', or you're gonna have some real problems in life."

Chapter 14

Trevor had a good friend named Khalil who moved from New York to Long Beach about three years before him. Khalil was handsome, sharp, musically gifted, and had family in the entertainment business. Within a year of landing on the west coast, Khalil had a number one hit song on the radio, his own fully-financed record label, and was making big money. The two hung out from time to time and Khalil promised to look out for Trevor when he started his own label. Khalil was at the club to check out Trevor's acts live.

Like a cop with radar, Dee spotted Khalil seated on the side of the stage sipping a drink and watching the performance. Khalil was a year older than Trevor and smooth as silk. He reminded everyone of JC in his heyday. He had JC's finesse, but he bore a striking resemblance to LL Cool J—rippled abs and all.

Dee nearly knocked a few customers over to get to him. "Hi, I'm Dee, the hostess."

"What's up," Khalil said. He nodded at Dee but didn't pay much attention to her.

"Let me know if you have any specific requirements," Dee said as she walked away, realizing that Khalil's attention was on the energetic show Trevor's act was putting on.

Trevor had gone all out. Three gorgeous girls flanked the rapper, 562-JazzyJ. The Hot Girlz performed a well-rehearsed dance routine dressed in sexy, but classy, attire. Lights flashed and smoke appeared to rise from the floor. Khalil studied the tightly choreographed performance, listened intently to the militant lyrics protesting police brutality, and was impressed by the positive response from the crowd. The young people danced, others tried to sing along, and old timers at the bar were bobbing their heads in enjoyment. The deal was cemented when one of the Hot Girlz broke into a rap solo that could have put Ice Cube to shame. The young ladies weren't just fine, they had serious lyrical talent.

Dee was determined not to let a rich, handsome, celebrity come through the doors of The Empire without getting to know her. She returned to Khalil's table with a drink. "This one is on me," she said. With the drink still in her hand, she leaned over far enough for Khalil to have a clear view of her only physical assets and whispered, "As I said, if you need anything, anything at all, let me know."

Khalil thanked her, took the drink and continued to watch the show. Dee didn't move. Khalil looked up at her and said, "You look familiar, do I know you?"

"Not yet."

"No, you really do look familiar, have we met before?"

Trevor and Felix walked up. Trevor shouted over the noise, "She's a porn queen. Paid ho."

Dee took off, angry as usual.

"Oh snap, that's it! That's where I know her from." Khalil said, laughing as he stood up to talk to Trevor. "Man, your acts are the bomb. We can work with them. Especially those fine ass girls."

"I knew you'd like them. They got serious skillz. Know what I mean?"

Felix stepped in as if he knew Khalil for years, "Yo, you think we can make somethin' happen?"

Khalil never acknowledged Felix. He continued talking to Trevor as if Felix wasn't there. Trevor eventually introduced Felix to Khalil, but Khalil still showed no love. Khalil was a lot like JC. It took him a while to warm up to strangers–he didn't trust them.

Khalil asked Trevor, "Yo, you got enough material for those girls to produce an entire CD?"

"You know me, dog. I got anuf shazit for twenty CDs right downstairs. I'm always writing."

"Can you get a demo for me to play for my peeps at the label?"

"Most definitely. I can get a package for you right now." Trevor asked Felix to go into the basement to get a package for the group. Felix disappeared into the crowd.

Khalil said, "I'mma talk to my team and see when we can get ya'll into the studio to put somethin' down."

"Cool. We're ready."

"Trevor, you know this is a cut-throat industry so do like I said and handle your business."

"You sound like my dad."

"Your dad is right. You have to handle business first," Khalil added.

While Khalil and Trevor were catching up on gossip from the Big Apple, JC walked by on his way to run off the man Candace had been engaged in conversation with for a little too long. Part of JC's existence was to make sure he blocked any possible action Candace could get. He knew she would eventually find a man, but it wouldn't be on his watch. Candace was shrewd enough to know what JC was up to. She also knew the real reason JC bought a condo for her. He knew she would never disrespect him and bring a man into a place he paid for.

Trevor grabbed JC before he made it to his post. "Dad, come meet my boy, Khalil. Khalil this is—"

"I know who this is." Khalil said reaching out to shake JC's hand. "Everybody in the LBC knows the man who put us on the map. I'm honored to meet you, Mr. Powell."

JC smiled and politely returned the compliment. "I'm just an old country boy trying to make a living. But you, I hear all those hit records you're putting out." JC stepped to the side so he'd have a better view of the events playing out at the bar. Candace was still engrossed in a conversation with a refined looking gentleman dressed in an eggshell-colored linen suit. The man was tall, dark and gorgeous. After closer examination, JC concluded that the brother was "too pretty" and resumed his conversation with Khalil. "I'm honored to meet you, young man."

"JC," a voice called. It was Tamara beckoning him to the front. "JC, I need you out front for a second."

"They can't live without me. I'd better go see what she needs. It was good to meet you, Khalil. Trevor has been bragging on you since high school." As JC strolled over to Tamara, he yelled out jokingly to her, "You kicked me to the curb. Now you need me?"

After a really long time, Felix returned and handed Khalil an envelope that held a folder with pictures of Trevor's groups, two CDs, and a couple of bios.

"I'll get at ya' Trevor," Khalil said, clutching Trevor's hand and pulling him closer. As they embraced, he whispered, "Handle your business homie and watch your back. There's a lot of snakes out here."

"I hear ya'. Thanks for coming out, homie."

Dee saw Khalil exiting the club and ran over to slip him her phone number. Trevor peeped her move from across the floor, laughed and shook his head.

JC had made it to the bar to block any possible action for Candace. He was sitting at the bar telling her about the three teens he saw standing near the entrance of the club. "One of them was doing the Crip walk to loud music blasting from a blue low-rider that was parked in front of them. There were some new faces and all of them looked like sho'nuff bangers."

"I've noticed a lot of new faces out there, too," Candace said.

"The one they call Havoc walked up to the kids and you would have thought Jesus returned. While he was talking to them, he kept pointing at the club. Payback better watch his back with that boy."

"Yeah, I really think something is up."

JC smiled flirtatiously. "Speaking of something being up, can I get a little Sex on the Beach?"

"Sure," Candace chuckled.

Sex on the beach was a daily ritual for JC. It started with him sneaking a quick peek of Candace's cleavage as she leaned down to get a can of pineapples from beneath the bar. She reached up and grabbed a highball glass from the rack above her head and stuck it into a tray of ice. JC watched intensely as she positioned the can in the can opener, pushed down on the handle until the sharp point entered the can. He was titillated when she pressed the button and the can began to slowly gyrate until there was a low pop. Candace poured the grapefruit, frozen cranberry juice, and a tad of coconut milk into a blender. She added about eight ice cubes, put the lid on and clicked the "on" button.

The blender rotated until a smooth, thick liquid formed. JC gawked as Candace slowly poured the creamy mixture into a chilled highball glass. She garnished it with a pink umbrella, laid a napkin on the bar in front of JC and gently placed the drink on the bar. JC propped his elbow on the bar and rested his chin in the palm of his hand. He was consumed with lust as she delicately dipped her index finger into the glass, wiggled it around, and then seductively licked the gelatinous potion from her finger.

"Umm, it's just right." Candace said, shooting JC a devilish grin.

JC was mesmerized. Candace was tickled. Performing her sensual dance each night for JC was a ritual for her as well.

A customer interrupted the intimate moment. "Hi, Candace," the customer said.

"Hey girl, what can I do you for?" Candace asked.

"Heineken." The young lady spoke to JC for a minute then turned back to Candace and asked, "Candace, who was that fine brotha' I saw you with at the mall?"

"Girl, he was just a friend."

"Looked like more than a friend the way ya'll was hugged up. He was F-I-N-E fine. If he has a brother, make sure you give him my number," the customer said and walked away, leaving JC agitated and uneasy.

There was a strained silence. Though he tried to hide it, JC was visibly upset. JC fidgeted for as long as he could. He ate a few peanuts from the bar, checked his watch a couple of times, and wiped his shoes with a napkin. He tried to stay calm but finally blurted out, "So you seeing somebody?"

"Oh, it's nothing," Candace nonchalantly replied.

JC waited for Candace to offer more information but she

never stopped preparing drinks. He ate a few more peanuts, took a toothpick from the bar, slid it in his mouth and then abruptly changed his tone. "Nothing? What do you mean nothing?"

The tension was mounting between the two. To keep from getting into a debate with JC, Candace never uttered a word. She just quietly continued working. JC took a sip of his Virgin Sex on the Beach and mumbled, "Picture that, a woman who would rather have nothing than everything."

He had finally pushed her button. "That's my low self-esteem. I don't think I'm good enough for the PERFECT man."

Candace stormed off to take an order from someone seated on the crowded patio. As soon as she stepped onto the patio, she noticed the blue low-rider roll up into the back lot, showcasing their hydraulics. The car bounced through the entire parking lot blasting loud music, exited the lot, and parked on the street. No one got out of the car.

When Candace returned to the bar, JC was gone but the handsome man she had been talking to earlier was back. When Paul took a seat at the bar, the man took off to the dance floor.

"Did I run your friend away?" Paul asked.

"Him?" Candace looked over at the man and said, "Nah, not my type. Be right back." She went to deliver the drink to a customer on the patio. Just as she leaned in to place the drink on the table, the low-rider quietly rolled toward the club, clicking switches. A voice in the crowd shouted, "Gun! He's got a gun!"

People in the crowd dove for cover. They knocked over tables and drinks. The car screeched off. Felix jumped up and stood amid the chaos announcing, "Everybody calm down, calm down. There's no gun. Everything's OK. Please, calm down."

Candace rolled her eyes at Felix then returned to the bar. Felix followed. "Candace, we need to give free refills. Candace. Candace, we should give these people free drinks."

"I heard you Felix." Candace never looked at him. She just continued preparing drinks.

"Attention everyone, your next drink is on the house," Felix announced in his most official voice and hurried back outside, making more announcements.

Paul was amazed by Felix's take-charge behavior. "I've got to leave this mess alone," Paul told Candace.

"Your brother needs you around."

"Why? He never listens to me, or anyone else for that matter." Paul took a gulp of his soda and added, "Anyway, you watch everybody's back, except the HO—I mean hostess."

"I don't trust that witch," Candace said.

"You know you don't have anything to worry about, baby girl. JC's merely passing time with her. He's waiting for you."

"It doesn't have anything to do with JC."

"Sure," Paul said chuckling. Candace was always trying to convince people that the problems she had with Dee weren't about JC; it was rooted in the score she needed to settle from the Rukus Room. Paul wasn't buying it, nor did he buy JC's story that they had to leave New York because of the violence. "Got all of us out here in California, following you. He should have just apologized."

"Not JC, he never apologizes. Why would he? JC does no wrong."

"He's just like our daddy, got a saying for everything, except sorry."

"JC won't change. But you really did change your life. I know it wasn't easy," Candace said, as she kept her eye on Dee who was now snuggled up in the corner with the good looking man that she had been talking with. Candace was all smiles when she saw Dee write her number on a napkin and hand it to the guy. As she cleaned the bar, she noticed a box and a card with her name on it. She opened the card and it read:

I know you like to keep it quiet, but I still remember and always will. Happy Birthday. You will always have a place in my heart.

Love JC

Candace opened the box to find a gold locket with a photo of her, JC, and two young children. Obviously moved, she stood staring at the locket. Numb.

Paul finished his drink and went to the back to speak with JC. He passed Trevor who had just heard about the uproar and was on his way to the patio to get the scoop on the ruckus. Paul warned Trevor to forget it. They could see the kids from the bar. They were still parked across the lot, but had gotten out and sat on the hood of the car.

When Paul entered the office, JC was quietly throwing darts. Paul leaned back against the table and announced, "I can't do this anymore. I got to give this up. Somebody's gonna to get hurt in here."

JC didn't look up or stop what he was doing. "Not now. I need you here. Something's not right. I feel it."

"For once, I gotta follow my own mind on this one."

JC stopped throwing the darts and turned to Paul. "You just don't have time for family anymore. You'd rather be running around with Akbar and promoting that broke ass politician. I don't know why 'cause he ain't doing shit for our community. What about the gangs? Where's the damn street signs?"

"JC, come on, why you got to act like this? When you said it was time to leave New York I thought YOU were crazy, but I listened."

"Good move, because they had a bullet with your name on it."

"Yeah, you saved my life and I love you for it. But I got it together."

"You did."

"Well baby brother, this time I'm telling you. You made plenty of money, now it's time to move on."

"I can't let those thugs run me out."

"You're just like Papa. And Trevor is just like you. It's gonna get the best of both you. Just like your daddy."

"Why you got to go there? Why?" JC walked away from Paul, then turned and said, "Maybe you're right about Trevor. But he's coming around. Look how he packed the house tonight. He's gonna make us proud, I know it."

Tired of JC's holier than thou attitude-never seeing his own faults-Paul just shook his head and proceeded to the door.

JC stopped him, "Paul, I do hear you. You think I don't want to do something else? You think I don't realize I'm too old for this shit? What am I suppose to do? I stayed on your back to change because you're intelligent. You can do anything you want. You know it ain't much I can do."

"JC, I've always told you, you're just as smart as me. You can do anything if you put your mind to it. It will be hard work, but let me help you. Deal?"

Just as Paul reached his hand out to JC, someone banged on the door yelling, "They got Trevor."

The two followed the loud voices outside where a crowd was gathered around watching the crew from the corner kick Trevor, who was on the ground. As JC and Paul made their way through the crowd, Felix hurled himself on top of Trevor to protect him from the attackers. During the tussle, Felix was hit in the head with a club. Blood splattered everywhere. Paul ran to Felix's aid while security chased the kids away. Aside from a rip in his jersey, Trevor was fine. He rushed Felix to an Urgent Care where they cleaned and bandaged the blow to his head near his temple.

Once the commotion died down in the club, JC went back in his office to finish his dart game. Playing games helped him think when he was frustrated. Between each dart, he studied the photos on the wall—his life story. Suddenly, he perked up as if he had an epiphany. He rummaged through a shelf of books and magazines. He grabbed a real estate guide. As he left the room, he hesitated, and then gently slid the switch down to turn off the lights.

Chapter 15

Empty packs of Zigzags and an ashtray filled with the remnants of marijuana joints leaned beside the engineering boards in a forty-eight track recording studio in Khalil's basement. Khalil, Trevor, and a four other young men in hip-hop gear were sitting in a single row in front of the controls. The Hot Girlz stood at separate microphones on the other side of the large double-glass window laying down a voice track.

Khalil took a long tote of a joint and coughed out a warning to Trevor. "Man, you gotta watch your back with Payback's crew. Word is you messin' with Havoc's wife—that's dangerous."

Trevor snapped, "You crazy? I don't want them kinda' problems. Havoc's wife a ho anyway."

"He wouldn't have to worry about her if she wasn't a ho." Khalil inhaled a hit of the joint and passed. "Didn't he catch a murder rap? How he get out so quick?" Khalil asked the young man working the boards.

Like JC, Trevor had an answer for everything. "Cops figure he helped them, just killed another brotha'. Long as you killing your own kind you don't have to worry about doing long time."

The room was in agreement; the system could care less about black on black crime. The music got louder. On the other side of the glass, the rappers engaged in a lyrical battle, showing off.

Khalil flung his index finger toward the girls in the booth. "You know we got a hit. This shit is slammin'. They're so on point I'd love to record them live."

Trevor thought for a minute, then suggested, "We could do it at my dad's club."

"Serious?" Khalil fanned the smoke from the joint he had just fired up. "Thatta work, an LBC thang."

Trevor's mind was ticking. "How about the night of the Playas Ball? Mad celebrities will be in the house."

"I could bring some acts from the label. If you can make it happen, we could shoot a video that night."

"A video at The Empire! My dad will love the idea. No doubt."

"Ah'ite, let's make this shit happen," Khalil said as he gave Trevor a pound. Khalil adjusted the knobs on the boards as the group continued to perform "Middle Passage," a song with hard-hitting lyrics reminiscent of The Last Poets/Gil Scott Heron era, detailing the horrific journey of 15 million Africans who traveled on slave ships from West Africa to the Americas.

Chapter 16

Trevor persuaded his uncle to play his artists' music at the bookstore during the Akbar Jones event. Like his dad, Trevor could be very convincing. He went on about how his uncle was the one who inspired him to write such revolutionary lyrics and suggested that this may be a way to reach the youth. "Just a different way to teach our history," he told Paul.

The music went over remarkably well. When the Hot Girlz debut single, "Book of Joshua," started playing, the casual conversations among the guests began to quiet. It was definitely hit-song material. The music track was so funky you could almost smell it. The crowd was even more impressed by the riveting lyrics that told the story of former slave, Denmark Vesey's failed revolt in 1822 and compared it to the Bible Book of Joshua.

In provocative hip-hop lingo, and exhibiting a lyrical dexterity akin to KRS One, the lead singer of the Hot Girlz delivered, "even back in the day, people tellin' for pay….a slave informant spoiled the plan, but Vesey died a man. …with the new slav-er-ry… they sellin an' tellin', and sellin' that tell.. it ain't easy for a black man to be free." The crowd roared.

JC, Candace and Tamara arrived a little late so one of the store clerks placed chairs for them in the back of the crowded bookstore. The two hundred and fifty folding chairs set up in the center of the room were all taken. Some of the widely Afrocentric audience stood shoulder-to-shoulder against the wall, others squatted in front of them, and several found a seat on the floor.

People lined the balcony that wrapped around the second floor loft. No one seemed bothered or uncomfortable. Nearly five hundred Blacks, Whites, Latino's, and others crammed into the small bookstore with no complaints. They were all focused on uplifting their community. Tables lined the room loaded with information on HIV/AIDS, voting, and other grassroots propaganda. A booth displaying promotional materials for Trevor's group was in the corner next to a table with stacks of Akbar's newest book, "Conspiracy."

Akbar was in front of the room at a microphone, running down the conspiracy against black people in America. Paul, who was seated on a couch to Akbar's right, facing the audience, cheered him on and kept the enthusiastic crowd roused up. Felix was propped in the front row co-signing on Akbar's every word.

After a few "hallelujahs" and "speak my brother's," Akbar ended with, "So if you're assed out, on drugs, no job, don't worry, they ain't thinking about you. But, if you get a little something, that's when it's time to watch your back."

By then everyone in the audience was on their feet including JC. Not that JC was into conspiracy theories, but Akbar and Paul had become close friends so he felt he should show respect. Actually, JC did respect Akbar and all of the people from the civil rights movement for being able to make a dollar off the whole race issue. At times he had thoughts of conjuring up and publishing his own conspiracy theory.

The audience became a bit disorderly as they moved forward to meet Akbar and get their books signed. Without warning or permission, Felix darted to the front of the room and started directing the crowd. He moved a table that had been set up for the signing to the side of the French doors that led to the patio. "Please everyone, form one line. One line over here." He pointed to the table. "Buy your book here and move forward so Mr. Jones can sign it."

It took nearly five minutes to navigate through the crowd to get to Paul in the front of the room. JC, Tamara and Candace wrestled through the eager activists to congratulate Paul on a successful event. Candace and Tamara exchanged cynical looks as they watched Felix dole out directions.

Paul hugged JC. "You made it."

"Of course, I wouldn't miss this for the world." JC nodded toward Akbar. "He really is deep."

"Yeah, heavy stuff."

Paul called over to Akbar, "Before you get busy, come meet my brother."

"The legendary JC Powell?" Akbar replied.

"That's me." JC blushed a little, feeling proud that his big brother had talked about him. "It's an honor to meet you Akbar. This is Tamara and Candace. They want their books signed."

"I'd be glad to. It's nice to finally meet you, JC. Ladies, come with me." Akbar guided them to the book signing area. Akbar stopped and turned to JC. "Young Powell, did you hear the message?"

"Yes sir. Righteous—"

"No response required. Do you hear me now my brother?" Akbar continued to the book signing area. Trevor appeared from nowhere, whipping his arms around Tamara and Candace.

"Trevor, I didn't know you were here," Candace said.

"Wooo, call the press, Candace missed something!" Trevor said.

Candace playfully poked Trevor in the arm. "Akbar, this is JC's son Trevor."

"The rap writer slash producer?"

Trevor smiled and lowered his head in a bashful way. "Yeah, I'm the one. Those are my lyrics playing now."

Akbar shook his hand and said, "You realize you have a duty to use your music to uplift black folks? Lyrics can be powerful. A song stays in your mind a long time—sometimes forever. Use your gift to be part of the solution."

"You're the one with the insight," Trevor responded.

"And I expect no less from you, young man. The books in here tell the real story." He pointed around the room. "Keep doing your homework, you hear me?"

"Uncle Paul stays on me. I'm working on some powerful material."

Felix was on the other side of the room smooth-talking a customer looking at home improvement books. "I'm a licensed contractor. I can help you get all of your work done. Call me, it's what I do," he said, as he handed them a business card with his name and number. Felix caught a glimpse of Paul and JC on the other side of the room engaged in a personal conversation. When he saw the brothers walking outside, he immediately began maneuvering his way through the crowd to get out to the patio where brothers had gone.

"I thought about what you said. What about real estate?" JC said.

"Not a bad idea."

"I found an apartment building. I want you to check it out after the reunion," JC said. They were less than fifty feet away from the ocean so they could hear the soothing sound of the waves washing ashore.

"Now that's a plan," Paul said. "The only work is collecting rent."

"Yeah, but you know you and Candace will have to deal with the paperwork. I'm not sure if it makes sense to get into something involving so much paperwork."

"You know we'll be here. But you have to step up your game and—" Paul felt a slap on the back and turned to see that Felix had made his way out on the patio. Paul was taken aback but remained cordial.

Felix said, "The program was excellent."

Paul slid a hand-rolled Montecristo cigar into the side of his mouth, lit it, and, as the smoke slowly seeped towards Felix, remarked, "I didn't expect to see you here."

"You know I've got to show support for my peeps," Felix said, surprised at Paul's comment. "I have to get back to the club now though. Nobody is there to make sure they set up right."

Paul studied Felix as he sauntered off to the parking lot. He spotted a new Movado watch on his wrist. "Something about him," Paul motioned toward Felix, nodding his head.

JC said, "He's okay. It's good for Trevor to be around a college graduate." They watched Felix until he disappeared into the darkness. JC continued, "I know you're keeping your distance, but the Playas Ball is the night before the family reunion."

"Wow, that's in two weeks, huh?"

"Yeah, and Trevor's group is going to film a music video at the club during the Ball."

"What, a music video? He didn't tell me about that. Don't even ask, you know I'll be there!"

Later that evening, Candace stood in front of the club, telling a worker where to hang a poster. There was a long line to enter the club. A string of cars were double-parked in front of the box office, causing a traffic jam. Trevor instructed his friend to drop him off at the end of block. A carload of thugs cruised by flashing gang signs. They noticed Trevor making his way through the crowd and immediately swung a quick U-turn at the corner. Trevor stopped to speak to a group of people in the line, but kept his eye on Dee as she strutted over to Candace. Dee had one hand on her hip, the other flailing, and a Kool cigarette dangling from the side of her simmering lavender-painted lips. With Trevor's attention on Dee, he never noticed the car cruising toward him.

Dee shouted to Candace, "Haven't I told you about leaving the bar?"

Candace didn't look at Dee, but she smelled the alcohol from a distance. Dee swerved closer to Candace and shrieked, "I'm talking to you."

Candace shoved her open hand in front of Dee's face. "Leave me alone, Dee. I'm working—something you know nothing about."

"You act like this is your club. You need to get a life."

"This family is my life." Candace turned back to Dee. "You know what? It's time for your ass to go."

"Don't even try it. If you don't stop putting that damn dirt in my things, your ass will be out of here in a hurry." Dee, who was merely a skeleton of her former self, continued to walk behind Candace, fussing and warning her that she was on her way out. She had lost so much weight over the previous months no one noticed the cleavage she tried to display by wearing tight, low cut blouses. Instead, the bones protruding from her chest drew more attention. Candace was now sure her suspicions that Dee was using drugs again were correct.

Dee crossed the line when she brushed up against Candace, knocking her slightly to the side. Candace lost it. "You don't get it do you, ho?"

Dee was so shocked to see Candace flip on her, she couldn't get the words out of her mouth. She talked mess constantly because she knew Candace tried to carry herself like a lady but, in reality, Dee knew she didn't want to go toe-to-toe with her. Candace stepped closer, "Look wench, you may think you got game, but trust me, I created it. On your best day, you can't compete with me on my worst day. Hear me now, PACK YOUR BAGS, HO. You are on your way out."

Trevor noticed the argument getting more physical and dashed over to give Candace a hand. Just as he reached the squabble, the car that had done the U-turn pulled to the front of the club. A gun appeared in the back window, haphazardly spewing gunshots in the direction of the crowd. Chaos erupted as bullets ricocheted off bricks and glass shattered everywhere. People in the line began to flee and others ran out of the club to find out what was going on.

A voice from the crowd yelled, "Help, help! Somebody help!" Another bystander shouted, "Oh God! Somebody call 911, call 911. We need an ambulance."

A mob had assembled around a body laying on the ground. When JC arrived on the scene, he didn't spot any familiar faces amid the chaos. He did notice a suspicious-looking brown sedan with two older men in it parked across the street. Sirens resonated in the background as a panicked JC ran into the center of the commotion yelling, "What's going on? What the hell happened? Where's Candace?"

JC attempted to push his way toward the center of the pandemonium but was knocked to the ground by a stampede of people running in the opposite direction. He tucked his chin to his chest and protected his head with his arms, but never tried to get up. He had learned that lesson the hard way. Back in the seventies he suffered a concussion trying to get up during a disturbance at a concert on Randall's Island.

After several stomps and a very long minute, JC felt a forceful hand jerk him from the ground. It was Felix. He grabbed JC and covered him like a bodyguard protecting the president. Felix quickly escorted JC inside the nearly empty club.

A while later, after the ambulance, police, and the last of the onlookers left, JC sat at a table inside the club, holding his head in his hands, drained and distraught. Tamara was at his side, trying to calm him down. Felix zipped out of the club, passing Dee at the back door. She sashayed over to JC, took her usual stance with her hand on her hip, and announced, "JC, a lot of these problems are from Trevor's bad attitude."

JC's cool, southern disposition got lost somewhere in the midst of the drama. "What the hell are you talking about?"

"Trevor. He shouldn't be working here. He goes off too easy and keeps mess going with those thugs. Trevor. He's the problem."

"Somebody just got shot here and this is what you have to offer? You just got to start some drama, don't you? You better take your frail ass the hell out of my face."

Tamara was shocked. She pleaded for JC to ignore Dee. Although people always said Trevor inherited his temper from his dad, she had never seen this side of JC. Normally Dee would know she had gone far enough, but the drugs and spirits had taken control. "Your thug ass son needs to go," Dee said.

"I ain't never gonna give up on my son. You'll go long before he does. Keep talking shit and it will be sooner than you think." At this point JC was standing yelling in Dee's face. "I'm not going to warn you again. You better get out my face."

Just as JC stepped closer to the raging drunk, Candace came into the club, rushed over and grabbed JC. With her arm around him, she led him back to his seat. "JC, Nate's okay. The bullet just grazed his arm. Just take it easy. Calm down, he's alright." Dee continued her rant. Candace turned to Dee and in her most lethal tone said, "You need to find somewhere to be."

JC asked, "Did he have to stay in the hospital?"

"No. JC, he's fine. He wanted to come back here but I took him home. He said to tell you to remember he's still walking around with a bullet fragments in his hip from Vietnam and survived being set-up by fellow LAPD officers. This is a walk in the park for him."

JC chuckled, "That sounds like Nate."

Outside the club, Trevor ran to catch up with Felix when he saw him headed to his car. He yelled, "Yo Felix, where you going?"

Felix turned and waited for Trevor to reach him. "This shit is getting out of hand, I got to do something," he said.

"What? What can you do? You know it was Havoc's boys."

"I'mma go to try to talk to Payback."

"Payback? Yo man, let me call some of my homies,"

"No I'm just going to talk. If a crew goes, there will be problems."

"You crazy? You know I can't let you go over there by yourself."

Felix lifted his shirt to reveal he was strapped. "I'm not alone. I never leave home without my fo-fo."

"Man, 5-0 is scared of them goons, what you gonna do with that?"

"Okay, you can go but you have to wait in the car. Any problems, you can call for help and be ready in case we need to leave quick." They laughed and jumped into Felix's brand new Porche he had purchased to drive when he was in Long Beach. According to Felix, he drove an e-class in Atlanta.

Trevor nervously waited in the car outside of Payback's house—not the best neighborhood. He was agonized by the midnight sounds, and spooked by each passing car or late night walker. After a few desperate attempts to make a call on his dead cell phone, Trevor started looking under the seats and in the glove compartment. He leaned to the driver's side, popped the trunk, and got out of the car. He fumbled in the trunk for a few moments, never noticing the label on the luggage revealing a Michigan address. He dug behind the luggage, emerged with a crowbar, and got back in the car.

Trevor jumped as the driver's door opened and Felix hopped in the car.

"What happened? Everything ah'ite?" Trevor asked.

"Everything's cool. He'll take care of it. We shouldn't have no more problems. Let's bounce."

Chapter 17

The "Second Annual Playas Ball" was expected to attract the largest crowd ever at the club. It surpassed all expectations.

JC called a two PM meeting in the office. Candace had to finish taking care of business with a couple of vendors who were delivering alcohol and supplies. She joined the meeting late and was shocked to see Felix in the family conference for the first time.

Candace leaned in and whispered, "JC, you're truly slippin'."

"Not now Candace. It's a big night. The Playas Ball, and they're filming a video. Plus my family is in town. I need all of you to be on your best behavior."

Trevor said, "Thank Felix for buyin' a truce. Haven't heard nothin' from Payback's boys since we went over there a few weeks ago. What'd you say, Felix?"

"Later Trevor." JC turned to Felix, "We do appreciate whatever you did Felix, big time. But right now, everyone needs to go out there and act like ya'll got some class. Let's get crackin'."

When the doors to The Empire opened that night, a camera crew was posted outside filming celebrities, hustlers, pimps and wanksta's—gangster hopefuls—as they arrived in limos and stepped onto the red carpet decked out for the Playas Ball. Big ballers represented their cities from coast-to-coast. Mack Daddy, Detroit Blue, Joe Valentine, Big Bama, Memphis Black, Chicago Black, DC Black, and After Midnight were all in the house.

The police blocked off the streets and security was everywhere so the crowd was able to mingle in front of the club without the threat of a drive-by. The long line for public entry had stopped moving but the people waited patiently; happy to be outside to watch the VIP arrivals. Khalil stepped out of a limo surrounded by four beautiful girls—one of the groups on his label. Two cameramen ran over to catch his every move since he was one of the stars of the video.

Inside the club, Trevor's groups were performing. Several cameras panned the room filming the crowd. Family, ballers, and celebrities greeted one another with love and caught up on what they had missed since they last saw each other. They danced and took lots of photos. JC was in heaven, constantly calling Candace over to take pictures with him.

Felix was dressed in his best threads. He had given up his bright colors and was wearing an upscale beige designer suit with brown and beige eel shoes to match. After running around making sure things were in order—coordinating the food line on the patio when it got a bit disorderly, running in and out of the basement getting things for the group, and making several trips to the store for film and other items—he eventually sat down inside the club to enjoy the show with the family.

Across town, at a cozy restaurant near the beach, Dee finished up an intimate dinner with Lynn, the handsome hunk she met at the club. She gulped down her Margarita and said, "I've got to get out of here, it's a busy night. You know they can't get anything right without me." She stood, tossing a fluffy pink boa around her neck, and leaned to kiss Lynn.

Lynn grabbed Dee, pulled her close, and looked into her eyes. He thought about how hideous she looked with her colorful makeup and outrageous feathers flung around her long, emaciated neck. He smiled and said, "As good as you look, umm, just forget work, stay with me and let's get freaky tonight."

"You know I'm incapable to do that."

"Why?" He pulled Dee toward him. She jerked back. He said, "Oh yeah, I forgot. Your other, other man is in town."

"My other, other man? Who are you talking about?

"Mr. Smooth."

"Oh, you talking about Felix? That snake is the last person you need to worry about."

"Snake?" Lynn questioned.

"Game recognizes game, okay? He can't run one on me." Dee gulped downed the remaining half of her date's drink. "Baby, I really have to go, I have to make a few stops. See you later?"

"Yeah, meet me at the spot I showed you by the beach. I told you, I'm feeling real freaky tonight," Lynn said.

"Freakin' ain't free these days," Dee said.

Lynn tapped Dee on the butt. "Baby, I'll dig as deep in my pockets as I need to, if I can get some of this." He wondered what man in his right mind would pay for sex from a used up, drug-addicted whore. Lynn pulled out his cell to make a call as he watched Dee switch out of the restaurant and hop behind the wheel of JC's brand new Benz.

Riding home, Dee passed Payback's house and saw the back of a Porche resembling the one that Felix drove. It was parked in an alley on the side of a one story bungalow in a rough neighborhood. Dee slowed down but couldn't see if it was actually Felix's car. She swung a U-turn only to find that she still could not get a view of the car or license plate. It didn't matter. Dee was convinced Felix was visiting Payback and raced home for a quick change of clothes before heading to the club, eager to tell JC what she discovered. *Surely*, she thought, *JC would recognize her worth with the delivery of this critical information.* She couldn't wait to get to the club.

Dee entered the club and sprinted over to the table where the family was seated. She acknowledged everyone then shouted at Felix, "Why were you at Payback's house?"

Felix realized Dee was drunk. He immediately got up from the table to lure her to the back. Dee followed him yelling, "I saw your car parked at Payback's house. What were you doing there? Huh, Felix?"

Felix stopped near the door of the office and calmly asked, "What are you talking about, Dee?"

"I saw your damn car."

"My car, what are you talking about?"

Dee screamed, "Don't play stupid with me Felix. It was your car. I know your car."

"Dee, calm down. This is a business. Don't be so damn ghetto. And you smell like a liquor factory," Felix said.

"Who you callin' ghetto?"

Trevor was behind JC as he rushed over and moved the spat into the back room. Candace finished preparing a drink for a customer then headed to the back.

JC asked Dee, "What's going on? Do you realize how loud you are?"

"I saw his car by Payback's house. I want to know what he was doing there. Tell us, Felix."

"I don't know what you're talking about, Dee. I've been here all night."

"He sure has." Trevor said. "Dee, you just mad 'cause Felix won't give your ho behind no play. You've been throwing yourself at him since he got here. You think people don't notice?"

"Trevor calm down." JC turned to Felix. "I'm sorry man, I don't know what's wrong with her,"

"That's OK, JC. She's drunk as usual," Felix said as he walked out of the room. Felix stood at the door, briefly listening to the conversation before going back into the club.

JC yelled, "Dee, take your drunk ass somewhere and sit down. You are just out of control. You need to get some help for that alcohol."

Felix walked away from the door, satisfied he had been vindicated. Candace had listened closely to both Dee and Felix, but did not say a word. Once Felix was gone, she said, "JC, hold it."

"Now what YOU got to say?" Dee said, huffing and glaring at Candace.

Candace rolled her eyes at Dee then turned to JC. "JC, I think you need to listen to her this time."

Dee was shocked that Candace would take her side. She crossed her arms, sucked her teeth, poked out her lips, and with her head leaned to the side, stared at JC without a blink.

Trevor jumped in, "Now here you go, Candace." He turned to JC, "Dad, since Uncle Paul left, they both got beef with Felix 'cause he's holding things down. They're just threatened by him."

"Threatened by Felix? You know what, JC? You don't have to listen to me. Go on and listen to that out of control kid of yours. I know what the hell I saw. I'm just tryin' to help your ass out," Dee screamed and walked back out to the club. Trevor started behind her but JC grabbed his arm and stopped him.

Tamara peeked in the door. "Did anyone happen to come across my gris-gris?" she asked as she placed her hand on her bare neck.

"Gris what?" JC asked.

"Nah, I haven't seen it." Candace leaned in a whispered, "She's talking about her necklace."

"Don't look too hard, that thing was creepy." JC said.

Tamara looked upset as she started back to the front of the club. "It was our only protection," she said.

Strange looks flew around the room. Candace called out and stopped her. "Tamara."

"What you need?" Tamara asked, looking back in the door.

"Where was Felix when you thought you saw him in LA?

"Felix?"

"When Trevor told you he had left for Atlanta. You said he must have had a twin."

"Oh yeah. Downtown. By the courthouse. It really did look like him. I really need to get back on the door. We're swamped," Tamara said and darted off.

Candace looked at JC. She was silent for a moment then said, "Come on JC. Twice is no coincidence. He has been in and out all night. Just like Paul said, something is not right with that boy."

"Don't get Uncle Paul in this. You're just hatin' Candace. Dad, he's been here at the club all night. He only left to go downstairs."

"I saw him roll up in the parking lot a while ago, so he left for something. Anyway, what's up in the basement? Does he live down there?" Candace said.

You know we're down there rehearsing."

"Ya'll cut it out. Just cut it out," JC yelled. He went to the back of the office and quietly started throwing darts. Trevor and

Candace knew JC was digesting everything that had happened so they stood in tense silence. After a few minutes, JC turned to them. "Trevor, call somebody to change the locks tomorrow morning while we're at the reunion. I'll deal with Felix next week."

"Because Candace and Dee are tripping? They're not even family. This don't make no sense."

"Calm your ass down. You're too hard headed to get it. Watch your back with him and don't say anything. Understand? Got it, young man?"

Trevor stormed out and Candace returned to the bar, keeping a watchful eye on Felix. JC stood in thought for a moment, picked up another dart, and threw it—bulls eye. He went back out to the club but didn't mingle. The revelation about Felix had ruined a wonderful night. Candace watched as JC stood off to the side looking preoccupied. She eventually went to JC, tenderly took his hand and led him onto the dance floor. Suddenly, JC had forgotten the drama of the day.

The fast record faded and a slow one started. JC quickly pulled Candace to him, holding tight for fear she'd slip away. The crowd piled off the dance floor when they heard the slow music start and only a few couples remained. JC and Candace danced slow and intense, oblivious to anyone around them. The female singer seemed to morph into Patti LaBelle. As she belted Patti's "Love, Need, and Want You," JC took his hand and gently put it on the back of Candace's neck and guided her head onto his shoulder. All eyes in the club were focused on the magnetic couple.

Dee watched until she could bear no more. Under normal circumstances she would have acted a fool, but Dee knew she had caused enough mess for the night so she decided it would be a good time to meet up with Lynn and make a little money.

After the club was closed, JC walked up to the bar as Candace hung up the phone. "You need a ride?" Candace asked.

JC looked down the bar at Trevor who was engaged in an animated conversation with Khalil. He knew Nate had taken some family back to the hotel. "I guess so, he looks busy. I hope he's making some money."

Khalil came over to shake JC's hand. "Thanks Mr. Powell, it was the bomb. The music, the video shoot—all went perfect. I know we got a hit."

"Am I going to see The Empire on TV?" JC asked.

"We hope so."

"Is this boy gonna make some money? Cherie is younger and she's almost finished college. I can't keep taking care of this one."

"I think he'll be ah'ite," Khalil said laughing.

"Okay now, I'm gonna hold you to it. He don't get paid, I'm sending him to your house."

As Trevor started to leave with Khalil, he turned to Candace and said, "Candace, I." He paused a second. "I just wanted to-"

"I love you too Trevor," Candace cut in.

❖   ❖

Candace took the long way home, alongside the Beach. The windows were down and the smooth jazz music played low enough to hear the water rolling up on the beach. JC cherished every opportunity to enjoy quiet time with Candace. When she pulled off her hat, JC was captivated by the way her hair seductively blew in her face from the ocean breeze. He just stared at her beauty.

He snapped out of his stupor when it dawned on him that they were riding a round-about way to his house; not that he really minded since he couldn't get enough time alone with Candace. "Candace why are you going this way?"

"Uh, I need to stop at the store," Candace said.

"This is way out the way."

"Not much is open this late."

The car fell silent again. JC wanted to ask Candace if she felt something that night. He wanted to ask if he stood a small chance of getting her back. He wanted to grab her hand and tell her how much he loved everything about her. Apologize for all of his past indiscretions. Beg for her to take him back.

JC said, "How's your mom coming along?"

Candace's mother suffered from drug and alcohol addiction most of her adult life. About a year before, she had reached an all-time low and was found in an alley where she had been living, nearly dead of an overdose.

"One day at a time. She really acts like she wants to get it together this time. She even found a job and an apartment."

"It will work itself out eventually. Everything does," JC said, staring at Candace as she drove. JC savored every move Candace made. He adored the way she talked slightly out of the side of her mouth, the way she neatly placed two strands of hair swirling down each temple, and the way she whispered personal things even when they were alone, as if there were someone around that could overhear their conversation.

They were cruising through Long Beach with the Pacific Ocean as their backdrop and Ramsey Lewis setting the mood. JC thought, *surely this is the best opportunity to plead my case to Candace. She can't walk away. A captive audience. Now is the perfect time to ask her to take me back. I'll just beg.*

Before he could get a word out he spotted his Benz. "Hold up Candace, is that my car? Slow down, Candace, slow down!" JC was hanging out of the window trying to see if anyone was in his car.

"I know you're not trying to check on Dee," Candace said.

"There she is, over there. You see her? Look out by the beach. Ain't that a bitch! You see her?"

Candace slowed down to a creep and looked but never stopped.

"Stop the car. Look over there, over by the beach. Look at that wench all out in public. Candace, stop the car."

Candace glanced at a silhouette of Dee and a man leaning against a fence kissing, about fifty feet away from the street. She kept driving. "You knew what you were dealing with so why are you tripping?"

"You haven't seen me trip."

"I don't get it. I thought you said she's not your woman and she can do whatever she wants to."

"She's not my woman. But there's a way you carry yourself if you're staying with someone and driving their car. If you want to continue staying with them, take your dirt to the next town. Show some respect. Even dogs won't shit where they sleep. She can't disrespect me like that. I got something for her ass."

A few hours later, Dee noticed four garbage bags in the driveway as she maneuvered the Mercedes into the garage next to the Rolls Royce. When JC walked into the garage to watch her park, he spotted a sedan similar to the one that was near the club parked across the street a few houses down from his house. This time the car looked empty.

Still a little inebriated, Dee parked so close to the wall she had to tussle to get out of the car. Using the wall for balance, she squeezed her way to the front of the car where JC was standing.

He snatched the garage remote, cell phone, and keys from her and pointed at the large green garbage bags. "Get your shit and get the hell on."

"What's wrong, JC? You still pissed about Felix?" Dee said still walking toward the entry to the house. JC stepped in front of her to block her way. Dee realized he was serious.

"You want to ho, huh? Well I ain't your damn trick," JC said.

"What did I do? Is this about Felix?"

"Just take your shit and go. And don't bring your slut ass back."

Dee tried to be sweet. "Where am I supposed to go? You just gonna kick me out on the street?"

"That's where I found you. Now go the hell on." JC stepped inside the garage and pushed the remote to close the garage door.

Dee stood in the driveway crying and screaming as the door lowered in front of her. She crammed clothes from one bag into another, snatched the lighter bag and took off on foot, yelling, "You'll be sorry, JC. I'm gonna get your ass."

In a humorous tone, JC yelled from behind the closed door. "Stop all that noise in this neighborhood. Take that shit back to the ghetto."

"Oh, it's funny, huh? You better watch your back asshole. I mean that shit. You're a marked man. You and that trifling son of yours. Watch your damn back."

Chapter 18

The Powell family reunion was more than an opportunity for the everyone to get together for fun and games. It was also a spiritual retreat. As president of the reunion committee for the past twenty years, Mama made sure that, in addition to the picnic and banquet, there was a mandatory meeting to find out how everyone was doing, what they had planned for the coming year, and how other family members could be of assistance to those in need. She also made sure time was allocated for prayer and, of course, the entire Powell clan attended church services together on Sunday morning.

The reunion gave Mama a chance to see all the people she prayed for throughout the year, and enabled Auntie to get enough gossip, once embellished, to last until the next reunion. Everyone, including Junior, the consummate mess-up in the family, was on their best behavior for the first five days of July each year. This year was the first time the reunion was held outside of Georgia. The state was on lock down because of the Olympics so JC was happy to host the family in Long Beach.

Tamara and Trevor picked Candace up at her condo. Just as Candace went to slide her foot into the back of Trevor's restored '72 Caddy, someone yelled out of the window of the condo next door to her "Candi, honey."

Candace looked up to see Lynn, the good-looking man from the club, hanging out the window. Looking prettier than ever, diamond stud earrings and all. He swung his arm out of the window and snapped his finger. "You owe me one, girlfriend."

"I owe you two!" Candace said sliding into the car laughing.

Trevor arrived at the parking area of the California State Park right behind JC and Paul. The lot was so full that the brown sedan that was parked near JC's house the night before went unnoticed. Paul headed toward the front of the park to where the valet parking attendants were busy parking cars. Trevor followed.

"Valet parking at a park. Only in LA," Paul said.

As soon as JC entered the park, he spotted about sixty members of the Powell family seated at picnic tables under a tent. They were garbed in T-shirts adorned with "Powell Family Reunion 1996." Beyond the picnic tables was a one hundred and fifty-foot pool built like a beach. Directly behind it, next to a forest-like area, was a large man-made lake with a small dock where you could rent Jet Ski's, kayaks and pedal boats. JC stopped to speak to some of the people lurking around the entrance before proceeding to the picnic tables.

A woman shouted, "JC." It was Dee marching toward him.

The word had already spread like wildfire about JC giving Dee the boot, so everyone was shocked to see her. A voice whispered. "I can't believe she got the nerve to come up in here. Ooh, she's getting ready to get cussed out."

Reeking of alcohol, Dee said, "JC, I need to talk to you."

"We don't have anything to talk about, Dee."

"But JC–"

"Don't come in here and show out in front of my family. I'm serious Dee, don't bring it here."

"I'm not leaving until we talk."

Trevor ran up. "Didn't my dad say go? Kick rocks ho!"

"Trevor, not now. Show some respect," JC said.

"Respect? She's dissin' our family being here."

Mama walked up and tapped her cane on Trevor's leg, interrupting the argument. Her expression let everyone know she was not in the mood for any confusion.

"Trevor," Mama said in a soft but stern voice.

"Ma'am," Trevor replied. No matter how angry anyone got in the family, they knew not to disrespect Mama or Auntie. They'd have to deal with them and the other sixty or so members of the Powell clan.

"You don't speak to people that way. Go over there and sit down."

"But she don't have no—"

Mama cut her eyes at Trevor. He shut up immediately, walked over to the picnic tables and sat down. Mama turned to Dee. "Young lady, you are not welcome here."

Dee didn't move. Never releasing eye contact with Dee, Mama continued, "Don't embarrass yourself; have some pride. Now act like you have a little sense for once and go on about your business."

When Dee tossed her hand on her hip and formed her lips to start her drama, Mama, with the family behind her in attack mode, raised her hand to stop her. "Dee, I don't know how, but, I know you've known the Lord in the past. That's why you avoid me. You need to pray for Him to save you from the demons inside of you. I will continue to pray for you. Now go on, Dee. Let us be."

Mama knew she had the final word. She turned to the group that was huddled around preparing to cuss Dee out and said, "Okay, let's have a Powell family reunion."

Dee knew not to respond. It would have been disrespectful and she knew no one in the Powell clan would allow Mama to be disrespected. She twirled around and charged off, angrier than she was the night before.

JC and the crew joined the other family who were playing cards and already engaged in the first argument of the reunion. This was the first meeting since the OJ Simpson verdict, so they continued the argument from last year's reunion. No one could agree on whodunit. Suspects ranged from his ex-wife's spurned lover to a hired Colombian hit man. What they all did agree on, after over an hour of debate, was that the verdict had nothing to do with race. The jury had to find OJ not guilty because there was too much reasonable doubt. Even those who thought OJ was guilty thought the prosecutor needed to show where the knife and blood went in order for the jury to come back with a guilty verdict. OJ could have been there, and everyone thought he knew who did it, but they were sure the murderer had to be soaked in blood.

Even though she couldn't swim, Candace had the fanciest bathing suit in the park. It was a classy solid black halter neck one-piece suit that formed a sexy low-hanging 'V' in the back. The material beneath the breast line was black sheer vertical stripes. She had a colorful wrap skirt tied in a knot at her hip. Her inability to swim kept her away from small boats. JC had lured her onto larger cruisers in New York – the Staten Island Ferry, the Omega Boat Ride, and the WBLS Cruise around Manhattan Island – but he could never convince her to get into a small vessel. After prodding and promising to stay near the edge of the lake, JC was able to persuade Candace to take a quick ride in a canoe.

Candace was not the only one who liked surprises. JC was the shock doctor. He had enlisted Paul's wife to prepare a goodie basket that was tucked under a blanket at the back of the canoe. JC steered the canoe out into the lake and around the bend, to a private area he had peeped out when he came to look at the park. JC and Candace were seated facing each other. He pulled the basket out and placed it between them. There was a small plate with cheese and crackers, a bowl of fruit, and two plastic long stemmed wine glasses. He pulled out the bottle of sparkling cider and filled each glass halfway. JC reached behind him and slid a CD into the portable player Tracy had thoughtfully included.

As the CD dragged trying to start, JC gently placed his hand on Candace's hand and tilted his drink in for a toast. "Here's to new beginnings," he said.

The glasses touched lightly.

"New beginnings?" Candace said in a sweet, enticing tone; her head slightly tilted.

"Candace, you have to know." JC paused. He seductively slid a chocolate covered cherry into her mouth, trying to buy a little time. He was never good at apologies or deep expressions of love. He labored to remember the words he had rehearsed time and time again. A soft voice finally emerged from the CD Player.

"I truly adore you" Prince belted, as if on cue.

JC was no Prince, but his voice could pass in a church choir.

He knew whatever Prince sang—even when the words were inaudible—had women and men around the world salivating over him. "Adore" happened to be one of the Prince songs JC knew most of the words to.

JC quickly redeemed himself and, like it was part of a master plan, joined Prince. As he sang, he moved the basket and glasses and knelt down in front of Candace. Hitting notes he never thought he could, he pressed tightly on her thighs. He began to rub her all over –from her thighs up her body to her bare back, and arms. He massaged her shoulders then slid his hands down her arms locking her fingers between his. He nibbled on her hands, wrists, and her sensitive neck. At "Truly adore you," Candace had totally forgotten about her fear of water.

Singing softy in her ear, JC took his tongue and gently rolled it around her earlobe. Candace placed her hand on JC's thigh and squeezed it so hard that JC could feel the love radiate from her body through his. JC gently placed her chin in his hand and turned her face to his. With a fiery passion that had built up over ten years, they kissed.

By the time JC and Candace got back to the picnic area they chummier than ever. They arrived just in time for the Soul Train line. Actually, the family held up the line until the two returned. It was a requirement that everyone dance down the line so there was no way Mama would let them start without JC and Candace. Paul had to pry the two apart to get them to join in. But, every single family member boogied down the line. Even Mama and Auntie wiggled from one end to the other. They had to. It was a Powell tradition.

While the family danced, Felix made his rounds, introducing himself to distant family members. Anyone twice removed or more heard the tale of his relationship by marriage. Felix was seated at a picnic table with cousins of cousins from Mississippi when Trevor approached from behind and overheard him bragging about his position with the airlines. Felix told them, "I can get you passes on United. I won't fly with anyone else. Take my number. I'll hook you up. It's what I do."

Surprised, Trevor turned around before reaching Felix and rushed over to report what he heard to his Uncle Paul.

At the end of the night, the family sang top-forty songs as they packed coolers and bags and prepared to leave. The word was out on Felix and everyone did their best to avoid him. He was at a picnic table alone, curled over, talking on his cell phone.

Candace and JC broke away from each other long enough for her to supervise the youngsters packing up the food. Paul walked over and took a seat by JC who was still in seventh heaven.

Paul asked JC, "Are we still going to see the apartment building Tuesday?"

JC jumped, he didn't notice Paul approaching. "Oh yeah. Definitely. Around eleven." JC hung his head and his voice grew serious. His gut was telling him something was wrong. "I'm so ready to move on. I dread going into the club anymore. It's getting worse than New York. I feel that typhoon stronger than ever."

"You back on that? I thought we left the typhoon in the Hudson River."

JC studied the family. He saw his daughter holding his niece's baby. "Sissy's baby sure is big. Cute as she can be." He noticed Junior walking over to join Felix who was alone at a table. He leaned in to Paul and whispered, "Junior don't look good. You think he's having one of them sick spells?"

Paul tucked a cigar into the side of his mouth and huffed, "Sick of smoking that mess."

JC looked startled.

"Come on JC, where have you been? He's been on and off that stuff for years. Why you think he keeps getting in trouble?"

"You think that's it?" JC Paused. "He likes to come out and work on Trevor's events, maybe we should keep him out here with us."

Paul looked at JC like he was crazy. "Even the Bible warns you to be careful of who you let in your house. That boy ain't nothing but trouble."

JC and Paul went over to join the singing, which had migrated to the valet parking area. Most of the family was parked in the regular the parking lot so the majority of them left on foot to their cars. No one thought anything when they passed Nate, who had gone ahead to get the truck for the coolers. He was leaning in the window of a brown sedan talking with the driver. The family just bid their farewells and exited the lot.

The Powell's were the last people in the park so, once the parking lot cleared out, JC and his crew of about twenty awaiting vehicles in the valet parking area were the only people left. To pass time as they waited for the attendants to surface, JC and Paul broke into their imitation of the Temptations, choreography included. When "Ain't No stopping Us Now" started playing on the boom box a cousin was holding, the brothers immediately turned into McFadden and Whitehead. They recruited other members to the stage to participate in the performance.

JC, Paul, Tracy and Candace were the lead singers and four cousins in matching reunion T-shirts served as the background singers. They all took their performance seriously. JC grabbed Mama's cane to use as a microphone and passed it around. Felix faced the group, playing conductor, while Auntie and Mama sat on a park bench enjoying the show.

Paul sang "Ain't No Stopping Us Now." He passed the "microphone" to JC.

"No Stopping." JC sang, passing the cane to Candace.

"No Stopping." Candace tried to pass the mike to Trevor but he refused. As the family continued to sing and dance, Nate finally drove up with the truck and the younger cousins quickly loaded the coolers and food onto the truck.

"Nate, what took you so long?" JC asked.

"I saw two dudes I used to work with, got to talking cop gossip," Nate responded. He looked back toward the lot. It dawned on him where they were. "They weren't just sitting there. They must be up to something."

Trevor asked, "What's up with the cars?"

By now at least a thirty-five minutes had gone by and there were still no park workers in sight. The atmosphere was very surreal. JC began to scrutinize the area and became suspicious of the inactivity. "Something's not right," he said.

"There you go with your feelings," Candace said.

"Scary thing is, he's usually right, and it really has been a long time," Paul said.

Trevor got tired of waiting. "I'mma go see what's taking so

long."

As Trevor walked toward the parking area, the ominous brown
sedan emerged, followed by an army of police cars and vans. Like
a typhoon plunging ashore, a torrent of gun toting police surged
on the Powell family, forcing everyone to the ground.

Yelling through bullhorns, police wearing jackets stamped
with "DEA" and "LAPD" advised everyone they were under
arrest. JC was sprawled on the gravel with police above him. He
looked over and saw Mama and Auntie lying out on the ground
in front of the bench surrounded by police with guns drawn. He
was screaming, "Leave them alone. What the hell is going on?"

Paul resisted a bit but was eventually forced to the ground
and cuffed by four officers. After his demands for an explanation
went unanswered, Paul began yelling to everyone, "Don't say a
word to anyone until we get a lawyer and find out what's going
on. Not a word. No one." This was something drilled into Paul's
memory during his early days in the civil rights movement. Trust
no one, I want a lawyer, and silence.

Most of the family—Mama, Candace, Auntie and Tracy—
were put into a van together, but JC, Paul, Felix, and Trevor were
each transported in separate vehicles. As the cars took off, Paul
could be heard yelling, "Don't say a word. JC, keep your mouth
shut."

Chapter 19

Over the next week the police seized everything. Candace's condo, cars, the bookstore, bank accounts—anything of value became property of the DEA. Yellow police tape surrounded the entire club, and all homes in the Powell name were bolt locked with poster-sized signs on the doors.

JC, Trevor, and Felix were charged with drug trafficking and related infractions. Paul, Nate, Mama, Auntie, Candace, and Tamara were charged with conspiracy and other minor charges. The women were able to get released on their own recognizance after two bail hearings and a little over a week in jail. JC, Trevor, and Felix had no bail. Paul's bail was set at a hundred thousand dollars, which might as well have been ten million since their assets were frozen, and they had no means of raising the cash.

After the threat of prison did not yield incriminating information on JC, the charges were eventually dropped against all but JC, Trevor, Felix and Paul.

Harry Smart, the federal public defender assigned to JC's case, only met with him one time for ten minutes in over two weeks. JC knew he had to do something to get back on the streets so he could straighten things out. He had no idea where they had taken Paul, and, with everything seized, he had no way to contact anyone. He gained his information from the recent arrestees who had heard the word from the streets. Some of the information came from news reports, but inebriated thugs with overzealous imaginations had filled in the details. When an entering crack-head informed him that "JC Powell" had been shot during the sting, he knew he couldn't trust most of what he heard.

After almost four weeks without communicating with anyone in the family, JC was sitting in a six by nine cell he shared with three other inmates when his name was announced over the loud speaker for a visit. He automatically assumed that it was his mindless court-appointed attorney finally returning with information on his bail. When he arrived at the visiting area, the Correctional Officer, or CO as they're called inside, ushered him to a small private room behind the main visiting area where two tall men stood talking and casually sipping on sodas. One was white, one was black. The men offered JC a seat, as if he had an option, and identified themselves as Drug Enforcement Agents.

Only one of the men spoke, Agent Talbert, while the other agent presented the evidence, operated the tape recorder, and took diligent notes. If he were to trade his dark suit for a sweat suit, on a city street Talbert would pass for just another brother going to shoot a few hoops. His walk and talk was street, not at all what JC envisioned a DEA agent to be like. He politely informed JC of the charges against him as well as the possible consequences.

Talbert said, "This meeting is to give you the opportunity to tell your side, Mr. Powell. To see if we can clear things up. This meeting is completely voluntary and you can end it at any time. And, of course, you have the right to have your attorney present."

JC never said a word as Talbert read the list of charges against him and then gave a quick summary. "You're accused of being the ringleader, along with your son Trevor, of a drug trafficking and distribution ring. You are charged with conspiracy to purchase and distribute crack cocaine."

Talbert was silent for a few seconds and when JC did not respond, he continued. "Although they are not facing charges as serious as yours, the other people working at the club were charged with conspiracy."

Once Agent Talbert finished his speech, the room fell silent, awaiting JC's response. Talbert sat next to JC, crossed his legs, and leaned back in his chair.

"Mr. Powell, we only want to talk—to see if we can straighten things out," Talbert said. "We have drugs and a reliable confidential informant who can confirm the drug operations at the club. He identifies you as the leader of the pack. It doesn't look good for you Mr. Powell. I just want to see how I can help."

JC remained silent as the second agent slid a copy of an evidence report for the drugs confiscated in a major bust. "According to the informant, the drugs were allegedly purchased for your organization." Talbert stood and paced the floor again.

"Mr. Powell." Talbert slowed his stride and turned to JC. "Mr. Powell, can I call you JC?"

JC nodded in the affirmative.

"JC, according to our informant, you made an agreement to buy large quantities of drugs from a man you know as Payback, for distribution out of state." Talbert stood still. "Man, are you sure you don't want a snack or a drink? I know the food is disgusting as hell in here."

JC eventually accepted a soda, since he had not yet acquired a taste for the colored water the prison passed off as juice. Never taking his eyes off Talbert, he popped the top of the can and took a long satisfying gulp. The two continued the mental chess game, but they both knew the DEA had the upper hand. They had taken down his empire and JC couldn't defend himself without his queen and knight.

"There is significant evidence of your guilt. That's why you have no bail. If I could just hear your side maybe I can work on getting a bail set for you. I'm trying to do what I can to help you, ya' feel me?"

"I don't have a side. I didn't have anything to do with any drugs and have no idea what you're talking about," JC said.

"Didn't you make some type of agreement with Payback? What about that?"

"It didn't have nothing to do with drugs."

"But you're saying there was an agreement between you and Payback?"

JC was silent.

"Was your brother aware of your agreement with Payback?"

Another silence followed, much longer than the other.

"JC, I just thought you might want explain the deal you had with Payback to help your brother. Right now, everyone is mixed up in this mess. We could work on getting him released if he didn't have anything to do with the agreement between you and Payback."

"He didn't."

"So there was an agreement?"

JC was silent again.

"JC, I'm trying to work with you so you can help your brother get out."

"I made an agreement with Payback to keep his gang-banging hood-rats away from the club in exchange for my word that I would make sure there were no drug sales in or near the club."

"Were you making drug sales other places?"

"Wasn't no drugs."

"So why the agreement?"

"I had to do something to keep them away from the club. Payback just needed to know nobody was at the club stepping on his toes, so I assured him of that."

"And your brother knew nothing about the deal?"

"Nope. I went to talk to Payback on my own."

"Well JC, I think I understand a little better. If your brother had nothing to do with it we will get to work right away on his release. We just need to get something official on paper. You can write it down in a short statement." The second agent pulled out a blank piece of paper. Agent Talbert raised his hand to stop his associate from handing JC the paper. "Better yet, to make it easier, we can type what you said into a short statement, is that okay?"

JC agreed. The two agents exited the room for about fifteen minutes and returned with a typewritten statement about two paragraphs long. They handed JC the statement explaining that the document covered the information they had just talked about. The agents left the room to give JC a few minutes to review the document and returned ten minutes later with an officer to witness the signing of the statement. They asked JC if he understood and agreed with his statement. JC, the witness, and the two agents signed and dated the document. The agents thanked JC for his cooperation and left.

JC tossed and turned all night, afraid that he may have acted impetuously. The next day, Saturday, JC heard his name announced over the PA for a visit. For the first time in nearly a month, a wide smile graced JC's face when he stepped into the visiting booth and saw his big brother on the other side of the glass window.

"Man, you're a sight for sore eyes. You don't know how good it is to see you out there," JC shouted into the phone.

"Yeah, I got out yesterday but couldn't get in here until this morning. Everyone is out except you, Trevor and Felix. But they got everything. Everything. They even froze all our bank accounts."

"I was worried. I didn't think they would keep their word."

"Who are you talking about?"

"The agents promised they were going to get you out."

"Get me out?" Paul looked puzzled. "Akbar made some calls, got some politicians working and they reduced my bail and he got me out. If it were up to them agents we'd all be sitting behind that glass. You didn't say anything to them did you?"

JC was quiet for a few seconds then replied, "I only explained about the agreement with Payback and that you had nothing to do with it."

Paul was on his feet enraged, shouting, "What did I tell you, JC? You got to listen. I said keep your mouth shut. You can't explain shit to those pricks. How did your lawyer let you talk to them?

"He wasn't there. They said it was voluntary."

"They said, they said? You're telling me what a bunch of conniving, scandalous liars said? Have you heard me at all over the years? Their job is to keep you locked up, by any means necessary."

JC lowered his head. He knew Paul was right this time.

Paul sat down and continued, "If they come back and try to get you to talk or sign anything—anything—just ask for your lawyer and shut up. You understand, JC? This is serious shit. Do you understand? Don't even tell them the weather or they'll find a way to use it against you." Paul noticed that JC would not look at him. He said, "JC, please tell me there's nothing else, please."

JC hesitated. "There was a short statement they had me sign," JC uttered.

Paul was back on his feet, so angry that tears formed in his eyes. He banged the phone against the glass yelling, "You don't ever listen. You don't know what the hell you signed. We both know that. You don't listen."

A guard warned Paul about his behavior. Paul flopped back in his seat taking a minute to gain his composure. JC couldn't say a word. He knew he had messed up. He was so desperate to get out he acted without thinking.

Although optimism wasn't his strong suit, the look of despair on his brother's face prompted Paul to be positive. He calmed down and said, "Okay, look. Akbar is helping me to get them to drop the charges and release the freeze on my assets. Once we get my money released, I can hire an attorney to handle all of this. The public defender is worthless. The government pays him."

"Is Trevor all right?"

"Trevor has the same charges as you with no bail, and I couldn't get any info on Felix."

JC perked up a little. "If they set a bail for me, call New York. Black will put some property up for me. And, Candace and Tamara have some cash I had them put away. You can use it to try to get the family settled in a place and get your charges worked out. Once you get straight, you can work on me and Trevor."

"Candace gave Akbar your money to help with my bail, but I'll get the money from Tamara. I just have to find out where she's staying. All of us are crammed in Candace's mother's one bedroom apartment right now. I'm not complaining. She's a life saver."

JC laughed. "Sounds too much like Georgia. I guess I should look at the bright side, I only have three roommates."

Candace and Paul spent the entire afternoon riding around

looking for Tamara. Paul was waiting in the car while Candace stood at the door of a house talking to Tamara's old neighbors. She turned and ran back to the car. "They haven't seen Tamara either, and I can't think of anywhere else to look."

"She couldn't have just disappeared," Paul said.

"Her and her mom." Candace was quiet for a minute. "You think she's the snitch?"

"Why would she make up all this mess? Nah, Tee wouldn't do anything like this."

"I wouldn't think so either, but where did she go?"

"I don't know, but it wasn't her. If Felix wasn't locked up, I'd think it was him. What about Nate? He used to be a cop, you know."

"Nate is just as worried as us. He tracked me down when he got out. It's not him." Candace said. "It doesn't seem right that we don't know who the informant is. Since we got arrested, don't we have a right to know who said these things?"

"Candace the laws are written in their favor. There is a law protecting the identity of an informant until you go to court. Even then, you can't get much more than their name. They usually seal their records. Most of the people that get fingered by a snitch take a deal and don't ever find out who told on them."

"How is this stuff legal?" Candace paused. "Paul, what are we going to do about a lawyer?"

"Akbar is in town. I'm going over to his hotel to talk it over. You got time?"

"That's about all I do have."

Paul and Candace drove into Los Angeles to meet with Akbar at a hotel on Sepulveda Boulevard right outside LAX. The three of them sat in the lobby of the modest hotel, reviewing the details of the arrest and charges.

Akbar tried to explain what went down in broader terms. "Prison is an industry and snitches are being used all over the place to keep the prisons stocked with their product—convicts. They call it a "War on Drugs," but it's really a war on the minority community."

Akbar leaned in, pointing for emphasis. "With the mandatory minimum sentencing guidelines, someone convicted of selling five grams of crack gets the same time as somebody selling five-hundred grams of powdered coke."

"Damn, that's a one hundred-to-one ratio," Paul responded.

"You hear me now?" Akbar replied. "These people are getting the same time as murderers. The only way to avoid the mandatory sentences is to be a snitch. So our community is full of informants desperate to rat anybody out."

"There weren't any drugs at the club. Who would say that? Don't they need proof?" Candace asked.

"Look, my sister. Some of these people are facing life sentences for drugs. There is so much pressure to snitch that a lot of them just make up accusations against people to reduce their time. Get two people to agree on the same thing and you got a charge."

Paul added, "Also, it's prestigious and profitable for the agencies to convict people—guilty or not."

"You're learning, my brother." Akbar said.

Paul was on a roll. "It's like the laws they passed back in the 1700's."

Akbar and Candace both shot Paul a perplexed look.

"You got to think. What about the Fugitive Slave Act? All the slave owners had to do was go before a judge and make an oral statement that they owned a slave. Slaves weren't given a trial or allowed to present evidence on their own behalf, not even proof that they had already earned their freedom. Same suit, just warmed over."

Akbar pointed at Paul. He smiled and nodded in agreement. "You did your homework. Don't be surprised if I use that in my next speech." He reached into his briefcase and pulled out a news article. Akbar never left home without documentation of the mind-boggling stories he would tell his audiences across the globe. They were true but so extreme they were hard to believe without back up.

He handed the newspaper to Candace as he summarized the story. "In 1989, a man with a construction business, a wife and a son, bought a pound of pot for $950 from a felon with thirty convictions on his record. The snitch was paid $200 by the police to sell the weed. That poor man, a Vietnam Vet, was sentenced to life-without-parole for trafficking in marijuana. Hear me now. He got life for buying one pound of marijuana from a paid snitch. He is still in jail now."

"That's crazy," Candace said as she continued to read the article. "Life for buying weed and the courts let these rapists and gang-bangers get out in no time so they can continue raping and killing? Can't they figure out who's lying?"

"They are not interested in the truth, my sister. Don't get me wrong; there are some good cops and agents. But, on the inside, informing translates to whistle blowing in government language, and whistle blowers don't last long. So, everyone walks around like the three monkeys. See no evil, hear no evil, speak no truth. They can't do anything else."

"You see what happened to Nate," Paul said.

"People are fighting to get the laws changed but it will take some time." Akbar handed a business card to Paul and continued, "Call this lawyer. I already spoke to him but it will cost a lot of money and the cards are stacked against JC."

Chapter 20

Dime–sized wads of sweat dripped from JC's forehead onto his pillow as he passed time stretched across his bed, tummy side down, with his chin resting on his hands. He had undressed down to his boxers but the heat was still excruciating. It was the hottest day JC could remember—ever. He had never suffered through that type of heat living in Long Beach where he had the benefit of the ocean breeze. In the middle of downtown Los Angeles, the week long October heat wave was brutal. Guards claimed the air was switched over each year in late September so nothing could be done. JC had heard of this in New York where building owners turned off the air and serviced the furnace for winter, but this was the middle of the desert and September and October were known to be the hottest months of the year in Southern California. *This had to be illegal,* he thought.

JC stayed inside as much as possible, determined to avoid the desert sun at all costs. Plus, he had been staying away from the yard since Tupac Shakur was gunned down in Vegas after a Mike Tyson fight in September. Rumors about the identity of the assassins created major tension among the inmates.

Normally, JC would play solitaire to pass the time but he feared the slightest activity would generate more heat. Instead, he spent the day sitting still, thinking and reflecting on what appeared to be a bleak future. All of his attempts to get released on bail had failed. His attorney left much to be desired but the family could not pull together the funds to hire a good attorney, so it was the best he could do. Quotes for a proper defense ranged from a low of $25,000 to $100,000 or more, with no guarantees.

JC thought about the two federal agents who had visited him three times in the past month. Unlike the agents playing nice that were sent to collect his statement when he was first arrested, these two showed no mercy. One was a tall handsome black man about thirty-five, in the prime of his upwardly mobile career. The other was short, portly, white, and looked to be at the end of his career, close to retirement. Both were arrogant, aggressive and on a mission to get JC to turn snitch.

JC never spoke; he only listened to the duo list out the charges against him. They slid a copy of the mandatory minimum sentencing guidelines in front of JC to review while they explained how the point system worked. They stressed the fact that the judge was bound by these guidelines regardless of extenuating circumstances. In other words, if JC was found guilty, the judge would be mandated to sentence him to at least fifteen years in prison and possibly more. They went on to tell him that the only chance he had to reduce his points was to assist them in making more arrests. The more help he offered that resulted in arrests, the more his points would be lowered, which, in turn, would decrease his sentence.

The agents drilled JC for the names of associates, friends or family JC knew who engaged in the drug trade. They suggested that Trevor was really the culprit and JC had no knowledge of what was going on. *Do they really think I would snitch on my son?* JC thought. They asked him about people he may have heard about, hustlers who had attended the Playas Ball, and a lot of high rollers from New York—some he knew and some he didn't. They also offered to allow him bail in order to help them set up someone he knew. Of course, each time the agents visited JC with their skillfully rehearsed sales pitch, JC stared silently at the two as if they were speaking a foreign language.

On their final visit, the duo came armed with ammunition to convince JC he had no chance to win in court. Just as Paul warned, they were using JC's statement against him. It confirmed a deal with Payback. There was also the witness statement from a confidential informant, photos, and the drugs. JC didn't flinch, although thoughts whirled inside his head wondering what photos they could possible have. The older agent was holding a folder they told JC was the drug evidence. JC thought, *how much crack can fit into that little envelope?* The agent pushed his horn-rimmed glasses to the top of his nose, dug into the folder and pulled out a picture of drugs found in the basement of The Empire. JC was dumbfounded. For one fleeting moment, he wondered whether the drugs belonged to Trevor. Knowing his son, he concluded that the police had planted the drugs.

Before JC could wrestle with the shock of seeing the drugs in his basement, like a man taking his last thrust before an orgasm, the older agent snatched several photos from a second envelope and slapped them across the table. This was JC's first realization that he had been followed for several months leading to his arrest. There were pictures of him everywhere. From sitting on the lawn at the Long Beach Jazz Festival, to a Whitney Houston concert in Las Vegas. Albeit completely innocent, the most damaging were: shots of JC and Payback on the street embracing; another of Trevor getting out of the car in front of Payback's house; JC, Payback and Havoc huddled in front of the club; a photo of Felix coming out of the basement with a package; and a shot of Felix handing the package to Trevor. Despite his shock, the two agents left without hearing a peep out of JC.

Perhaps it was the heat in the prison that day, but JC thought about contacting the agents to tell them he would work with them. It could get him back on the streets so he could see his family and breathe again. He never considered setting anyone up since, even on the hottest day of the year, he would not stoop to snitching. He figured he could take as long as they gave him on the streets to put some money together for an attorney. He could, at least, try to get Trevor out. If he pulled that trick, JC knew he'd be looking at the maximum of the maximum sentence if he were convicted. At this point, twenty-five years didn't sound much longer than fifteen to JC.

JC thought more about the point system. It was a clearly a game that could only be won if you master the art of snitching. *Snitchcraft*, JC thought. The snitch game was like a game of tag.

The agents had used their bag of tricks to get points on someone; they gave JC some of their points. Now, JC needed to forget everything he was taught about loyalty and set-up friends and family in order to pass on his points. If he was crafty and lowered his points enough, he could buy his own freedom and let the next person worry about reducing their points by getting somebody else. Someone else gets the next mark, and so on, and so on, and so on, keeping those prisons stocked with fresh new healthy workers.

For a brief moment he thought about the real drug dealers on the street; people he had problems with. Perhaps he could set one of them up. With what he knew on some of the big time hustlers, he could probably earn enough points to buy his freedom—but that was snitching. It was dangerous and he wouldn't last long on the streets, nor could he live with himself.

Dusk brought some relief from the heat of the sun and by ten that night JC could feel a chill in the air. He started thinking more clearly. Now able to move about, he used his last hour of light to play solitaire and think of a plan of action. He was sure his lawyer was not giving much thought to his defense.

Chapter 21

A CO escorted JC to a small, drab room with square tables slightly bigger than elementary school desks. The room was packed with inmates exchanging information with their lawyers, most of whom were paid by the government. Just as JC reached the corner booth where a slovenly public defender was flipping through a stack of papers, he spotted Manny, an old timer he knew from back in New York. He immediately went over to talk to him.

"Yo, what's up man?" JC said.

Manny hopped up and gave JC a bear hug. "JC Powell, I heard what happened man. How ya' holdin' out?"

"They got me fighting for my life man."

Manny looked over at JC's lawyer. "That's your lawyer?" He said shaking his head. "Take a deal man. Take a deal! You can't beat the system."

The guard gestured for JC to take a seat. He went over and sat directly across from his attorney, Harry Smart. JC offered no greetings or small talk—he just got straight to business. "What's the plan?"

Harry Smart said, "Well JC, I've looked over the case in great detail and the evidence is overwhelming."

"Overwhelming?"

"Well, it will be hard to convince a jury that two people would lie for no reason. Why would they make all this up?"

"I don't know. When it all started they only had one witness.

Did you find out who the witnesses are?"

JC watched as the lawyer dug through piles of papers inside his briefcase in search of his file. He had no faith in Harry Smart, but this man was his only means of getting information on the case. The family was still hoping for a miracle and the rest of Paul's cash to be released. They found out it takes a lot more time for the Fed's to release personal assets than it takes to seize them. The federal agents explained to Paul that it was a "process," which could take some time.

The family was able to retain a lawyer to get back Candace's condo and the bookstore because they were no longer in JC's name. The Fed's kept a freeze on all of JC's bank accounts, the house where Mama and Auntie lived, and JC's house. They did eventually allow Paul to retrieve JC's personal property from inside his house. The government agents had no idea of the value of some of the flashy items JC had adorning the house. When they let Paul inside, in addition to removing the crystal chandelier and wall sconces, he replaced all of the designer faucets and light fixtures with cheaper items.

Against Paul's wishes, rather than try to retain a cheap private attorney, JC instructed Paul to use the proceeds from the sale of his belongings to pay on Cherie's college tuition. They never found Tamara so the money she had was in the wind. Consequently, the court assigned Harry Smart to represent JC.

Harry emerged with a manila folder labeled "Powell, J.C." He proudly said, "Here it is. The witness is—" He ruffled through the papers. "Uh, Jason Green. Yes Jason Green. What can Mr. Green reveal?"

JC said, "Jason Green? I don't know no Jason Green."

The lawyer looked back at the file. "Oh here it is. He goes by the name of Payback. What can Payback tell them about your operations?"

"Operations? You talk like you believe I did something. What can he tell them? Not a damn thing because I wasn't in the drug business. There was no operation." JC calmed himself down. "Payback is a gangster I had some problems with in the past, but he don't know me to know my business."

"The other witness is Felix Calhoun. I told you about him,

didn't I?" Harry Smart looked up at JC as he stood and walked around the room, deep in thought.

"Damn." JC paced the floor in intense silence for a few minutes. "Felix! That's it! Why didn't I put this shit together? Now it adds up."

Harry Smart asked, "What adds up?"

"That's why that boy went back and forth to Atlanta—selling drugs. The punk was probably down with Payback the whole time. Get what you can on Felix. He got arrested too. He must be lying to cover his own ass. They had to be Felix's drugs."

Harry Smart said, "I checked. Jason Green, or Payback, has a long record, but I can't find anything on Felix Calhoun. It doesn't mean he doesn't have a record. It could be sealed."

"He's from Atlanta, that's all I know. I'll see what I can find out."

"About bail. Well, uh, still no luck on the bail hearing."

"I'm looking at twenty years and can't get bail. That ought to be illegal."

"It's a tactic the government uses to make people take a deal."

"Not me."

"JC, I really think you should consider the deal. They've got a solid case against you."

JC slammed a chair against the table. "I ain't takin' no damn deal. I had nothing to do with Felix's shit. Anyway, what case? Two people saying I did it? They can't convict me on that."

"With a conspiracy charge they don't have to present anymore evidence. The witnesses are enough. But Jason was busted after a drug deal with Felix the night after Players Ball. They say you set it up—that's conspiracy. The drugs were later found in the basement of the club. Even though it wasn't a massive quantity of drugs, it's still hard evidence."

"Those were Felix's drugs, not mine." JC paused. "They got a thug named Payback and Felix? No deal."

"And the photos."

"I explained them to you."

"There's also the assets they seized. They'll all be converted to drugs."

"Converted?" JC said.

"They take the dollar value of your personal assets and convert it to an amount in drug sales," Smart said.

"Hard work bought everything I got. They can check the books."

"JC, you will never get a jury to believe you went from a major loss to making millions in less than two years. It doesn't make sense to average people, true or not. And they also have your statement."

"But they changed my words in that statement. That's not what I said."

"But you signed it." Harry Smart closed his briefcase, "Look JC, this is a federal case. If you're found guilty, the judge has no leeway. He has to go by the guidelines. The minimum time you will get is fifteen years. The only way to reduce your time is to offer the government what they call 'substantial assistance'—help them bust someone else."

"I ain't no snitch."

"I advise you to cooperate with the agents."

JC yelled, "Who do you work for? Are you my lawyer or what? I told you I'm not taking a deal."

"Okay. Okay. I'll call Paul so he can help me get in contact with your witnesses."

"You said that the last time you were here. Do you do anything when you leave?" His demeanor calmed. "Please, find something on Felix. And don't bother my mother. She's too old for this drama."

JC stood, waiting to be escorted out of the visiting area. The evidence they had troubled him. Ever since the federal agent showed him the photos, he had been racking his brain, trying to figure out who took the pictures. He knew anyone could have captured the shots taken in public places. But, there were so many photos taken at family gatherings in the club it had to be a regular. He concluded that Felix couldn't have taken pictures to incriminate himself, so the question remained, *who was close enough to take the photos?* He couldn't think of regulars who would have had that kind of access, so the finger pointed back to the people around him.

Thoughts whirled through JC's head. As much as he hated himself for thinking the way he did, JC began to suspect everyone. *Nate was a former cop,* JC thought, *perhaps he was trying to get back on their good side or, even worse, maybe he was working undercover the whole time. And what about Dee? She was in and out of trouble and everyone knew she'd do anything for a dollar. Then there was Tamara. Maybe she wasn't as sweet and innocent as everyone thought. No one had heard a peep from her.*

JC decided it wasn't Nate, who was constantly calling Candace to check on JC. Tamara would never be that vicious, he knew her too well. It couldn't be anyone around him, he thought. Finally, a light bulb went off. He remembered the mysterious old man who sat at the bar every Thursday, Friday, and Saturday night. He sat through all the family events and never spoke beyond whispering his drink preference. After all this time, there was probably no one who could identify him in a line-up since he kept his large brimmed hat covering his face all the time. That was it! They had an in-house federal agent watching them the whole time.

Chapter 22

The trial lasted only three days. In those few days, JC Powell catapulted from a simple country boy determined to make a living to take care of his family to a "gangster legend" in Long Beach. By day two of the media-frenzied trial, all hope in convincing the jury of JC's innocence was shattered; everyone could see that JC's "panel of peers" was sure of his guilt.

Without many objections from Harry Smart, the prosecutor called cunning Felix Calhoun to tell the tale of how Jason Green, AKA Payback, and JC conspired to take over the drug trade in Southern California and various urban cities across the nation. They had a couple of witnesses JC never saw before to verify the story, but Felix was the only one from the club. Paul had warned JC that Dee might use the trial as an opportunity to retaliate against him, but, as JC thought, she didn't turn out to be that vicious. She was nowhere to be seen.

The federal prosecutor played a videotape of Felix buying the drugs from Payback the night of the last Playas Ball. Payback had taken a deal for his testimony so he confirmed his own participation in the scheme. They also offered into evidence the cocaine confiscated during a search of the basement of the club, the photos, and JC's statement.

Even though they followed JC for months, aside from the drugs seized upon arrest, the sole basis for JC's "Kingpin" status was DEA estimates, not actual drugs found or evidence of any other drug transactions. The prosecutor offered up JC's material acquisitions—converted to drug sales—as evidence. This time, JC's flamboyance worked against him in and out of the courtroom. With no mention by any media of how JC and his family worked tirelessly to build the club into a million dollar enterprise, the public couldn't help but think that all the cars, jewelry, and other assets were ill-gotten gains.

The tale of the Powell enterprise had taken on a life of its own. It became big enough to gain international media attention, glorifying the DEA for bringing down one of the largest drug operations in California—perhaps in the country.

The prosecutor held a press conference at the beginning and end of the trial praising the work of the DEA and other law enforcement agencies that collaborated in the efforts to topple a major Kingpin in the drug trade. JC's enterprise was reported to be a fifty thousand dollar a day operation. The prosecutor repeatedly announced, "This bust prevented millions of dollars worth of drugs from infiltrating neighborhoods across the country."

It took less than an hour for the jury to return with a guilty verdict. In accordance with the mandatory minimum sentencing guidelines, JC was sentenced to fifteen years and eight months in a federal penitentiary.

Chapter 23

Four inmates covered in prison-issued orange jumpsuits, played bid whist at a picnic table. The orange identified the federal prisoners who were housed in the LA County Jail until they were sentenced and transferred to a federal penitentiary. The jailhouse gospel singer, Church, was seated at the end of the table singing Howard Hewitt's "Say Amen." An exercise-addicted inmate pumping iron a few feet away, urged Church on.

JC's friend, Manny, was engaged in a vigorous legal debate with another inmate, Twin. Manny and Twin were prison veterans and experts on the system. Manny had just taken a deal for twenty years on a drug trafficking charge and Twin was doing a stiff three for the sale of a firearm. Both were awaiting transfers to a federal penitentiary. They were discussing legal strategies for the young, first-timer, playing cards with them.

Sadly enough, better advice came from the jailhouse educated legal experts than the inmates could get from their court-appointed representatives. Fellow prisoners took the time, which they had plenty of, to research relevant cases. Inmates would pay with cigarettes and clothes and have girlfriends on the outside send money to the families of the legal experts. It was normally a money making business, but they also offered free advice, which they had done in JC's case.

"Bid man," said Twin. He yelled, "Church, shut that noise up, don't you know nothing' but gospel songs?"

Manny replied laughing, "Dumb ass, why you think they call him Church?" He looked back at his hand and said, "Six low."

"You got it." Twin looked across the yard, "Hey, look who's back."

Everyone turned and watched JC drag across the yard toward them. He looked frail. It was a combination of stress and the fact that he had lost fifteen pounds since his arrest. Manny whispered as he arranged the cards in his hand, "He don't look like he got good news." Then he asked JC, who had made it to the table, "Yo' JC, how did it go in court?"

JC propped one foot up on the edge of the bench, leaned in, and, looking drained and distraught, mumbled "Fifteen." He sighed, "They gave me fifteen years."

The younger inmate cried out, "Damn! They did you bad." The inmates shot the youngster the evil eye. They all knew from experience, sentencing day was not a good day, so they were trying to be as cool as possible – for a few minutes, that is. They just wanted to give JC time to pull himself together and vent a little, before they hurled around their I-told-you-so's. The jailhouse lawyers had warned JC of this outcome and urged him to take a deal. Against their expert advice, JC demanded his day in court. Of course, the penitentiary legal team was eagerly awaiting their opportunity to validate their adept knowledge of the system.

JC went on, "The lies. Felix lied so bad. And Harry Smart never questioned him. I can't believe he has a law degree. The first day, he had me confused with another client."

Manny decided JC had vented enough. It was time for him to man up, and take his blows from his fellow inmates. "What did I advise? I told you to take the damn deal. You were tripping, thinking you could prove something. It's their system, not ours." Manny pulled the toothpick from the crease of his mouth and pointed around the yard, "We keep their system working so they can stay employed. A criminal is a commodity in America."

JC whined, "Yeah, they sure got it down. They take your money so you can't get a real lawyer."

Manny threw a card from his hand. "Once again, their system—they make it work for them. They got all kinds of games." He tossed another card and asked, "How much time did that boy get?"

"Felix?" JC said quizzically. "I don't know but he was clean, didn't look like he been locked down at all."

Twin added, "He probably wasn't. They offered me probation if I set somebody up. But that ain't me, so now the state's takin' care of my five kids."

"I just don't believe it," JC's voice faded. "I can't go out like this, I can't."

"We told you to take the deal. You can't beat 'em," said Manny.

Out of nowhere, Church shouted, "Yes you can. You just have to pray about it."

All heads turned to stare at Church, the resident psycho. Manny said, "Man, you crazy as hell. You on you way to do life, set up by your baby's mama, and you walking around singing gospel songs and praying."

The men laughed. JC said, "You talk to the Lord for me, Church. I'm gonna talk to another lawyer." He looked at Manny. "Manny you know Paul is a former panther and activist from way back. He has even more connections than when you hung out with him. He's working on getting his money released and then we'll appeal. Believe me, the Powell family will not go out like this!"

Manny jumped up, slammed his cards on the table and yelled, "BOSTON!" He turned to JC who was seated next to him with his head in his hands. "You can't beat a man at his own game, JC."

Chapter 24

"Hello. Hello. JC are you there?" Paul said into the phone after accepting the collect call from an inmate in the federal penitentiary in Lompoc.

"Yeah I'm here. What's up?"

"It's all good," Paul said.

"Man don't mess with me. You know what I mean, what happened in court?"

"JC, they counted the prior convictions—"

"Come on, what did he get?"

"Twenty four years."

"Twenty four? How did we get into this shit?" JC cried out.

"JC you have to be patient. I'll work this out. Trust me."

"You're telling me my son got twenty-four years in prison and I should be patient? Patient? That's what you have to say?"

"I know what you're going through—"

"You know? How do you know?"

"Come on JC. You know this is killing us out here. It's killing me."

JC paused for a minute. "I know Paul. I'm just glad you're out there to hold it down. I know you're doing what you can. I have to get off, but you know what to tell everyone. Thanks for everything."

The next few months turned to years. JC realized that what

he thought were his hardest times—building the club—were a walk in the park compared to the challenge ahead of him. He was initially sent up north to Lompoc, California for his first year. He frequently talked with his brother and they worked diligently to get an appeal and a transfer to a facility closer to home. Going into the second year, JC's energy began to wane. By the time he got transferred to the federal penitentiary in Victorville, he only left his cell when he was ordered to. He called family less frequently. By year three, he stopped calling home at all. Cards and letters, all unopened, piled up. He refused visits.

JC could not bear to hear another motivational speech from well-meaning friends and family, especially Paul, who had joined their mother in preaching that "faith and prayer are the answer." *Paul could be thankful that he had the freedom to go to church every Sunday to give thanks.* JC figured, *if there was a God, or, as people always said, an angel watching over him, his angel got lost somewhere in the City of Angels, and it certainly would not find a way to the federal pen Victorville.* He knew he was on his own for this one. Beaten.

Paul continued to visit for about a month, but when JC would not see him, he stopped going. Candace persevered. Since she could no longer ride with Paul, she took the train and a bus. That worked out just fine since she had reentered the nursing field and worked until six AM.

Rain or shine, Candace started her three-hour journey to Victorville every Saturday morning at seven AM. She would sit quietly in the visiting booth, hoping that it would be the week JC would find the strength to get up and fight. She figured JC would hear them call his name on the PA system and know that she was still there for him.

Three months passed with no JC. Candace continued to visit. The ritual was just as much for Candace as JC; they did have over twenty years invested in each other. JC was the only man she ever loved and the PA system in Victorville had become her only means of communicating that message to him.

Six months later, eleven AM came and went without JC hearing his name on the PA system. He listened intently the next two Saturday's— just in case— but as he thought, Candace had finally given up and moved on with her life. Although he missed the weekly announcement, he knew it was best.

JC's spirit deteriorated day by day. Eventually his depression took a toll on him physically. He lost over thirty pounds and appeared at least two shades lighter. His eyes were sunken in and his lips resembled a pair of his alligator shoes. He was rushed to the prison infirmary three times for dehydration and once for a severe virus. JC was on a slow path toward death.

After over a year of gloom, JC was spread across his bed late one night, playing over his life in his head like a movie, trying endlessly to press stop at the point he went in the wrong direction. His normal bedtime routine—determining the size and amount of rats he heard lurking in the darkness—had been interrupted by the violent rain smashing against the roof, and the noise emanating from the prison block.

It was New Year's Eve. The inmates had been pleading with the CO to take JC for his periodic trip to the prison infirmary to get his liquid fix. He was severely dehydrated, lethargic, and experiencing short bouts of confusion—a sure sign that he needed intravenous therapy to replenish his body fluids.

JC was, once again, without a cellmate. It suited him just fine. His prison family was convinced that he had lost it once he stopped speaking, but JC heard and understood everything and wasn't up to ignoring fifty questions that night. He already had to endure inmates yelling to him from their cells imploring him to snap out of it. A cellmate only made it worse. Like on the outside, everybody liked JC. They couldn't stand seeing him speechless, emaciated, and broken.

The lights didn't go out at eleven PM as usual. The guards allowed the inmates to stay up to bring in the New Year. Loud music played and the inmates used whatever they had in their cell to create a cacophony of celebratory noises.

JC changed his position, turning flat on his back, his hands behind his head, awaiting the dark silence he had come to enjoy. Finally, it was midnight. The guards endured a few verses of Old Ag'zine and allowed about twenty minutes of merrymaking before the lights faded. To JC's dismay, the noise continued in the black of night without admonishment from the overseers. As the prisoners settled down, a light tapping sound emerged from the darkness. *That damn Church*, JC thought. When they were locked up in LA, Church assured everyone that the Lord would send him to Victorville to serve his time. It was less than fifteen miles from his family. Church was the only person in their group that was sent to the prison of his choice. Of course, Church saw it as a sign from the Almighty.

As Church continued to tap, a few prisoners began to hum, clap, or thump lightly to the beat. In a melodic falsetto Church sang,

> *"Amazing grace! How sweet the sound, that saved a wretch like me. I once was lost, but now I'm found, was blind, but now I see."*

By the second verse of "Amazing Grace" even the guards were praising the Lord. JC was moved. He struggled to sit upright on his bed, closer to the heavenly sound flowing through the air. He grabbed the post of the bed for leverage but still could not muster the strength to get up.

Suddenly, as if someone offered a helping hand to lift the weight of his heavy head, JC found the strength to rise up. The uplifting music seemed to resuscitate him. The gospel was so powerful, it penetrated throughout JC's body causing him to shiver—like someone had opened a window to let the real air from the outside world inside. He could even hear the sounds of the wind blowing against the prison bars. Church continued,

> *"Through many dangers, toils and snares I have already come. 'Tis grace hath brought me safe thus far, and grace will lead me home."*

JC was more alert and energized. Renewed. That short verse of Amazing Grace had opened his heart to give heed to the quenching of his spiritual thirst. Before JC could fully process the refreshing feeling overwhelming his body, Church started tapping again. The musicians in residence added their instruments in the background and voices from the darkness urged Church on. "Take your time, Church...talk to me, Church...preach brother," the men yelled.

Out of nowhere, Church softly whispered, "This one is for you, JC." He startled JC, who listened intently but never responded. A faint voice sang:

> *"There will be mountains that I will have to climb*
> *And there will be battles that I will have to fight*
> *But victory or defeat, it's up to me to decide*
> *But how can I expect to win If I never try.*
> *I just can't give up now*
> *I've come too far from where I started from*
> *Nobody told me the road would be easy*
> *and I don't believe he brought me this far to leave me*
> *I said I don't believe he brought me this far,*
> *JC, I don't believe he brought you this far to leave you."*

About mid-song JC swung around, knelt on the floor and, for the first time since his father died, he prayed.

Chapter 25

"E ff—" JC struggled to read the next word.

"Sound it out," the instructor said. "You've seen this word before."

"Eff," JC paused. "Eff–a–ca–c." JC proudly said, as he flipped the page of "Are Prisons Obsolete?" by former Black Panther and political prisoner Angela Davis. Paul had sent him the book the day JC announced that he was finally tackling a major stumbling block in his life-his inability to read.

"Good. Now read the full sentence."

"We should ask how it is that so many people could end up in prison without major debates re-gard-ing the eff-i-ca-cy of incarceration."

"Excellent. You're a fast learner JC. I don't know why you waited so long to learn to read. Angela Davis is a college professor. This is not easy reading material."

"I had such a hard time as I kid, I just figured I couldn't learn. My brother tried to teach me but it was too embarrassing, even with him."

"Try to finish the book this week. It's only one more chapter. I look forward to hearing what you think about it. I'll see you next week," said the diminutive old man. The volunteer, a member of Guardian Angels Prison Ministry, was the perfect person to help JC get over his reading block. He was soft spoken, patient, and non-threatening.

JC left the training room satisfied that, at last, he could mark off the number two issue on his mental list of goals. He could read.

As he traveled back to his dismal jail cell, focused on staying positive, JC thought, *it's a shame that it took prison to face up to the real John Cornelius Powell.* Paul had convinced JC that admitting that he couldn't read could be instrumental in gaining an appeal. The truth was, he really had no idea what he was signing when they put his statement in front of him. Once he worked up enough nerve to ask for help, he realized that he was not alone. Plenty of intelligent men had trouble learning to read. Like them, JC took classes and tackled his problem word by word.

Eventually JC learned to read well enough to help work on his appeal. He passed time working out, reading, and even visited the Prison Chaplain on occasion. But, most of his spare time was spent in the law library where the librarian and jailhouse lawyers would help him research information related to his case. Paul was still working on the outside, sending letters to congressmen and rallying the support of activist groups.

A series of articles by a journalist named George Curry brought national attention to the bias in the criminal justice system and was instrumental in President Clinton's pardon of Kemba Smith, a young college student sentenced to twenty-four years based on the mandatory minimum sentencing guidelines. The pardon spawned major controversy, resulting in even more discussion of the prison system and the sentencing guidelines. Groups like the Hip-Hop Summit Action Network, NAACP Legal Defense Fund, and the Sentencing Project were vigorously fighting for reforms in the sentencing guidelines.

Paul attended a criminal justice conference in Atlanta held by the Georgia Coalition for the Peoples' Agenda and made enough noise for Lawrence Giles, a prominent civil rights attorney, to take the case pro bono. Giles and Akbar were friends and had marched with Dr. Martin Luther King, Jr. in the '60's. Giles was very active in the prison reform movement. During their first meeting, Giles assured JC he would be granted an appeal. Things were starting to look brighter. Almost.

There was still weakness number one: Candace. A few months back, Paul told JC she was seeing someone and he thought it was a serious relationship. JC expected to hear that news one day, in or out of prison. He knew she would eventually have to move on with her life. JC was surprised that this news didn't crush him as he feared it would. Actually, he was happy for her. Candace was a good loyal woman and deserved to have a strong man by her side. JC knew he didn't lose Candace when he went to prison; he lost her when he returned home and found that she had left him in New York. Candace was the type of woman that would stick with her man through thick and thin, but when she had enough, it was over.

When Candace left New York, it took a while for her to contact JC. He waited patiently, knowing she would call eventually. They did have a daughter together. A few months later, she called and informed him she was in Long Beach. She offered no explanation for leaving, and JC never asked why she left. They both avoided the issue. The family urged JC to go after her, promise to be faithful and beg for her forgiveness. Deep down, JC knew it wasn't other women that disrupted their perfect world and ran Candace off. Candace knew JC would never love anyone but her. Their problem was a lot deeper than other women.

JC stuck with the philandering story over the years because he was embarrassed to admit he had done the one thing Candace could not accept. He had deserted her when she needed him most. Their relationship was unique. They were friends, lovers, and truly respected each other. They always promised that, no matter what was going on in each of their lives, they would be there to support the other in time of need, just like Candace had been there for JC throughout this ordeal. But JC knew he had reneged on the deal, fell short of his responsibilities as a man, and abandoned his best friend, the mother of his child, in the most challenging time of her life. He was ashamed.

He also had to admit that his inability to commit to Candace had nothing to do with his desire to be with other women. It was his own low self-esteem. He admired Candace; she was perfect. He always thought HE wasn't good enough for her and eventually she would figure that out and leave him. His response to that fear was—once again—avoidance. If he didn't commit, she couldn't leave him. Looking at how his life turned out, he figured things worked out for the best after all. All he could do was to be happy for Candace.

JC required more time than the year left on his sentence to tackle additional demons he needed to address.

Chapter 26

"Powell, you have a new roommate," the CO said, interrupting JC's game of solitaire.

In walked Manny, fully gray and at least ten pounds heavier. The two were pleasantly surprised and hugged. Manny said, "JC, it's been what, seven or eight years? I thought you got parole by now."

"I'm short man. I get out in three months. Where you been?" JC said.

"Traveling. When I left Lompoc, I went to Leavenworth for a year, then to the Federal Pen in Beaumont. Finally, I asked for a transfer to New York and I ended up here."

"Beat them at their own game?"

Manny laughed. "You know I didn't want no parts of New York!" He stepped back and gave JC a once over, "Look at ya, you been working out! You look good. Last time I saw you, I was worried. You were looking mighty glum."

Manny put his belongings away and the two talked for hours, catching up on gossip in and out of prison. Manny started checking out the photos that covered the entire wall on one side of the cell. "I met your son, real respectful kid and talented as hell. Every time I saw him, he was singing a new song he had written."

At the end of JC's bed, Manny stumbled on a stack of papers— letters to congress, judges, the governor, and a reading book. He moved a few letters over, grabbed two photo albums from the side of the pile and sat down to look at the pictures.

"Yo, you was doing it back in the day! You sure got a rep. I heard you were the biggest dealer in Cali. You a Ghetto Superstar."

"An urban myth."

Manny said, "Look at this, a Mercedes, Rolls. Uh! You were puttin' it down."

JC replied, "Yeah, I had to keep women around because I don't even drive." Manny looked at him curiously. JC waved his hands and said, "Long story, don't ask."

Manny flipped to a picture of a pool party at a large two-story brick house. "This was your house?"

"Yeah, it wasn't nothing extravagant."

"It sho' ain't low income housing."

Manny continued admiring JC's past. He laughed at outdated hairstyles and clothes, and was fascinated by the horde of material acquisitions.

All of a sudden, a serious expression took over Manny's face as he scrutinized a photo. He held the album closer and leaned under the light. He screamed, "Oh shit! I don't believe it. That's Larry Cook, all grown up."

JC jumped up and looked over Manny's shoulder at the photo. JC snatched the photo out of the book and said, "Larry? His name is not Larry. That's Felix, the snitch who lied on me."

"Felix?" Manny took the photo from JC and examined it closely for a few seconds. "Then Felix is Larry Cook, because this is definitely Larry. My son went to school with him in Detroit. They were friends for a minute but they had a serious falling out over some lies Larry told. Almost got my son killed. I had to go to Detroit and handle things."

"Detroit? Cook? Nah this boy is from Atlanta."

"I'm telling you JC, I know that boy, no question. That's Larry Cook."

"How could he testify under a bogus name?" JC asked as he sat back down.

"I don't know. But I do know he's a chronic liar for sure. I heard he was under investigation in New York for perjury."

"Perjury? Is that right?"

"The way I heard it, he lied on the wrong crew. People with

big time connections."

"Perjury. That could help me get an appeal."

"An appeal? Are you crazy? Didn't you say you were on your way out? Let this shit go."

"I can't. They took my life. My money. Destroyed my family."

"I feel you but—"

"I still have nightmares replaying the cops putting my mother in handcuffs. I lost too much. I ain't never gonna let this shit go."

Chapter 27

Dressed in his best suit, JC pulled the photos from the wall of his cell, took a quick look at each photo, then delicately placed each one in a box on the bed.

An inmate pushed a cart in front of the cell and handed JC his final mail at his Victorville address— two letters. The first one was his weekly prayer from his mother. The other was a letter from his attorney, Mr. Lawrence Giles. JC slipped his glasses to the middle of his nose and proudly opened the letter. Using his finger as a guide, and his lips to sound out each word, he read the letter. Although Manny was eager to find out what JC was smiling about, it was apparent to him that JC could barely read. He waited patiently as JC slowly absorbed every word in the short document.

JC looked up and said, "I'll be damn. They granted me a new trial."

"A new trial. What good is it now?" Manny asked.

"I told you, I'm going to prove Felix lied. My lawyer found out he—"

"Prove it? Haven't you heard anything I've said to you? They knew he was a liar from the jump. It's a prerequisite. JC you're free. Just leave it alone."

"A broke man ain't free. What am I suppose to do at my age? I'm going to expose some shit and get my money back. Watch me." He tucked the letter into his pants, closed the box, and continued to talk with Manny about meeting up on the outside when he was released.

JC's heart throbbed when he heard his name announced over the PA system for the last time. His excitement increased when the CO appeared to escort him out.

He hugged Manny. Without saying a word, he picked up the box and started his last journey down the dark, dismal halls of the Victorville prison complex. He stopped briefly at each cell to bid farewell to his housemates who were cheering him on and banging on the bars to their cells. By the time he reached the end of corridor, he had given away almost all of the mementoes from the box to inmates along the way. He figured they would have more use for them than him. The only items left were the family pictures people had sent over the years and a special Bible Mama sent him when he was first arrested.

When JC reached the last cell, just before the locked gate leading to the main building, Church stepped out of his cell. JC placed the box on the floor and raised his arms to hug him.

"I'm praying for you, JC," Church said.

"And me you." JC said as he reached into the box and emerged with The Original African Heritage Study Bible that he cherished. Mama had made Paul drive her all the way to Eso Wan Books in Los Angeles to buy JC that Bible. Over the years, Church spent a lot of time reading JC's Bible, sometimes to himself and eventually to JC. Church's own Bible was so tattered and worn, the inmates teased him constantly about finding loose pages scattered around the cellblock. JC knew Church was fascinated by the Afrocentric approach to the Bible.

"This is for you, Church," JC said.

"Oh no JC, you need that with you, I've got a Bible. Your mother gave that to you."

"Believe me, Mama would make you take it. Here, take it, it's the least I can do." The two embraced again.

Outside the prison, the sky was the same color of the debilitating walls of the prison complex. It was a cloudy day in the desert. No rain was expected, just clouds passing through en route to a place more worthy of their fertile droppings.

Despite the weather, the heavens seemed to radiate when, after eight very long years, JC walked out of the Federal Detention Center in Victorville a free man. A survivor.

A quick moment of sadness and reality swept over JC when Candace was not at the door to greet him. But, Paul was waiting. His mustache had earned a few more gray hairs and, something JC couldn't see during visits, he was wearing a few too many of Tracy's notorious sweet potato pies.

There was a long silence as the two just stood, face-to-face, staring at each other. They embraced, stepped back and took another glimpse and JC said, "I can't believe it, you're on time."

"Good to see you too, baby brother."

JC immediately pulled the letter out and handed it to Paul. "It's on now. I told everybody, this ain't over."

Part II

Chapter 28

It was another Powell family reunion and, for the first time in eight years, aside from Trevor, everyone was present. This one, however, was not held in a state park, but the Los Angeles Federal Courthouse. At last, the Powell family was having their day in court.

This trial was nothing like the first one. The great Lawrence Giles came armed with co-counsel, a legal researcher attached to a laptop computer, a jury consultant, and a high-profile Hollywood publicist from the Jazzmyne Agency. In addition to convincing several A-list celebrities to help bring media attention to the trial, the publicist coordinated daily press conferences and distributed a statement from Giles to newsrooms every afternoon.

This case was not about money for Attorney Lawrence Giles, a tall, slim, very light-skinned man with wavy jet-black hair. Although both of his parents were black, Giles could easily have passed for white. Giles had marched across the Edmund Pettus Bridge with Martin Luther King, Jr., helped plan the '63 March on Washington, represented victims of the MOVE bombing in Philadelphia, and made millions winning some of the largest race discrimination class-action suits in America. Now, the charismatic attorney was determined to expose the corrupt environment the government created by bartering for testimony in order to fill up prison cells across the country.

Akbar had convinced Giles this was the perfect trial to bring national attention to the serious injustices black people were suffering at the hands of the perverted system. Giles was brilliant in the courtroom and a real media darling. The national media attention would enable the activists to expose the Prison Industrial Complex for what it really was –the new slavery.

Of course, through his trials and tribulations, JC had become of believer of conspiracy theories, but he was not quite convinced the entire system knowingly participated, as black activists constantly eschewed. While he sympathized with their quest and understood his brother's militant tirades better, JC wasn't really concerned with the big picture; he was focused on clearing his name and getting his money back.

The voir dire only took two days. Aside from the Arian Nation-looking twenty-eight-year-old white guy who slipped by when all the preemptive challenges were exhausted, the defense was satisfied with the outcome. According to the high-priced jury consultant paid for by Akbar's organization, barring any major twists, the worst possible scenario would be a hung jury. She was convinced the thirty-five-year-old black female homemaker and the fifty-four-year-old black male postal worker would favor JC. She was also confident about the sixty-six-year-old Hispanic woman, who she thought would appreciate the fact that JC took care of his family. In total, there were six whites, three blacks, one Asian, and two Hispanics on the jury. Both alternates were white males.

Herbert Walker, the fifty-two-year-old, reasonably handsome black Assistant U.S. Attorney who tried the case was a bit cocky, but likeable. Although Giles was older than Walker, the two knew each other from college. Giles was Walker's "big brother" when he was pledging Omega during his undergraduate studies at Howard University. And, like Giles, Walker received his law degree from Harvard Law School. The two were friendly for years but just pursued different directions in their careers.

Giles was not the only who came prepared for battle. Since 2004 was an election year, Walker was under a lot of pressure to win the case. The prosecution's case lasted over a week. JC's defense team had banked on some of the witnesses not being available after so many years, but they all showed except one – Jason Green, also known as Payback. This was a major coup for the defense, since his crew was caught in the drug exchange and Payback was the only one to corroborate Felix's story that he was buying the drugs for JC. Payback's absence forced the prosecutor to work harder to convince the jury of Felix's truthfulness.

The prosecutor did attempt to call two witnesses who did not testify in the original trial. One was a crack head who said that he heard JC admit to the crimes while he was locked down. The other was a former cellmate who claimed JC tried to hire him to kill Felix. After a verbal battle between lawyers, which JC's attorney won by a landslide, neither witness was allowed to testify. Watching Giles wage war against Walker reinforced JC's notion that he was sitting on the side with the star players.

The strongest witness was Felix. Even with the government report the defense had obtained that proved Felix had lied on the stand in the past, the high-priced jury consultant was positive that his testimony had a major impact on the jury. Felix came off sincere and likeable. According to the consultant, most pathological liars have a knack for ingratiating themselves with the masses.

There was also the curve ball the prosecutor pitched when Felix testified that he had not participated in the bust for any type of deal for a reduction in prison time. He was just an honest citizen that approached the DEA when he found out what JC was up to. Felix went on to talk about how hard it was to make the decision to turn JC in, since he really loved the Powell family. His testimony was certainly bad news for the defense. Their theory of the case was predicated very much on the fact that Felix and Payback had something to gain by testifying. Specifically, the two were bartering freedom for testimony.

First up for the defense was Paul, who was seated on the witness stand reviewing a document. He already testified for the defense, denying any illegal activities whatsoever, and was now being cross-examined by Walker. Paul looked up from the document he was reviewing and said, "Yes, this was my statement."

"Mr. Powell, after all of the testimony the past week, are you still saying you had no knowledge of the drug activity?" Walker raised an arm in a sympathetic gesture. "Please keep in mind that you are under oath, Mr. Powell."

"There was no drug activity," Paul replied, never missing a beat.

"Mr. Calhoun testified that you stopped going to the club because of the drugs, isn't that the case?"

"No." Paul followed Giles instructions, one word answers on yes or no questions and offer no explanations or theories.

"Why would he lie?" Walker asked.

Paul could not pass up the opportunity to strike a blow at Felix, "It's what he does," he said.

"I have no further questions of this witness, Your Honor."

The defense called Candace Banks to the stand. JC was mesmerized as she gracefully glided to the witness box. She had on a simple black dress, a Gucci bag dangling from her shoulder, and a string of pearls nestled comfortably across her breast. Her four-inch black-and-white Ferragamo Alabama leather slingbacks accentuated her seductively contoured calf muscles.

As Giles questioned her from his seat, Candace convincingly took the jury through her history with JC in New York, her return to Long Beach, how she persuaded JC to purchase the Rukus Room, and some early challenges. Her testimony was delivered with confidence. The consultant thought the jury believed most of what she said.

JC didn't hear Candace's testimony. He was so focused on the love of his life, he could barely concentrate on the trial. He was amazed at how well she had aged. Candace was just as gorgeous as she was when he met her at nineteen. He knew she had a man but, that didn't stop JC from lusting for her. She was still there, by his side, every single day. *That had to mean something*, he thought. Plus, JC had noticed Candace's man was dropping her off and picking her up the first week of the trial. *A smart move*, JC concluded. But this week, Candace was catching a ride with Tracy or driving herself. JC thought perhaps there were problems at home, or, maybe Candace was honest with the brother and had let the man know that she was destined to be with JC.

JC snapped out of his trance when Giles stood up and asked

Candace, "So you were at the club from the day it opened, Miss Banks?"

"Yes I was."

"Could the Powell's have operated a drug ring from the club without your knowledge?"

"Absolutely not. There were no drugs. As a matter of fact, JC had ongoing battle with the local drug dealers. He went to great lengths to keep the drugs and gang members away from the club."

"Thank you, Miss Banks."

Walker questioned Candace from his seat.

"Are you Mr. Powell's girlfriend?" Walker asked.

"No sir." Candace's answers were short and succinct.

Walker stood with a confused look on his face, he looked at the jury as he asked Candace, "But you do have a child by him, so you must have been his girlfriend at one time correct?"

"As I said earlier, that was decades ago."

"Would it be fair to say, after all those years, that you love JC Powell?"

"Well," she looked at JC. "Yes, I suppose."

"Would you do anything for Mr. Powell, even lie for him?"

"I don't know. I've never had to lie for him. He did nothing wrong."

Walker turned to the jury. "How can we take your word for it? I have no more questions of this witness." He took his seat.

Tamara was the next person to testify for the defense. Giles called her to the stand to quickly confirm that, to her knowledge, there was never any illegal activity going on at the club.

Walker was eager to talk to Tamara. As soon as Giles finished he jumped up and said, "Miss. Bastille."

Tamara leaned to the microphone and said, "Mrs. Du'bois."

Walker apologized and explained that he was going by old records. "You were not married when you worked at the club were you Mrs. Du'bois?"

"No." Giles had prepped his witnesses well. One word answers when possible.

"You were also JC's girlfriend, weren't you?"

Giles had covered this question. "We were friends."

"Friends?" Walker said. "Isn't it a fact that you lived in an apartment paid for by Mr. Powell?"

"Sir, I worked for Mr. Powell, so yes, he did pay my rent."

Walker changed direction. "Did you testify in the first trial?"

"No sir."

"Why is that Mrs. Du'bois?"

Tamara displayed much more confidence than she had in the past. "I was never asked to testify."

"Was it because you fled?"

"I moved," Tamara said.

"When people flee during an investigation it's usually because they're guilty or know something. Isn't that the reason you ran?"

"As I said, I moved, I did not flee. I was arrested and held in jail for a week. They questioned me three different times. The first time they questioned me for at least sixteen hours straight." Tamara got choked up and emotional. "When I got out they had seized the condo I was living in and put my mother, who was dying from cancer, into a filthy state institution because of her Alzheimer's. I had to track her down. When I did find her I still had nowhere to take her."

Tamara pulled out a tissue and dabbed her teary eyes. She reached up and rubbed the sack dangling from her neck, sat erect, and continued with power and conviction. "So no sir, I did not run because of guilt. God watched over me and sent my family to take me home, back to Louisiana where my mother could die in peace."

Tamara's testimony was so moving, even the prosecutor froze for a second. He caught himself and said, "No further questions."

Tamara had scored one for defense. The jury, the judge and everyone else in the courtroom sympathized with her. Her statement about her mother was used as the teaser for the evening news; and the front-page headline in the morning paper read, "DEA EVICTED DYING WOMAN TO SEIZE JC POWELL'S ASSETS."

As Tamara, still emotional, slowly stepped down from the witness box, Giles called Reverend Akbar Jones to the stand. When Akbar entered the room escorted by a guard, the spectators became disorderly. A few made negative gestures, but others clapped. A man seated in an aisle seat on the left side of the room reached out to shake Akbar's hand. The room settled down when Judge Sullivan banged the gavel and urged everyone to behave or risk ejection from the courtroom. Even the jury appeared impressed as Akbar slowly strutted to the witness stand—milking the moment for as long as possible. He stepped into the witness box, and proudly placed one hand on the Bible, the other in the air.

Once Akbar was seated, Giles walked toward him, stopped, then turned and approached the jury, smiling. Walker squirmed in his seat. He had been warned about the dog-and-pony show these militants ran when they got together in the courtroom. The jury was already spellbound and testimony hadn't even started.

"Please state your name for the jury," Giles said.

"Reverend Akbar Jones."

The family looked around. They knew he was officially a reverend, but no one knew they'd pull that rabbit out of the hat.

"And Reverend Jones, what is your occupation?"

"In addition to ministering to my flock, I am the Chairman of the organization, 'For My People', and will be releasing my eighth book next month. It's about how I survived my fathers lynching and made it from being a field hand to graduating with honors from Morehouse College." The jury didn't know that the release of this book had been imminent for the last thirty years. This was a shrewd strategy the two came up with to introduce background information on Akbar.

Giles smiled. He knew Walker wanted to object but couldn't for fear of appearing insensitive. He leaned his head slightly to the side and replied, "Very impressive." Then threw another jab. "I can relate Reverend. I picked cotton before going to college." Walker was twisting in his seat—right where Giles wanted him.

Giles walked the floor a bit to allow the jury to absorb what they had just heard. He picked up a stack of papers and held them in the air. "Reverend Jones, I have here exhibits twenty-six and twenty-seven." He turned to the judge, "Already entered into evidence Your Honor." After a brief pause he continued, "Reverend Jones, please explain exhibit twenty-six to the jury." He laid down an article in front of jury. The headline read "40 Tulia Residents Exonerated."

Akbar's timing was impeccable. He started his answer before Walker could object. "A cop set up forty-six people who were convicted on drug charges."

Walker jumped to his feet yelling, "Objection, relevance."

Akbar never lost eye contact with the jury, nor did he stop talking until he got his point across. He was at home on the stand. "They later found out the officer had fabricated the charges."

Walker continued to object and finally Judge Sullivan interrupted. He put his hand up to stop Akbar. "Reverend Jones, when there is an objection you have to wait until I rule before you answer."

"I apologize, Your Honor," Akbar replied, as if he was embarrassed of his ignorance of courtroom procedure.

The Judge entered his ruling, "Sustained. The jury will disregard the response."

Giles strutted a little harder, oozing confidence. He prowled the courtroom like a newly crowned Mr. Universe taking a cat walk. They had made two major coups. First, Akbar was able to get the information in and, second, Judge Sullivan called Akbar Reverend. They were on a roll. He knew, however, the stunt would not work again.

The next article had all the pertinent details in the headline, so he quickly read it aloud. "Undercover agent uses chalk to set up seventy innocent people." Walker objected immediately, but Giles still slapped the article in front of the jury.

"Objection. Objection, Your Honor."

Giles argued to the Judge— really performing for the jury— that the twenty unrelated incidents of innocent people being set up illustrated the rampant corruption in the criminal justice system.

Judge Sullivan banged his gavel and said, "Sustained. Mr. Giles, the defendant is Mr. Powell, not the criminal justice system. Let's move on, Mr. Giles."

"Reverend Jones, in your expert opinion, what has caused

such widespread abuse of the system by government agents?"

Walker was back on his feet shouting, "Objection. He is not an expert."

At this point Walker was working for the defense. The more he yelled objection, the more convinced the jury became that the government was trying to hide something. Giles softly stated, "Your Honor, the Reverend's organization publishes an annual report on police misconduct and—"

Judge Sullivan raised his hand to stop Giles, "Overruled. I'll allow it. Continue."

"Why the widespread abuse, Reverend?"

"It's simple, money and power. The money from seizures goes back to the agencies—that's a problem in itself. Informants are paid with money or freedom. Agency officials get their names in the news. And there's also the money being made from the prison industry itself. They have to lock somebody up; it's their business. Money and power have driven things out of control."

"Thank you, Reverend Jones." Giles took a seat.

"Any questions of this witness Mr. Walker?" The Judge asked.

"Just a couple, Your Honor," Walker responded. He questioned Akbar from his seat. "Mr. Jones, were you ever at the club?"

"No." Akbar said.

"So you have no knowledge of what was going on in John Powell's organization?"

"No."

Walker was aware of this tag team's antics and would not take too much of a chance with Akbar. "No further questions for Mr. Jones."

Giles announced, "The defense rests, Your Honor."

"Your Honor, I do have a few rebuttal witnesses," Walker said as he stood.

Judge Sullivan said, "This would be a good time to end for the day." He turned to the jury, "We need you to report back here by nine tomorrow morning."

Chapter 29

The next morning, there was chaos outside the courthouse. Activists promoting various causes marched in circles with protest signs chanting "end mandatory minimums" and "kill the death penalty," while others rallied for stricter punishment for criminals. Sentencing guidelines had become a major debate in America with people challenging prison terms from Washington State to Washington DC. Volunteers from Families Against Mandatory Minimums, The November Coalition and the Sentencing Project circulated through the mob, handing out flyers and signing up new members. Organizers representing "Black Youth Vote" came all the way from Drew University in Watts to register citizens to vote. Street vendors raked in big bucks selling T-shirts and refreshments, and the media continued to demand entry into the courtroom. It was a circus.

One amusing protester attracted the attention of both sides. He was a clean cut, African American gentleman. He actually could have passed for a cop. He was wearing a T-shirt that read, "If You See the Police" on the front. On the back, in bold black capital letters, was "WARN A BROTHER." The T-shirt even elicited snickers from the police who were trying to keep the crowd calm and behind the barricades.

A rude reporter from a small town paper in the middle of nowhere had angered the judge the first day of the trial, so the media was banned from the courtroom. The ban proved beneficial to the defense team; it allowed them to spin the story in their favor. Each afternoon, in time for the evening news, Akbar and Giles made sure they were outside the courthouse to provide the media with an update on the day's activities.

JC pushed his way through the morning madness unnoticed. Just as he reached the door to the courthouse, he heard someone call out his name. It was Tamara, about twenty-five pounds heavier with a new short haircut. She ran to catch up with him. "JC, can I talk to you for a minute?"

"Of course, I wanted to speak to you earlier but you left out so fast. Thank you so much for coming."

"I'd do it anytime for you, JC." Tamara put her head down for a quick second then looked up and said, "I wanted to apologize for leaving. I didn't know what else to do. They were trying to force me to testify against you. They threatened to lock me up."

"You did the right thing Tamara. I understand why you left, and I appreciate everything." He hugged her. "Hey, you got married, huh? Congratulations."

"Yeah, I have three kids." They walked in silence a minute. Tamara still needed to clear the air. "JC, I used the money to—"

"Tamara, you did what you had to do." The two embraced again.

Once court was brought to order, Walker called Mrs. Delilah Ogden to the stand. Everyone in the courtroom was shocked. She hadn't been seen since Mama gave her the boot at the family reunion. The collective whispers became earsplitting as Dee hobbled to the witness stand wearing a matted wig, black stretch pants and a tattered orange shirt with spaghetti straps. It was obvious that no one had convinced her that her corn-ridden toes were not fit for public viewing; she was still squeezing her wide feet into unsuitable open-toe sandals she thought were sexy.

Candace ogled Dee as she went by. She whispered to Paul, "It would take a carton of pumice stones, a ton of Vaseline, and at least two months of daily paraffin wax treatments before she could apply for sandal privileges." The two snickered.

Dee hadn't aged well. When she turned to slide her hand on the Bible, the bags beneath her eyes and the gaping crows-feet lining their edges made her appear over fifty, even though she was just a year shy of forty.

Giles rose to his feet quickly, "Objection. She didn't testify in this trial, Your Honor."

Before Giles could complete his objection, Walker cut in, "May we approach, Your Honor?"

The Judge motioned for them to approach the bench.

Walker said, "I have three rebuttal witnesses. Two of them did not testify in this trial, but they can directly contradict defense testimony. Delilah Ogden and Jason Green." Mr. Green's statement is in evidence and he is on the witness list, but we couldn't locate him earlier to testify. I assure you, Your Honor, both witnesses can rebut testimony offered by defense witnesses."

"Your honor, this is unfair. We've had no time to prepare for Mrs. Ogden."

Judge Sullivan motioned Giles to stop. "Mrs. Ogden can testify and I will give you a couple of hours to prepare for cross-examination."

Giles took a seat and the prosecutor walked over to Dee. "Mrs. Ogden, you were JC Powell's live-in girlfriend, correct?"

"Yes I was," Dee responded.

"Were you aware of any illegal drug activity at the club?"

"Not at the outset. After a while, I suspected illicit circumstances with the extensive amount of money circulating, but I wasn't sure. When I realized they were transacting drugs, I absconded."

"So when you realized they were selling drugs, you left?"

"Objection, leading," said Giles.

"Sustained."

Walker looked at the jury. "Mrs. Ogden, there has been testimony stating that there were no drugs at the club. How do you know for a fact that JC Powell was selling drugs?"

"I went in the basement to inventory supplies and I encountered drugs—lots of drugs. I was so afraid I went home and moved out immediately."

JC was flabbergasted. The family glanced at each other.

"So Mrs. Ogden, you can corroborate Felix Calhoun's testimony that drugs were stored at the club?"

"Yes."

"When exactly did you see the drugs?"

Dee thought for a minute. "The night of the last Playas Ball. After the club was closed. It was the day before everyone got apprehended."

"Mrs. Ogden, you're absolutely sure you saw the drugs?"

"Undisputably. In packages about this big." She held her hand about twelve inches apart. "I saw the drugs. And, JC was always in the basement, so he had to know."

"Thank you, Mrs. Ogden. I have no more questions." Walker took a seat.

Judge Sullivan said, "It's ten now. Let's say we meet back here at two PM? Will that give you enough time to prepare for this witness, Mr. Giles?"

Giles wanted to buy as much time as possible. "Two-thirty would be better Your Honor. I would like to sneak a bite to eat."

"Two thirty it is." Judge Sullivan looked at the jury. "Please report back at two-thirty this afternoon."

JC and the family waited at the back of the courtroom while his lawyer talked to the prosecutor in the front. Auntie, now in her eighties, grabbed her chest and plopped down in a seat. She didn't look good. Mama rushed to tend to her.

JC followed. He asked, "Auntie, what's wrong, are you okay?"

Forcing words between heavy pants, Auntie replied, "I'm fine baby, it's just indigestion. Don't worry 'bout Auntie."

JC turned to Paul's wife. "Tracy, can you take her and Mama home?" He leaned in to Paul, "I been telling everybody they're too old for this. They needed to stay home."

JC and Paul were on each side of Auntie but could barely get her out of her seat. The former security guard from the club, the larger one, came to their aid.

Mama said, "You're going to the doctor right now. This has been going on all week."

"All week?" JC said. "Paul, you go with them. It could be serious."

"No. Paul, you stay with your brother. Don't worry, the Lord is with us," Mama said.

Auntie caught her breath, balanced herself and, with Tracy on one side and the security guard on the other, she flung her head in the air and walked out of the courtroom. Her performance didn't calm the family.

Giles walked up and whispered to JC. "Bad news." He grasped JC's arm to lead him away from the family. Candace and Paul followed. "Dee really hurt our case. The prosecutor offered you a deal. If you plead guilty now, they'll give time served and you won't have to do your parole."

"That's not a deal. I don't have nothing to hide. I can do ten years parole if I have to. No deal."

"Here's the catch. If you don't take the plea agreement and lose the trial, Walker will seek the maximum sentence— what Trevor got."

Paul asked, "What's that mean?"

"It means you could have to serve ten more years if we lose, JC."

Candace stepped in closer to Giles. "Can they put him back in jail?"

"It's what I explained before we started. The prosecutor filed a cross appeal. They're saying, based on the guidelines, you should have gotten twenty-four years because of your assault conviction from New York."

"I was only eighteen years old. Anyway, I was never in jail. All I had to do was pay a fine."

"It doesn't matter, you pled guilty and the guidelines say it should be counted as a prior conviction. The Fed's will slap it to you in order to stop other victims from filing appeals. Up to this point, my reputation has worked in our favor. Not anymore. They know I specialize in class action litigation and they fear a major suit from anyone who had a case involving a questionable snitch. This could be a major catastrophe for the government. As an activist, I would like to stay in it on principle. But, as your attorney, I must strongly encourage you to take the deal."

"I'll take principle," said JC.

Paul said, "JC, your freedom is on the line."

"No deal. Okay Mr. Activist. What's next?" JC asked.

"Come on JC, are you crazy? He's saying they can lock you

back up," Paul exclaimed.

"Actually, JC, I need to make myself clear. I am saying they WILL lock you up. Giving you more time is their only deterrent to other people filing lawsuits," Giles said.

JC smiled at Paul, and gave him a taste of his own medicine, "Isn't it you who always said if you don't stand for something, you'll fall for anything? What about the big picture?"

Candace massaged her temples, shaking her head in disbelief. Paul was so upset he walked away for a second. He wondered, *how he could preach about doing the right thing but, when facing his brother's incarceration, he wanted him to give in. Did he believe the black power messages he'd been spewing all these years? Perhaps JC was right about black activists using their oppression as an excuse.* Paul pulled himself together and walked back over to JC, prepared to proudly stand by his brother's side and see the battle through to the end.

Giles said, "JC, the strength of this case was based on the theory that Felix lied to get a deal for himself. Felix didn't get a deal. To be honest, most of the jury has probably lied about a job or their level of education at some time in their life so we're not gaining many points for his minor lies. Now, Dee has corroborated his story about the drugs. The jury, and most of the courtroom, is convinced something illegal was going on. The question is: why would Felix just set you up for no reason?"

JC lowered his head. "Now my own attorney doesn't believe me."

"I didn't say that, JC. I know Paul and Akbar and trust what I've been told. I have to put on a defense and right now we don't have one. We need to answer that question. At this point the jury thinks Felix is an honest Joe for exposing a major drug operation. He has Dee and Jason to back him up. If we can't counter their testimony, you're better off taking the deal."

"Mr. Giles, I respect your advice, but I will go back to prison before I admit to something I didn't do. So what's the plan?"

"Well, the key right now is to stop the enemy from gaining ground. We need to discredit Dee. I'll focus on why she didn't come forward earlier, but that's not enough. We already know Jason's testimony is damaging, but he has a long criminal history.

Felix's name change is legal so all I have on him are the minor lies, which the jury already knows about. I called in every favor I could to get Felix's record unsealed and the missing pages from the report but nobody could get a hold of his actual record. I'm sure it would help. Usually when the government goes to these lengths to seal a record and pull pages from a report, they're concealing the name of an informant. JC do you think anyone else you know could be involved in this?"

"No, there is no one else."

"JC, you really need to consider—"

"No deal." JC stepped to Paul, "I have to make a run. Let me hold your car keys."

Paul looked puzzled. JC hadn't driven since they lived in New York. The only reason he kept his license updated was to register his cars that other people drove him in. "You need me to take you somewhere?" Paul asked.

He shook his head, "I need to do this, please. The keys, man."

Still stunned, Paul stared JC directly in the eyes and tightly gripped his hand as he passed him the keys. JC dashed off toward the exit.

JC ran all the way to Paul's car. He jumped in, jammed the key into the ignition, and froze. Every few seconds he lifted his hand to turn the key but could not bring himself start the car. He closed his eyes, and pounded his fists on the steering wheel in frustration. He grabbed the steering wheel with his left hand firmly resting at nine o'clock and his right hand at three, his head lowered, and sweat seeping from his forehead.

JC inhaled a few deep gulps of air and relaxed enough to let his mind wander all the way back to a time in New York when he was maneuvering his brand new white Cadillac Seville through the madness of rush hour traffic. Candace was in the passenger seat beside him. He could still feel the thrill he got each time he glanced over and she was still there at his side. By then, Candace had joined the list of people JC was duty bound to protect. It was his mission, his reason for existence.

Sinking deeper and deeper into this hypnotic state, JC clutched the car wheel for dear life. He could hear the sounds from the drivers laying on their horns seconds before the light changed that rainy day in New York City. The grinding noises created by bumpers as they scraped the pavement spinning out of deep potholes were still unnerving. He even smelled the scent of street vendors roasting peanuts on the sidewalk.

He remembered admiring Candace as she laughed robustly while they were stopped at the traffic light. They peered into the back seat at the children, the subject of their laughter. A horn blew. The light changed. JC took off into the intersection. Suddenly, a car crashed into the side of JC's vehicle. JC was nearly in tears as he envisioned his lifeless child sprawled on the wet city street, the steam from the subway rising on either side of him.

JC snapped back to reality. He banged on the steering wheel in frustration but stopped himself when he thought about the trauma he had endured over the past decade. The thought of his mother and aunt on the ground surrounded by cops with guns gave him the strength to confront another demon haunting him. He turned the key, and, for the first time since the accident that killed his son, he drove.

After the break, Paul and Candace waited for JC in the hallway outside of the courtroom, which was standing room only. JC didn't make it back to court by the time Judge Sullivan entered. After a few minutes, the two went inside and took their seats. The lawyers were at the bench talking with the Judge. Giles watched the door as he attempted to buy a little time.

"Where is JC? You think he had an accident?" Candace asked.

Paul tried to assure Candace that nothing was wrong, but he was just as concerned about JC's whereabouts. "He'll be here. He just had to make a run."

Candace blurted out, "This is too stressful—all of it. And why doesn't he just take the deal? Just let it go. It's over."

"He's stubborn like papa. That's what killed him." Paul said.

"What do you mean?" Candace asked.

Paul shook his head sadly. "Papa loved games. One evening he walked five miles after work to get us a new game. Dr. King had just been assassinated and folks were cutting up so Mama told him to wait until the unrest died down to walk at night. But Papa never listened. Just stubborn. On his way home, three white teenagers tried to take the game from him. Papa came in that night bloody and bruised, but he had that damn dartboard under his arm."

Paul paused and took a deep breath. "He bled to death in his sleep. JC always felt guilty because he had begged papa for that damn dartboard."

Candace was moved by the story. It explained a lot about JC, Paul and the Powell family. Once the Judge instructed the lawyers to proceed without JC, Candace was certain something bad had happened. She continued to watch the door, looking for JC. He was all the way in Long Beach standing on a street corner talking to Nate, who, due to his injury in Vietnam, was now in a wheelchair.

Nate searched his pockets and pulled out an address book. JC handed Nate his phone, Nate flipped through the book, located a number, and punched it into the phone. After a few minutes of animated conversation Nate clicked the phone shut, pulled a red sign reading 'STOP' from the side of his wheelchair, and rolled to the middle of the street proudly elevating the sign. About six young children crossed the street and Nate rolled back to the curb to exchange a few more words with JC. The two shook hands and JC took off running, back to the car. He had to make one more stop.

This time he went deep in the hood where drug slinging, constant squabbles, and nookie for sale, day and night, ruled.

JC jumped out of the car and approached three scantily dressed "working girls" manning the day shift on Long Beach Boulevard. They curtly waved him off and walk away. A cashier at a drive-thru cleaners saw the encounter from across the street. It was the old barmaid from The Empire. She darted across the street and embraced JC. After talking with him a few seconds, she beckoned the women back over and convinced them to give JC all the information he needed. As she walked away, she turned and thanked JC for paying for her mother's funeral; she always knew he was the only person that would do something like that without telling anyone.

Meanwhile, back in the courtroom, they recalled Dee for her cross-examination. She sauntered back up to the witness stand, throwing piercing looks at the Powell family. Candace continued to watch the door but JC was nowhere to be seen. While JC was intently engaged in conversation with the friendly felines on the boulevard, Dee sat upright in the witness stand and churned out a string of lies that severely damaged JC's character. She was so convincing, even the twenty-five-year-old black male jurist the defense considered a sure bet showed compassion for Dee and the life-threatening abuse she had to endure under the strong arm of JC Powell. JC's absence from the courtroom certainly did not help.

During his cross-examination of Dee, Giles frequently glanced back at the door looking for JC. The trial was taking a turn for the worse and his client was MIA. Giles knew Dee had scored a home run for the prosecution and he had to refute her testimony. To do so, he needed to convey to the jury Dee's incentive for lying about JC. He also needed ammunition from JC to counter Dee's abuse accusations.

A bit anxious and desperate to stall for time, Giles rambled through some papers on the defense table. Although he knew it was not a compelling rationale, with no alternative theory, he accused Dee of conjuring up her story because she was a vindictive woman—a woman scorned.

Giles asked Dee, "If what you say is true, why didn't you testify in the first trial?"

Still erect with steady eye contact, Dee responded, "After I saw the drugs, I left town. I was afraid of what JC might do to me for leaving. By the time I heard what happened, JC was already convicted."

"Isn't it true that Mr. Powell actually put you out of his house and you're testifying today to get back at him?"

JC hurried into the courtroom and slid into his assigned seat.

Dee paused. She sat up very proper and convincingly said, "He never put me out. Never. But even if he did, that was nearly ten years ago, I'd have to be crazy to hold a grudge that long. I'm married with four wonderful children now."

Once again, Dee had scored for the prosecution. JC caught Giles' eye, then waved a slip of paper he was holding. Giles requested a second from the Judge. Giles quickly reviewed the slip of paper, had a few words with JC, and then approached Dee with renewed confidence.

"Mrs. Ogden, were you arrested in the past week?"

"Arrested?"

"Yes, arrested. Taken into custody by the police, Mrs. Ogden. Were you arrested?"

Dee's entire demeanor changed. "Uh…. Umm..Yes."

"What were you charged with?"

"Objection, your honor. Mrs. Ogden is not on trial," said Walker.

"I'll allow it."

"But, I haven't been found guilty."

"Your charges, Mrs. Ogden?" Giles said.

"Possession."

"Drugs?" Giles looked at the jury, then turned back to Dee. "Anything else, Mrs. Ogden?"

Dee hesitated.

"Mrs. Ogden?"

"Solicitation," Dee replied.

"Prostitution?" Giles asked.

"Yes, prostitution, "Dee responded lowering her head in embarrassment.

The courtroom erupted. Candace nudged Paul on the shoulder and whispered, "I told ya'll she was selling nookie."

Giles let the charge sink in then asked, "Were you offered a deal to testify against JC Powell?"

"Yes but—"

Giles interrupted her. "So you stand to benefit from your testimony?"

"I guess you can say that."

"No further questions. This is just more of the prosecution's manure."

Judge Sullivan pounded his gavel.

Chapter 30

A toilet flushed from behind a door in the courthouse bathroom. Tamara exited a stall and started washing her hands in the sink next to Dee, who was in the mirror applying a new coat of bright red lipstick. They carried on in silence until Dee pressed her lips together making a puckering sound, then cut her eyes at Tamara in a menacing way.

Tamara said, "I don't know how you could come in here and tell all those lies after all JC did for you."

Dee stepped to Tamara pointing, "Dee looks out for Dee."

Candace walked in and quickly scoped the room. "What's going on?"

Convinced that Candace was the one who found out about her arrest, Dee turned to Candace, one hand on her hip, one flailing, and said, "Oh, here comes miss know-it-all. Always whobangin'. You ain't the only who can get information, Miss Candace. I heard your Mama was a drug ho and has no idea who your daddy really is. I heard she got so high she threw boiling water on your ass thinkin' you was a rat. Fried that damn arm didn't she? That's why you was in and out of foster homes. Yeah, you ain't the only one who can get information. I got the 411 on you."

The vicious words immobilized Candace. Before she could pull herself together, Tamara stepped up to Dee and, at the loudest level her meek voice could muster, shouted, "Hold up! Your dad was a minister and your mother was a teacher and you ended up being a whore. YOU have no excuse." Tamara threw her hand on her hip, "That's right, I heard a few things myself, Miss Delilah."

"All these years and you're still a spineless bitch," Dee said.

At bitch, Tamara swung and punched Dee with such might, Dee slipped backwards into a stall and landed on the floor next to a clogged toilet. Tamara and Candace stared down at the balding Dee slumped on the floor, crying. Her lip was busted and her wig hung in the bowl with wads of used toilet paper and week-old dung. They chuckled a bit and left Dee to bask in her own drama.

Although the defense was successful in challenging Dee's lies, they still had a major hurdle to climb. Jason "Payback" Green was up next. The plan was to focus on his gang lifestyle and the fact that he became a cooperating witness and agreed to testify against JC in order to get a reduced sentence.

When Walker called Jason Green to the stand, the person who entered the courtroom bore a resemblance to Payback, but this man was clean cut and wearing a very conservative dark-colored suit. As he sat in the witness stand, JC could see that it was clearly Payback, and was sure the new choirboy look would sway the jury.

Walker stood and asked Jason a few "small-talk" questions about how much time he served and his charges before getting to the meat of his testimony. Jason came off genuinely likeable, especially when he elaborated on his prior life as a thug and the fact that he "got saved" while in prison.

Walker looked over at the jury and asked Jason, "Is it true that JC Powell made a deal to buy drugs from you?"

"No," Jason responded.

Everyone was stunned, especially Walker. He flung around and rushed over to Jason, and became aggressive. "No? Didn't you testify in the previous trial that he was buying the drugs you were arrested with?"

"Yes, I did."

"Are you changing your testimony?"

"No. I'm just saying I don't know what JC agreed to. Felix told me JC—"

"Mr. Green, please tell the court what you testified to in the previous trial."

"Objection," said Giles. " Mr. Walker can't tell the witness what to say, Your Honor."

"Overruled."

"I have no more questions of this witness."

The courtroom was still roused up and trying to figure out what had just happened. Giles thought he could leave it be, certainly any lawyer worth his salt does not ask a question if he doesn't already know the answer. He decided to take a chance and give Jason the opportunity to finish his testimony.

He jumped up and asked Jason, "What did Felix Calhoun tell you, Mr. Green?"

"Felix came by one night with JC's son, Trevor, waiting in the car. He said he had convinced JC on a truce. Felix explained that JC was not interested in corner drug sales, only volume. Felix said they had hook-ups in Atlanta and some other cities. Felix told me that JC agreed to cop volume from me at a discount and he wouldn't put in any street work in Long Beach."

"Cop?"

"Buy drugs." Jason turned to the jury. "As I said earlier, before I gave my life to Christ, I was a drug dealing gangster—a confused, vicious person." He faced Giles and continued, "Anyway, the night the deal went down, I got busted. I was convinced that JC had set me up."

"Why didn't you say this before?"

"I didn't put it together until I was locked down. The word inside was that my right hand man, Havoc, got out because he was a snitch. So, I started putting two and two together and things added up."

"What did you figure out about JC's role in the drug deal?"

"When I thought about it, me and JC never had problems until Havoc got out. He introduced me to Felix. It was Havoc and Felix that said JC was stealin' my business. Plus, something I thought was odd back then, with all the money JC had, I couldn't figure out why he was paying me premium prices for a kilo. He paid more on credit. Felix could only give five grand upfront. I knew JC was making money, so credit wasn't a problem. Looking back, that made no sense. JC had no need for credit."

"In other words, the only money that exchanged hands was five thousand dollars that came from Felix?"

"Yes. I never had any dealings whatsoever with JC. That was strange too, since I know JC talks man-to-man. But I was doing drugs back then so my mind wasn't focused."

"Mr. Green, the prosecutor talks about an agreement between you and Mr. Powell. What was the agreement?"

"Back when The Empire first started, JC asked me to keep my crew a block away from the club and, in return, he assured me that no drug sales would go on in the club. I agreed and everything was fine until Havoc reappeared."

JC called the attorney over and whispered in his ear. Giles asked, "Mr. Green, do you know where this "Havoc" is now?"

"He's down on murder again. He can't deal his way out this time; he shot a white nurse," Jason said.

"Thank you very much for your testimony, Mr. Green."

Candace got word that they had taken Auntie to the emergency room so she rushed off to the hospital as soon as court ended for the day. JC and Paul met with Giles for a few minutes to debrief and consider what additional information Felix could offer in testimony the following day. The federal report they offered into evidence had already established Felix was a liar so Giles didn't understand why the prosecutor would want to end with a questionable witness, especially after the twist of events that day. He surmised that allowing Felix to restate the story at the end of the trial would have worked if Jason and Dee corroborated Felix's account. Giles speculated that by the next morning, Walker would decide not to recall Felix after all.

That evening, carrying large vases filled with flowers, JC and Paul walked down a long hallway, looking for Auntie's room. As they neared the room, as if he'd been holding the secret as long as he could, Paul blurted out, "He left."

JC asked, "Who left?"

"Candace's man."

"Is that right?" JC grinned with delight. He pushed the door to the room open and saw Candace, Tracy and Mama huddled around Auntie's bed, talking just above a whisper. The television braced on the wall above was playing with muted sound.

JC was shocked when he realized Auntie was unconscious. "What happened?"

Tracy softly said, "We got her in the car headed home. She was talking, a little short-winded, but she was talking. All of a sudden she stopped just blacked out. She hasn't come to since."

Mama leaned over and whispered to JC, "The doctor thinks it's her body's way of dealing with the stress. He can't find anything wrong. Said we should talk to her like she hears us. So we've been telling her all the good news about the trial."

JC chuckled, "If she does hear us, it won't be long before she'll have to wake up to put her two cents in."

Mama laughed, "I know that's right." She watched JC for a minute then placed her hand on his hand. "JC don't go feeling guilty, you have to learn that some things are out of your control. Let God handle this."

The room was silent for a moment then Candace shouted, "Look, it's on the news."

Everyone looked up at the TV on the wall above. A reporter was standing amid the protesters outside of the courthouse. Paul and JC stood and moved close to the TV, turning the volume up a little.

There was a whisper, "I can't hear it."

They all turned to see auntie's eyes wide open and rushed to her. Paul said, "Auntie, you're back."

"Shhh, turn it up and let me watch my baby on TV."

JC laughed and turned up the TV.

The anchor was on camera in the studio. She said, "The case of JC Powell has gained the support of civil rights leaders across the nation. Thousands showed up in New York today for a rally held by hip-hop star and activist J-Money in support of JC Powell."

The visual on the TV cut to the rally in New York. J-Money was on the stage with Queen Latifa, Russell Simmons, Li'l Kim and P-Diddy. J-Money was standing at a podium yelling above the cheering crowd. "It's a money making industry. In America, a prisoner is worth more than a student. That's the reality. The system is flawed and the laws are biased. That's why we're working so hard to get black youth involved in the political process before they get arrested and lose their right to vote. Like my partner here said, we got to Vote or Die." The audience roared in unity.

After brief sound bites from the usual suspects – Dr. Joseph Lowery, Jesse Jackson, and Al Sharpton— the visual cut to Akbar in front of the courthouse with Angela Davis and Afeni Shakur at his side. Akbar declared, "The criminal justice system needs a complete overhaul. Mandatory minimum sentencing, paid informants—it's just a present-day form of the Fugitive Slave Act. They set them up to bust them. Then, after they do their time, they set them up to fail. With a drug conviction ex-cons can't get a job, housing, or financial aid for an education, so many of them wind up back in the system."

The visual cut to the anchor in the studio. She announced, "Powell can't get back the years he spent in prison, but, if he wins, his money will be returned. A guilty verdict could send him back to prison for up to ten years."

The camera showed footage from the front of the courthouse earlier that day. Reporters rammed microphones into JC's face as he entered the courthouse. When he wouldn't comment, the reporter shoved the microphone into Giles' face and asked, "Mr. Giles, how can you allow your client to risk being locked up? Are you sacrificing your client to promote yourself and your cause?"

Giles responded, "Mr. Powell gambled with his freedom to show the world the corruption that exists within our criminal justice system. The black community must realize that our struggle continues. We have to hold the police and the politicians accountable. The voters put the individuals who made these laws into office. That's why it's important for minorities and the poor to register and vote these people out of office when they are not working in our best interest. We can't only vote in a presidential election. We have to vote in state and local elections. Those elected officials are allowing these biased laws to pass."

The news went to the next story.

Chapter 31

Giles was surprised when Walker stuck to his guns and called Felix Calhoun back to the stand. Felix entered the court and slithered to the witness stand wearing a cheap suit and no jewelry. He seemed to like the attention he was getting and was well prepped for his encore performance. Lying was natural for Felix; it was a habit he started at a young age. Determined to get away from the small town in Mississippi where he lived with his mother and stepfather, Felix made up a story to tell local police about his stepfather's physical and mental abuse. When the police questioned him about any family he could stay with for a while, he suggested they call his father who lived in Detroit. The thirteen-year-old was shipped off to the big city. When Felix tired of his dad's rules, he reported his constant drug binges and alcoholic rages – another lie – to his school counselor. As a result, instead of getting the free ride back to his mother as he expected, the state placed him in foster care. Felix ended up running away a month later and he's been on his own ever since.

Walker approached Felix and thanked him for taking the time to return to clear up a few questions. He asked Felix about the drug operations at The Empire.

"Like I said," Felix said. "From my observations, I estimate that JC Powell ran a two million dollar a year drug ring."

"Defense witnesses deny any drug activity. Did they know about it?"

As if he was amazed they would deny the accusation, Felix

responded, "Yes, they knew, sir. Everybody knew."

"The defense introduced a government report that said you lied on the stand. Can you explain the report?"

Felix talked directly to the jury, in a soft slow southern drawl he perfected just for the trial. "An attorney asked me if I graduated from high school, I said yes. I attended classes, took and passed the GED test, and was awarded my GED, so I didn't think they would consider what I said a lie."

"So you weren't intentionally lying?

"No sir," Felix said, glaring at the jury. "I was not lying. I worked hard to earn my GED so I could proudly say I was a high school graduate."

"Mr. Calhoun, the report also mentions your record. Why were you charged with impersonating a federal agent?"

"I was caught in the middle of a local drug sting in a small town back east. Once they put me into the back of the police car, I informed the officer I worked for the DEA. I didn't have a badge number and, since my assignments had to remain secret, I couldn't give him more information, so the officer didn't believe me."

It became evident that Walker's strategy was to have Felix explain away his lies to restore his integrity with the jury. Since Dee corroborated Felix's story, Walker thought he could salvage his credibility in the final hour. Although it didn't have the impact it would have had if Jason's testimony had backed him up, Felix did a brilliant job of winning more than a few jurors over.

"Mr. Calhoun, you were arrested with Mr. Powell, correct?

"Yes, but it was only to keep my cover. I was never really charged."

"So we make sure we're clear. You are not testifying against Mr. Powell in return for a deal?"

"No, I never got a deal for my testimony."

"No further questions," Walker announced.

Giles stood to question Felix but was distracted, along with the rest of the courtroom, by the rattling of the entrance doors on the extreme left side of the room. A guard pulled open the door and there stood an elderly gentleman, cane in hand. He had on a decent old suit with a matching hat. He slowly moseyed up the left isle to the front of the room and squeezed into a seat in the front row next to JC's cousin Junior. Everyone watched in silence as the old man placed his jacket over his lap and his cane between his legs. JC recognized the hat. It was the fedora-wearing man from the bar.

JC's heart dropped. *A surprise witness – the agent. I should have known they'd pull out all stops,* he thought. But before JC could completely bury himself in misery, the old man removed his hat. JC and Paul exchanged shocked looks when they realized the old man bore a striking resemblance to Philip, the hustler that showed them the ropes in New York. When the old man saw JC staring, he lifted his fisted right hand, put it to his heart and bowed his head. JC reciprocated. Amazingly, Philip used to show love with a similar gesture. Instead of the fist, Philip touched his heart with the peace sign.

The judge instructed Giles to begin questioning.

"Mr. Calhoun, you say you didn't know you lied about your education. Didn't you say that you graduated from college?" Giles asked.

"I did, but—"

"So was that a lie?"

"I guess so," Felix responded.

"You guess so? Are you saying you can't tell the truth from a lie?"

"I know the difference."

"Do you have any witnesses to any of the drug transactions you claim to have observed Mr. Powell engaging in?"

"No."

"Do you have video, audio, anything?"

"No."

"So Mr. Calhoun, we have to take your word for it?"

"I have no reason to lie."

"But you have lied on the stand in the past haven't you?" Giles stepped closer to Felix. "Mr. Calhoun, have you ever perjured yourself?"

Felix cried out, "Why would I lie on these people? I loved the whole family. They were my family. But I had to stop them from putting those drugs in our community. Drugs killed my father and left me a ward of the state. I was obligated to do something to stop JC."

The gallery got noisy. At the crack of his gavel, Judge Sullivan announced a twenty-minute break. Giles immediately turned to JC. "They've got the upper hand. Even though we know he's lying, the jury believes him. The report is all I have to impeach Felix and it's not strong enough."

Before his attorney finished talking, JC took off, making a mad dash for the door. He hurried out of the courthouse, down the ramp, and turned the corner onto a street on the side of the courthouse where Nate was at the curb looking as if he was waiting for someone. JC yelled to him. "Nate, I need it now. Felix is on the stand."

"He's on his way right now JC. I'm telling you, he won't stop if you're here."

JC went back to the front of the courthouse, paced a bit, and then sat on a bench. He kept checking his watch. After waiting fifteen minutes, he headed back inside.

A brown sedan with a police emblem on the side window pulled up to Nate. The person in the car leaned through the passenger window from the drivers seat to hand Nate an inter-office folder labeled "confidential." The car sped off. Nate quickly rolled around the building, spotted JC and yelled for him to stop. JC ran to Nate and the two briefly reviewed the papers in the folder.

JC hurried inside to deliver the information to his defense team. Giles read the information from the envelope, frequently glancing at JC in amazement. Felix, who took the twenty-minute break to re-work his story, strutted back to the witness stand, cocky as ever. He stepped into the box, took a seat, and tilted back in the chair while the attorney was still reviewing the documents. Giles stood and approached Felix with vigor, papers in hand. His co-counsel continued to review the documents from the folder and made notes on yellow sticky paper.

As the attorney's haggled over the introduction of the new evidence, Felix sat back, swung his left leg over his right knee and placed his hands in his lap. He had a smug expression on his face.

Giles said, "Your Honor, this is the same report that was

already entered into evidence. It's just the complete report. For some reason, we were given a report with several pages missing."

"Those pages contain confidential information Your Honor," Walker argued.

The judge ruled to admit the new information into evidence. Giles had the court clerk read back Felix's response before the break. He ruffled through a few pages of the government report, clipped back a sheet and handed it to Felix.

"Before our break you asked, why you would lie on these people. Mr. Calhoun, that's a good question. Let's see what the government report said about you. Please, read what's outlined in yellow."

Felix read very slowly. No one could tell if it was a reading problem or another one of his acts. "Felix Calhoun is a chronic liar corrupted by money and addicted to power."

By now, Giles was leaning on the jury box. He looked at the jurors and said, "A chronic liar corrupted by money and addicted to power."

While the jury digested the powerful statement, Giles took a moment to walk over and get a note from his co-counsel. He stepped up his pace. "Is it true that you instigated the problems that existed between JC Powell and local gangs?"

Felix leaned his head to the side like a professional witness. "Some. We have to use creative techniques to infiltrate an organization and gain their trust."

"We? What we? What do you do?"

"I'm a special agent."

"Special agent? You work for the FBI?"

"No."

"DEA, undercover cop? Who do you work for?"

"I'm a freelance agent."

"Are you on salary?"

"No."

"So you're a paid snitch." Giles made eye contact with the jury.

"Informant." Felix said.

"Okay, paid informant. If no one is arrested, do you still get paid Mr. Calhoun?"

"No."

"So, being paid on commission, you must be very motivated to get people arrested?"

"Only if they are breaking the law!" Felix arrogantly responded.

Bingo. Giles turned and walked briskly over to Felix; his tone was sarcastic. "Breaking the law? How many times have you been arrested?"

"Objection, Mr. Calhoun is not on trial," Walker said.

"He opened the door, Your Honor," Giles said.

"I'll allow it. Please answer the question, Mr. Calhoun," Judge Sullivan said to Felix. At that point even the judge was curious about Felix.

Felix was silent a second. Giles added, "Before you answer, I'd like to enter this arrest record into evidence."

"Objection."

"Overruled." Judge Sullivan said, waving Walker down.

Giles approached Felix with his record. "How many times, Mr. Calhoun?"

"About ten."

"And what crimes were you convicted of?"

Felix's voice lowered. "Fraud."

Giles repeated, "Fraud." He looked around the courtroom. "Ten counts?"

"No. I got charged with drug possession and, uh, like I said, impersonating a federal agent."

"Weren't YOU breaking the law?"

"No. I was working."

"Are we to believe that you were working undercover when you received all of these charges?"

Felix proudly answered, "Yes sir."

Giles stopped dead in his tracks glaring directly into Felix's eyes. He knew Felix had perjured himself. Walker and Judge Sullivan probably questioned the veracity of his testimony as well, but the jury was buying it. It was too late to present documented evidence to refute his statement. The silence lasted long enough for the fast-thinking attorney to notice Felix's shirt was buttoned incorrectly, which he concluded was a ploy by the prosecution – or Felix himself – to gain favor with the jury, making them think the boy was too backwards and country to put on his clothes correctly.

Giles knew he had to quickly annul Felix's testimony. Felix was an expert liar—likely pathological—but he needed time to think of his stories. Giles trotted over to the evidence table, snatched the government report and, waving the report in his hand, asked, "You are testifying under oath that you were charged and convicted of crimes committed in the line of duty?"

"Yes."

"Why would your employers, the federal government, allow you to be charged and convicted if you were working for them?"

"I can't say," Felix replied.

"Can't say because it's top secret, or can't say because you don't know?"

"I don't know."

"Mr. Calhoun, are we to believe that the federal government published a report about your lies, charged you with crimes, and you never asked why they would do that to you?"

"Objection, asked and answered," Walker shouted.

Giles shifted gears. "JC Powell was your first case—your proving ground, correct?"

"Yes."

"How much money have you made since John Powell launched your career?"

Felix shrugged. "I'm not sure."

The attorney went back over and picked up a piece of paper from the defense table and entered it into evidence. He approached Felix and questioned him as he was reading. "Does over four million dollars sound correct?"

Sighs echoed throughout the courtroom. Felix was losing his arrogant stance. His eyes lowered and studied the floor. "I guess that's about right."

Giles moved toward to the jury, looking each one dead in the eye, one by one. "That's about four hundred thousand a year—without graduating from high school."

"I got a GED."

"Mr. Calhoun, you have no proof that your story is true. We just have to take your word for it? A convicted felon?"

"Just like I said, I have no reason to lie."

Giles became aggressive. "How much were you paid for THIS particular sting? YOUR FIRST CASE."

Felix hesitated; all signs of the confidence he wore into the courtroom had disappeared. He pulled a napkin from his pocket and wiped the perspiration that poured down his forehead. He mumbled, "Three hundred thousand dollars."

Giles looked at the jury. "During the period in question, you were an unemployed laborer and your first sting netted you three hundred thousand dollars. Isn't that three hundred thousand reasons to lie?"

Felix just stared.

"I'm finished with him," Giles said.

Both lawyers presented very short uneventful closing statements. Walker focused on the photos, the statement, and the drugs confiscated. "The only thing the defense has proved is that Felix Calhoun exaggerated a little when it came to his education. We all know good people who may fudge a bit when it comes to personal issues. But the facts of the case are irrefutable." Walker approached the jury and held up one finger. "Fact number one, Felix Calhoun gave detailed testimony about JC Powell's drug operation. Two, his testimony was corroborated by witness testimony, and photos. Fact number three." Walker was holding up three fingers. "The drugs were found in the basement of the club owned by JC Powell." He walked from one end of the jury box to the other, looking into the eyes of each juror, then continued, "Unfortunately, in the world of drugs and crime, many of the people who witness the criminal activity may have a record – it's the nature of the beast. The background of the witness does not change the facts." He counted by finger again. "Testimony, witnesses, drugs, and millions of dollars. Ladies and gentlemen of the jury, we all know that when it looks like a duck and quacks like a duck, it's a duck. Do not focus on the minutia; deliberate the facts."

Cliché as it was, Giles knew Walker's closing had scored big time with the jury. Immediately on cue from the judge,

Giles stood and addressed the jury. He paced the floor with slow, measured steps. "Mr. Walker is right. Your job is to weigh the facts and the evidence. He just failed to mention that his case was laden with lies and innuendo, and short on facts and evidence. I must apologize to you ladies and gentlemen. Instead of performing your civic duty watching the prosecutor and defense attorney present opposing evidence related to the case, you spent the past two weeks attending Snitching-101. You've learned first-hand how government-financed informants lie, deceive, and manipulate for gain. Some snitches work for a get out of jail free card, and others, many of whom are borderline criminals, make a hefty salary living the criminal lifestyle they enjoy, legally. They're playing both sides."

"We all want to put an end to the rampant drugs and violence in America. The times we're living in create a host of challenges when it comes to catching and convicting criminals versus upholding the Constitution. But paying someone, in this case, a man with a GED, no work history and a criminal record, paying him $300,000? Many of us work forty hours a week for years to make that much. He's made four million dollars that we know of. Four million taxpayer dollars was paid to someone they branded a liar." Giles sashayed back and forth in front of the jury to allow the number to sink in. The slow taps of his footsteps echoed throughout the room.

"Consider these two facts:" Giles held up his fingers one at a time. "One. The government considers him a liar. They even documented the lies. And two. The only witness to corroborate his story is also a convicted felon. Paying for testimony, whether it is with a reduced sentence or money, creates a slippery slope none of us want to consider in America. Lies, money, and lack of evidence. Ladies and gentlemen, the prosecutor is right. If it quacks like a duck, it is a duck. Felix Calhoun is a liar and the only evidence—the drugs—were admittedly put in the basement by him. Quack. Quack. Quack, went the duck."

Judge Sullivan read his instructions to the jury then sent them to deliberate. The court recessed for the day. Paul and JC searched both inside and outside the courtroom, but the fedora wearing man from the club had disappeared.

Chapter 32

The Powell family awaited the verdict at Auntie's bedside in the hospital. The room was packed. They were just a bunch of country folk from South Georgia and could not stick to the absurd rule allowing only two visitors. Another rule they found hard to follow was the one prohibiting outside food for patients. They knew Auntie was not going to eat that awful institutional food, so they were forced to bring her something to eat from home. Auntie wasn't happy with the pickings—not once had they brought her pork and nothing she ate had enough seasoning. Auntie begged Mama for just a taste of some real ham hocks. Mama agreed. That evening she brought Auntie doctor-approved baked chicken, yams, and other salt-free dishes. She told Auntie to imagine that she was eating ham hocks.

Everyone was laughing and joking, reminiscing about New York. JC jumped up, grabbed Paul's cane, and began imitating his walk. "Paul walked around Harlem like he owned it. Thought he was tough." JC bopped across the floor a few times then fell into his seat laughing.

Candace was sitting next to JC and slid forward in her chair. "Speaking of tough. Can ya'll believe Tamara punched Dee? She turned into Evander Holifield. Dee's hair went one way and she went the other." Candace continued, "Did I ever tell you she had a voodoo doll for Dee?"

"Tamara? Get out of here." JC said.

"But this is even better. Ya'll know how Dee was always

tripping about the dirt in her purse and jacket pockets? Well, guess who again?"

"Tamara?" JC was shocked.

"Yep. She said it was graveyard dirt."

"Get outta here. Graveyard dirt?"

"Mmm-hmm. And that sack around her neck was a gris-gris, some concoction she put together to ward off evil spirits."

"I can't believe it. Tamara. I'm glad I didn't get her mad. That's why I say you got to respect people; you never know what's up with them," JC said.

Candace laughed. "Maybe that's why Dee was looking so old and haggard in court."

"That poison is what had her looking so bad," Paul said.

They were all hysterical, except JC. Paul noticed he had drifted into one of his quiet moods. "What's wrong, baby brother?"

JC's silence caught the attention of the rest of the family. "All the money in the world can't buy what I have right here. All of you are so special. I never say it, but thanks for looking out for me and my kids. I appreciate everything. Everything. I'm just sorry I couldn't do better to look out for all of you." He paused a moment, a little choked up. "If things don't go in my favor with this case —"

"Stop talking like that, JC. I told you, we must have faith," Mama said.

"But Mama, I do. I really do. That's why I know if it doesn't go my way, God's got something else in store for me. Are you forgetting Romans 8:28?"

"That's right, baby. All things work together for good to them that love the Lord!"

"I just wanted the chance to fight a good fight. Paul, you understand? If you were getting in the ring with an opponent and before you could get your bearings, he knocked you out— that's not a fair fight. You'd want to fight him again. But if you fought a good battle and lost, you still have your pride, know what I mean?"

Paul was silent but nodded in agreement. JC started to get emotional and Candace quickly came to his rescue. She leaned toward him, squeezed his hand and said, "We're always gonna look out for you because we all know you ain't too quick."

The room became jolly again and JC, being the butt of the laughter, was forced to make a comeback. He leaned in to Candace and said, "Oh, you got jokes, huh? Did I ever thank you for getting rid of Dee for me?"

With a look of confusion Candace replied, "Dee? You kicked her out. I didn't—"

JC cut her off mid sentence. "We haven't stopped at the store yet." He leaned back real cool in his seat, crossed his legs and slid his hands behind his head. "Ain't too quick? Well I was quick enough to see that the boy she was hugged up with on the beach lived next door to you. You know, the one you were talking to in the club the night Dee met him? I might not have watched Dee, but I never took my eyes off of you."

Candace stared with raised eyebrows and her mouth wide open as JC continued, "And the next time you want to set somebody up, don't ask your gay friends to help you out. You think I couldn't tell he was gay?" They busted out laughing. JC asked, "What I really need to know is what took you so long to get rid of Dee? She was driving me crazy." JC sat back in his chair and continued, "I ain't too swift. Girl, you know I was the slickest brother in Harlem when you started chasing me."

"Chasing you? Chasing you? Now you know you came after me."

"That's what you wanted me to think. What you didn't realize was that I was schooled by strong black women. My mama didn't raise no fool."

"Oh, you know you wanted me," Candace said in a seductive tone.

"I got you, too, didn't I?"

They laughed for a tender moment, then JC got serious again. He leaned in and caressed her hand. "Candace, I'm sorry."

"What?" Candace asked.

"I should have been there for you after the accident. I felt guilty. I got so hung up in my own misery I forgot you lost a son, too. I abandoned you at the worst possible time. I'm so sorry. Please forgive me. I really am sorry."

They exchanged a loving gaze. Candace took a deep breath.

"For a long time I felt like you abandoned me and you were supposed to be my protector. But I understand now. JC, it was an accident. You can't control everything. There is a higher power."

As the two hugged, Paul hung up the hospital phone and announced, "It's time. We have to get back."

JC stood and started putting his jacket on. He suddenly stopped and looked around the room. JC reached his arms out to his side, grabbing Candace's hand on one side and Mama's on the other. The family followed suit, taking the hand of the person next to them. Sounding more like a minister than himself, JC gave thanks.

"Oh Father, watch over this family as we seek justice, knowing that no matter what the decision today, only you can judge. Grant us the wisdom to understand why you chose this path for the Powell family. Psalms tells us 'the steps of a good man are ordered by the Lord, and he delighteth in his way.' The Powell family will follow your lead on this one. Lord, we thank you for watching over me, your son, John Cornelius and the entire Powell family for all these years and we pray that you continue to shine your light on Trevor. We thank you Lord for bringing us this far on faith. In Jesus name, we pray."

And the family said, "Amen."

Chapter 33

Just about everyone from The Empire was in the courtroom to hear the verdict except Mama and Auntie, who watched the coverage on the local news. Actually, it seemed as though all of Long Beach showed up to support JC. Those who did not make it into the packed courtroom stood among the huge crowd outside. A SWAT team armed with trained attack dogs was on hand just in case the crowd became unruly. Reporters from local and national news programs—including CNN and FOX News—were strategically placed on the stairs of the courthouse for live feeds offering no new information but building the tension surrounding the verdict. Giles pulled a few strings and got a crew from BET News into the hallway of the courthouse so they would be first to report the verdict. The defense team decided that since BET worked diligently over the years to expose the corrupt criminal justice system, they would be the first and only station to interview JC after the verdict.

Seated at the defense table, JC motioned for Paul, who leaned forward to hear what his brother had to say. JC whispered to him. Paul just smiled and nodded in agreement.

JC waved for Candace. She leaned forward, confused. "Let's wake up together on Sunday—every Sunday."

Candace stared at JC. They stood for Judge Sullivan to enter but never took their eyes off each other. "No other women. Just you." He pointed to Candace. "I love you, Candace. I've always loved you. Will you marry me?"

The spectators sat down, leaving JC and Candace standing, their eyes still locked. Candace leaned her head slightly to the side and whispered, "Sounds like a plan." The two quickly sat down.

Judge Sullivan asked, "Mr. Powell, are you finished? Can we proceed?"

JC replied, "Yes, Your Honor."

Judge Sullivan felt like giving him a hard time, lightening up the mood. "Are you sure?" He joked.

"Absolutely."

The Judge instructed the bailiff to bring the jury into the courtroom. As the jury piled into the jury box, eleven of the twelve jurors looked directly at JC, a good sign according to Giles. Once they were settled in their seats, Judge Sullivan ordered JC to stand. He looked at the jury and said, "Ladies and gentlemen of the jury, have you reached a verdict?"

The Jury Foreman stood and announced, "The jury is hopelessly deadlocked, Your Honor."

The entire courtroom became disruptive. After the litany of lies exposed, everyone believed JC would be exonerated, although the defense team was not shocked about the verdict. The jury specialist had already warned them that one juror may have decided before ever hearing the evidence. The culprit was obvious. Giles worried about him from the beginning of the trial. However, he was forced to use all their strikes to eliminate the most threatening people from the jury pool. They were all convinced that the young, militant, shaved head, white guy refused to give in.

"Are you sure that you are incapable of reaching a unanimous verdict?"

"We're certain, Your Honor," the Foreman said, glancing toward the only juror that never looked JC's way—a middle-aged black postal worker who, going into the trial, the defense thought was a sure thing. Once a few other jurors grimaced at the man, it became obvious that the Hitler wanna-be was not the problem. The everyday brother from the hood was the holdout. *Things are never as they seem*, JC thought to himself. He figured the postal worker probably never believed a black man could acquire so much through hard work alone. *A House Negro.* JC thought, *while the field Negroes were escaping for a better life, the House Negro thought his life was as good as it gets.* All JC could feel is pity for the man.

"I have no alternative but to declare a mistrial. Court is adjourned." Judge Sullivan pounded his gavel.

After a few words with Walker, Giles joined the family in the back of the courtroom. "Jurors can be bought, too," he said. "We need to meet with the prosecutor immediately."

JC raised his hand to stop Giles. "Everyone knows Felix lied. It's not like I lived a squeaky clean life. I've hustled right, and I've hustled wrong. You got to pay someday. Take whatever they offer and call it even. Let them keep the money, I got what I need." JC smiled at Candace.

Paul said, "Let's use all this attention to work on getting Trevor out."

The lawyer looked at JC for direction. JC pointed to Paul and grabbed Candace's hand to leave. Nate rolled up and handed JC an envelope. "I know it's late but maybe it can help Trevor."

JC knelt down beside Nate, put his hand on Nate's shoulder and said, "Man, what can I say? Words aren't enough. You came through big time for me. You're my top cop. How can I ever thank you? You saved my life."

Nate put his hand over JC's and smiled, "No JC, you saved my life."

The two embraced. JC slid the folder under his arm, gently gripped Candace's hand, and headed out of the courtroom. JC made a brief on-camera comment for BET News, then headed outside where the crowd had turned rowdy upon hearing the verdict. Reporters who had anxiously awaited JC's arrival swarmed the family, poking microphones in JC's face, shouting questions. If there was anyone in the crowd that wanted a guilty verdict, they were drowned out by the mob of activists chanting and yelling encouraging words to JC. JC maneuvered through the crowd at the top of the stairs shaking hands and thanking the community for supporting him.

With the euphoric smile on his face, any sane person would have thought JC had won his battle against the government. Amid all the hoopla, all JC could think about was his big win of the day. He whispered to Candace, "You know I'm broke. Are you sure you want to marry me?"

Candace stepped back and gave him a "don't even try to get out of it" look. The two kissed.

Khalil ran up to them. "JC, I was hoping I would catch you."

"You got me." He turned to the family, "Ya'll remember Khalil, the record label executive? Those kids sure are making good music."

Paul added, "Real positive messages. Positive, my brother."

"That's Trevor's work," Khalil said. "That's why I'm here, to give you this check." Khalil handed JC an envelope.

"Check?" JC asked.

"Yeah, profits from the music."

JC pulled the check from the envelope. Everyone leaned in to look at it.

Paul yelled, "Oh my goodness!"

"A half million dollars!" JC said, shocked. He tried to hand the check back to Khalil, "This is Trevor's money, not mine."

Khalil said, "No JC, that's your money. Trevor made you part owner of his company. That is your profit. He made a lot more than you."

JC waved the check. "This is mine?"

"Yep." Khalil said laughing. "But I think you'll appreciate this more than the money."

JC held up the check. "More than this? What is it?"

"The money was just released because I've been in and out of court with Felix," Khalil said.

"Felix Calhoun? For what?"

"He sued us for royalties saying he was Trevor's partner. He had Trevor's lyric book and also claimed he wrote the songs. He was shocked when we had copies of all the copyright forms Trevor had filed and he couldn't get a dime."

JC poked his chest out a bit. "I always told that boy to handle his business! I don't believe it." JC eyed Paul. "I told you he would make us proud. Ain't God alright!"

Chapter 34

Paul and Tracy were sitting in front, with JC and Candace in the back seat of the car. Paul turned onto Long Beach Boulevard. Caressing Candace's thigh with one hand, JC used the other hand to look inside the envelope Nate had given him. There was a file labeled "POWELL, John Cornelius AKA JC." The radio was playing in the background. The deejay on the radio—Porsha the Deliverer—announced, "The LBC's own Hot Girlz, taped live at The Empire, number one on the charts nine years ago this week."

JC chuckled, "I wish Trevor was out to enjoy it."

"After all of this attention on your trial, Trevor will be out in no time," Paul said.

"You got lucky big broh, I thought I was gonna have to come work at the bookstore."

They all laughed as the militant lyrics of the Hot Girlz thumped in the background. Paul turned up the volume. JC put on his reading glasses to glance through the brown file. A manila folder with several 8 X 11 photos inside caught his attention. He pulled out the folder to look at the pictures. The first one, marked Photo I, was a shot of JC going into the club alone. The label below the photo read: JC POWELL CASE #8846298. JC slid the photo to the back of the pile.

The second picture, marked Photo II, was a mug shot of Felix Calhoun, the label beneath read:

Felix Calhoun, AKA Larry Cook

CHARGES: FRAUD, DRUG POSSESSION, LARCENY... (CON'T ON BACK)
DISPOSITION: Sealed 2/94
CONFIDENTIAL INFORMANT

JC slid the photo to the back of the stack to reveal the next photo. Photo III was a mug shot of Havoc, the label read:

Bruce Taylor AKA Havoc, Little Soul
CHARGES: MURDER, POSSESSION OF A FIREARM, DISTRIBUTION (CON'T)
DISPOSITION: Early Parole 4/96
CONFIDENTIAL INFORMANT

Paul slowed down as he approached The Empire. They all looked over and stared at the dilapidated building. The car stopped across the street directly in front of the club. The Empire was shabby and vacant. Thugs loitered up and down the block. Most of the businesses had closed down, and buildings were boarded up and abandoned. The glass on the marquee was broken and the trim had fallen off. Sheets of wood were nailed to the building to cover the entry doors.

All exposed walls, wood, bricks, and the floor around the boarded up box-office was tagged with gang graffiti. The place was barely recognizable. They were so mesmerized, no one realized Paul had come to a complete stop until a driver behind them honked his horn relentlessly and jarred them back to reality. As Paul took off, a news report about the trial came on the radio.

A female reporter said, "The trial of JC Powell ended with a hung jury today. According to an anonymous source, the government may charge snitch, Felix Calhoun, with over twenty counts of perjury and will dismiss all charges against Powell and his son, Trevor. Also, an official from Daughters 2 Feed Film Studio announced they're trying to contact JC Powell to tell his story. Tell us what you think. Call 562-555-7843 or log on to www.snitchcraft.com. That's Snitch Craft.com."

They listened to a series of callers to the show.

"Caller one you're on with Porsha."

"This is Robin from Inglewood. I just want to say the government is more criminal than the criminals. They're just gangsters. They should give JC his money back."

Porsha said, "Thank you Robin. Next we have Cedric all the way down in San Diego."

"Dey outta give dat JC a movie deal 'cause this (BLEEP) is unbelievable. By the way, baby I love your show."

"Thank you Cedric. Caller three is listening online all the way in New York. What's on your mind Shaba?"

"What's up Cali? JC if you're listening, we're with ya' up here in the boogie down Bronx. I know some people, who know some people, who know Felix and trust me, that trick Felix, he'll get his. The way this went down we gotta' ask, is this America? Do we still have rights?" the caller exclaimed.

"This is 'Porsha the Deliverer' bringing it to you live on KLIE, 102.3 on your radio dial. In honor of JC Powell, here's the Hot Girlz newest hit song, "Snitchcraft," number one on the charts this week. Produced by Khalil Major and written by none other than the talented Trevor Powell. Keep your head up, Trevor."

JC was beaming with pride. He peered out of the back window for a long final glimpse of The Empire as Paul turned off Long Beach Boulevard. Bouncing to the beat of the Hot Girlz, JC continued to peruse the file in his lap. JC slowly slid the third photo—Havoc's mug shot—to the back of the stack to reveal the last picture. JC froze in shock. He sat staring at the picture in his lap. JC's heartbeat hastened, and his brain slipped into overdrive. Thoughts swirled through his head —the family reunions, the pictures, friends and family. He was overcome by hurt, outrage, and betrayal. All of his questions were answered when he read the caption below the last photo. Photo IV was a mug shot of Junior. Beneath the photo, he read:

David Powell, Jr. AKA "Junior"
CHARGES: Drug possession, sale of a firearm
DISPOSITION: 11/94 Probation
CONFIDENTIAL INFORMANT

Epilogue

The 2005 family reunion was held back in South Georgia where it had been ever since JC's arrest. The family vowed to always meet up during the first week in July in Phillipsburg, Georgia where the Powell family was given a heroes welcome from the town officials. In Phillipsburg, they were home grown celebrities and the entire city showed up to celebrate. The Hot Girlz stopped in Phillipsburg to perform for the reunion on their way to a concert in France. They had just accepted a BET award for the hit song "The Road to Freedom," written and produced by Trevor.

As usual, the family celebrated their coming together with good food, dance, games, and gossip. Everyone was amused to hear that a toothless Dee had been released to a halfway house after doing time for drug possession and was working as a waitress at the Denny's on Alameda. The word on Felix was he was locked up and still awaiting trial for perjury. Akbar and Giles were busy with a class action suit against the government on behalf of all prisoners who had been set up by commissioned snitches.

It was time for the traditional Soul Train line. Everyone assembled to participate. Although it took a little longer, Auntie and Mama were first to shuffle down the line. Nate's wheelchair served as a walker for Auntie. After a minor heart attack the doctors finally convinced Auntie to give up her pork. She was eating healthier food and had lost nearly fifty pounds. Since

Mama was Auntie's primary caretaker, she declared that this reunion would be "swine free dining" to help Auntie in her dietary goals. The truth was, Mama knew Auntie would sneak a piece of pork when she wasn't watching her so she figured she'd ban it altogether to make the day easier for herself. When Mama wasn't caring for Auntie, she was contacting government officials on her issue of the day. That month she was working on getting the water cleaned up in the Long Beach Harbor.

JC used some of the money Khalil gave him to buy a small apartment building to provide low-cost housing for homeless families. Nate was the live-in building manager. Nate was also working on his case against the police department with one of Akbar's associates who agreed to help him for free.

Moonwalking down the line behind Mama was JC's daughter Cherie and her fiancé. Cherie had graduated from law school, was practicing entertainment law, and was planning a huge Hollywood wedding for her marriage to recording star and label owner Khalil Major.

Chunky and very pregnant, Tamara wobbled down the line with her husband and children – all of them wearing some form of gris-gris. They were living outside of New Orleans where Tamara had followed in her mother's footsteps as a Voodoo Queen. She assured everyone that she didn't bring any graveyard dirt and only used her powers for positive outcomes.

Paul and Tracy danced down the line with their two-year-old great-niece. Paul was dealing with health problems so one of his nephews—Mary's son—had taken over management of the bookstore. Paul still coordinated special events there, mostly hosting political events that attracted conscious people from all backgrounds and nationalities. He and JC had purchased the entire plaza where the bookstore was located and their sisters opened a restaurant, "Sisters Barbecue," next door to the bookstore.

Trevor and his girlfriend of the week did the Harlem Shake down the line. JC figured the time in jail had Trevor behind schedule on letting go of his philandering ways. (As if JC could talk.) Trevor was released from prison less than two months after JC's trial when the government dropped all charges against father and son. Trevor was still writing hit songs, running his own label, and had three new acts.

JC came hustling down the Soul Train line. His partner, of course, was his partner for life, Candace. Three days after JC's trial the couple semi-eloped to Las Vegas. They did not quite elope because JC made the mistake of telling Paul the plan. When they arrived at the chapel in Vegas, Paul had brought Tracy, Mama, Auntie, and Candace's mother to witness the nuptials.

Although nearly a year had passed, the government still had a team of specialists assigned to negotiating a fair return of assets that were taken from the family. Of course, they no longer thought the assets were worth the $3 million they bragged about in their press conferences immediately after the arrest. They had miscalculated. The specialists needed time to determine the actual value. It didn't matter that those assets were "converted" to drugs and used against JC during the trial and for sentencing.

The money was insignificant to JC, who was living comfortably off the royalties from Trevor's work. He offered advice to Trevor and occasionally traveled with him on tour dates to keep the rappers in check, but he didn't play a day-to-day role in the business. He spent most of his time catering to Candace. In addition to traveling, they had bought a beachfront condo they were renovating. Candace got over her fear of the water and JC taught her to swim. JC also held monthly discussions at the bookstore for at-risk youth and worked with the Ben Mays Center to get the kids into job training programs and help them find employment.

The family cheered at the sight of JC and Candace.

"Go JC, Go JC, Go JC," the crowd yelled.

Just as the O'Jays sang, "It's so nice to see all the folks you love together" JC tossed Candace out for the infamous spin. When he twirled her back to his chest, he froze. His eyes were fixed on the front of the line—the next person. The family looked in shock. There, standing at the head of the official "Powell Family Soul Train Line" stood Junior. He was emaciated, unshaven, and appeared weary. Junior had not been seen since he got the word that the family knew he was a snitch. Verdict day.

JC walked up and stood face-to-face for the first time since his arrest with the man who had set the whole scheme in motion. The two stared at each other in silence. The family, especially Trevor, wanted to attack but they waited for a sign from JC. But he just stood frozen, gazing at the mole. A man he provided for from birth. A man he protected, bailed out of jail and welcomed in his home time after time. His family. A snitch.

As the details of his arrest, trial, and incarceration flashed in JC's head, Junior stepped closer. "Cousin JC, I'm so sorry. I haven't been able to live with myself since all this happened."

JC just stared at Junior.

"I was so caught up, I didn't realize what Felix was really up to. I was looking at twenty years and set up some corner thugs, but they wanted more. When I told them about you and cousin Paul and all the hustlers you knew in New York, they were interested. They put me with Felix. I thought he was supposed to go after one of them. I was just in too deep to see what was going on. I was scared and doing drugs. I didn't know. I swear. I didn't know."

JC and the family stared silently at Junior. Of course, Trevor was just waiting until his dad got finished before he went into attack mode. Although Trevor had become a little calmer over the years, Junior had caused a lot of turmoil. There was no excuse Junior could give for what he did. Paul was also ready to physically boot Junior out of the park.

Junior fell to his knees, begging for everyone's forgiveness. "Aunt Ester, Auntie, I'm so sorry for putting ya'll through this. I'm so sorry. You know I love my family. I swear, I didn't know all this would go down. I'm so sorry," he cried out.

JC battled the voices in his head that were screaming, kick him, beat his ass, spit on him. He just stood over the pitiful soul, staring down at him. Finally, after Junior sobbed to a silent crowd for at least five minutes, JC reached down and grabbed Junior's upper arm and tried to pull him up off his knees.

"Stand up and be a man," JC said. He was quiet for a few seconds while Junior continued to cry. He pulled harder and brought Junior to his feet. "Get off your knees and stop all that noise, this is a family reunion."

Before Paul or Trevor could say a word, JC put his hand up

to stop them. He shook his head, looked at his mother, then at Candace and said, "Forgiven people become forgiving people."

After the Book

- Readers Discussion Guide
- Take Action
- Resource Round-Up

Questions for Discussion

We hope the following questions will stimulate discussion for reading groups and provide a deeper understanding of Snitch-Craft for every reader.

1. SnitchCraft deals with the corrupt environment created by paying people for testimony. What do you think about the government paying large sums of money to criminals for them to work as confidential informants? If allowed, should the jury be informed of the payments? How about allowing bonuses to go back to agencies when assets are seized in large busts, do you think this promotes corruption?

2. If you served on a jury, how much weight would you give to the testimony of a paid informant? Do you believe that paid informants have an incentive to lie and fabricate?

3. If you served on the jury in JC's case would you have found him innocent or guilty, why?

4. Why was Candace determined not to become intimate with JC again?

5. JC has two women and is still after Candace, how does that make you feel about him? Does it make a difference that he is honest about it with Tamara and Dee?

6. JC initially thought money was the answer to all problems. How did his view change?

7. How does this book make you feel about family? What is the significance of the family reunion?

8. How did JC's attitude toward spirituality change over the course of the book?

9. The misdeeds of rogue snitches and police officers are constant

subjects in the news. How can the government create a balance to get citizens to report illegal activity without offering excessive incentives enticing people to make up stories? Is the government crossing the line into illegal activity in the so-called "War on Drugs"?

10. Do you think it's right that people are serving more time in prison for petty drug offenses than for violent crimes like rape and murder?

11. What was the significance of the mysterious fedora-wearing old man in the club? Why do you think he reappeared in the courtroom?

12. Slavery is mentioned a few times in the book. How does slavery relate to JC's ordeal?

13. JC makes the statement "forgiven people are forgiving people." Where did that statement come from? How does it apply to JC?

14. Do you think that it is fair that personal information on some informants is kept confidential?

15. What scenes demonstrate JC's thought that things are never as they appear?

16. When you think about the fact that elected officials pass laws enabling corruption in the criminal justice system, does that make your vote more valuable to you?

Take Action

Quick Facts:

• The Federal average cost per year to incarcerate an inmate is $23,542 annually. (Source: www.whitehousedrugpolicy.org)

• The US currently incarcerates more than 2.2 million inmates, at a rate of one in 143 people. (Source: www.prisonsucks.com)

• At the end of 2002, 6.7 million people in the US were on probation, in jail or prison, or on parole. (Source: Bureau of Justice)

• Since mandatory minimum sentencing first began for drug offenders, the Federal Bureau of Prisons' budget has increased by more than 2,100%, from $220 million in 1986 to about $4.4 billion in 2004. (Source: Unitarian Universalist Association)

• Among the more than 2.1 million offenders incarcerated on June 30, 2004, an estimated 576,600 were black males between ages 20 and 39. (Source: Bureau of Justice Statistics)

• Among males age 25 to 29, 12.6% of blacks were in prison or jail, compared to 3.6% of Hispanics and about 1.7% of whites. (Source: Drug War Facts)

• 1.46 million black men out of a total voting population of 10.4 million have lost their right to vote due to felony convictions. (Source: National Coalition on Black Civic Participation)

NOTE: Since 2004 the laws have changed to give judges more leeway in sentencing.

What you can do today

1. Educate yourself on the issues.

2. Register to vote.

3. Call, write or email your state representatives

4. Organize a church congregation, college club, or community action committee.

5. Go online to tell your members of Congress to oppose mandatory minimums.
   (www.mandatorymadness.org or www.famm.org)

6. Write a letter-to-the-editor of your local newspaper. Be sure to include your full name and contact information.

7. Donate to a nonprofit organization working to reform the criminal justice system.

8. Participate in a campaign or project with the November Coalition. Go to: www.november.org/projects

9. Monitor, evaluate, and weigh in on the Drug Sentencing Reform Act (S.3725), a bill introduced by a Bipartisan group of Senators to Reduce Cocaine Sentencing Disparities

10. Volunteer your time with a worthwhile organization.

11. Vote early and often.

Resources Online

Prison Activist Resource Center (prisonactivist.org)
The source for progressive and radical information on prisons
and the criminal prosecution system. PARC is committed
to exposing and challenging the institutionalized racism of
the criminal injustice system and to further developing anti-
racism as individuals and throughout our organization. They
provide support for educators, activists, prisoners, and prisoners'
families. This work includes building networks for action and
producing materials that expose human rights violations while
fundamentally challenging the rapid expansion of the prison
industrial complex.

Drug War Facts (www.drugwarfacts.org)
Facts and statistics on the drug war. A valuable resource for
anyone concerned with drug policy.

Common Sense for Drug Policy (www.csdp.org)
Common Sense for Drug Policy is a nonprofit organization
dedicated to reforming drug policy and expanding harm
reduction. CSDP disseminates factual information and comments
on existing laws, policies and practices. CSDP provides advice
and assistance to individuals and organizations and facilitates
coalition building.

The Drug Reform Coordination Network (www.stopthedrugwar.
org)
DRCNet was founded in 1993 and has quickly grown into a
major national and global network including parents, educators,
students, lawyers, health care professionals, academics, and others
working for drug policy reform from a variety of perspectives,
including harm reduction, reform of sentencing and forfeiture
laws, medicalization of currently schedule I drugs, and promotion
of an open debate on drug prohibition. DRCNet opposes the
prison-building frenzy and supports rational policies consistent
with the principles of peace, justice, freedom, compassion and
truth. Each of these has been compromised in the name of the
Drug War.

The Drug Policy Alliance (www.drugpolicy.org)
The Drug Policy Alliance is the leading organization in the
United States promoting alternatives to the war on drugs. On
July 1, 2000, The Lindesmith Center merged with the Drug

218

Policy Foundation to form the Alliance. Created in 1994, The Lindesmith Center was the first U.S. project of the Open Society Institute and the leading independent drug policy reform institute in the United States.

The November Coalition (www.november.org)

The November Coalition is a non-profit organization of grassroots volunteers educating the public about the destructive increase in prison population in the US due to our current drug laws. We alert our fellow citizens about the present and impending dangers of an overly powerful federal authority acting far beyond its constitutional constraints. The drug war is an assault and steady erosion of our civil rights and freedoms by federal and state governments. The drug war does not reduce drug use. Choosing to wage a 'war' on drugs stimulates a violent, underground economy, an economy which would collapse if drug prohibition ended. Our country, our world should be safer, not simply less free.

Families Against Mandatory Minimums (www.famm.org)

Families Against Mandatory Minimums Foundation (FAMM) is a national nonprofit organization founded in March of 1991 by attorneys, judges, criminal justice experts, and the families of inmates in response to the excessive penalties triggered by mandatory minimum sentencing policies for nonviolent offenses.

NAACP Legal Defense and Educational Fund

(www.naacpldf.org)

The NAACP Legal Defense and Educational Fund, Inc. (LDF) was founded in 1940 under the leadership of Thurgood Marshall. Although LDF's primary purpose was to provide legal assistance to poor African Americans, its work over the years has brought greater justice to all Americans. Racism in the criminal justice system is one of the greatest concerns of the African-American community and other communities of color. The nation seems to have two separate, unequal standards of justice for whites and minorities. LDF is working to reform this system by combating often brutal police practices, prosecutorial misconduct, inadequate legal counsel for indigent defendants, judicial bias, and sentencing and incarceration disparities. Since 1965, LDF has published Death Row USA, the most widely cited national listing of death-row inmates.

The Sentencing Project (www.sentencingproject.org)

The Sentencing Project is a non-profit organization which

promotes reduced reliance on incarceration and increased use of more effective and humane alternatives to deal with crime. It is a nationally recognized source of criminal justice policy analysis, data, and program information. Its reports, publications, and staff are relied upon by the public, policymakers and the media.

Human Rights Watch (www.hrw.org)

Human Rights Watch is the largest human rights organization based in the United States. Human Rights Watch researchers conduct fact-finding investigations into human rights abuses in all regions of the world. Human Rights Watch then publishes those findings in dozens of books and reports every year, generating extensive coverage in local and international media. This publicity helps to embarrass abusive governments in the eyes of their citizens and the world.

The Peoples' Agenda (www.gcpagenda.org)

The People....The Coalition conducted eleven public hearings around the state seeking to define and determine the concerns, needs and hopes of the people, particularly related to government. We continue to hold town halls meetings, seminars and forums to update the concerns, needs and hopes of the people. The Agenda....The findings of these hearings, etc., are compiled into a document called The Agenda. The Coalition... the coalition consists of representatives of the major advocacy groups in the state: civil rights/human rights/peace and justice. This body is charged with programmatically addressing the concerns, needs and hopes of the People as delineated in The Agenda.

FEAR (www.fear.org)

Forfeiture Endangers American Rights (FEAR) is a national nonprofit organization dedicated to reform of federal and state asset forfeiture laws to restore due process and protect property rights in the forfeiture process.

Human Rights and the Drug War (www.hr95.org)

HRDW is a multi-media project that combines the stories and photos of Drug War POWs with facts and figures about the US Drug War, to confront the conscience of the American people and encourage individuals to take action for social justice.

Leadership Conference on Civil Rights (www.civilrights.org)

The Leadership Conference on Civil Rights (LCCR) was founded in 1950 by three giants of the civil rights movement —A. Philip Randolph, founder of the Brotherhood of Sleeping Car Porters;

Roy Wilkins, Executive Secretary of the NAACP; and Arnold Aronson, a leader of the National Jewish Community Relations Advisory Council. It is the nation's premier civil rights coalition, and has coordinated the national legislative campaign on behalf of every major civil rights law since 1957.

Mandatory Madness Coalition (www.mandatorymadness.org)
Mandatory Madness is a project of a grassroots coalition of victims of unjust sentences, their families, and activists who—like U.S. Supreme Court Justice Anthony Kennedy—believe that in too many cases, mandatory minimum sentences are unwise and unjust.

Criminal Justice Foundation (www.cjpf.org)
CJPF's mission is to educate the public about the impact of drug policy and the problems of policing on the criminal justice system. We provide information and advice to policy makers, criminal justice professionals, and the public through consultation, education programs, conferences, publications, the news media and the Internet. The foundation assists drug policy reform organizations with advice on legal organization, management, outreach, research, media relations, and coalition building. CJPF also provides speakers to educational institutions and organizations of all kinds.

The ACLU Freedom Files (www.aclu.tv)
The American Civil Liberties Union and Robert Greenwald (Outfoxed, Unconstitutional) present The ACLU Freedom Files, a revolutionary, 10-part series that tells the stories of real people in America whose civil liberties have been threatened, and how they fought back.

Southern Christian Leadership Conference
(www.sclcnational.org)
The SCLC is a nonprofit, non-sectarian, inter-faith, advocacy organization that is committed to non-violent action to achieve social, economic, and political justice.

National Coalition on Black Civic Participation
(www.ncbcp.org)
The mission of the National Coalition is to create an enlightened community by building institutional capacity that provides and develops leadership. By educating, motivating, organizing, and mobilizing citizens in the African American community, the National Coalition seeks to encourage full participation

in a barrier-free democratic process. Through educational programs and leadership training, the coalition works to expand, strengthen, and empower our communities to make voting and civic participation a cultural responsibility and tradition.

Black Youth Vote! (www.bigvote.org)

Black Youth Vote! is a broad based coalition of organizations and individuals committed to increasing political and civic involvement among black men and women aged 18-35. BYV! is youth led and dedicated to educating young voters in the Black community who are increasingly disenfranchised and alienated from the electoral and legislative process. Through civic education, leadership development and training, BYV! works to educate youth and young adults on how to identify issues and ways to influence public policy.

The Joint Center for Political and Economic Studies
The Dellums Commission: Analyses and Action Plan to Reform Public Policies that Limit Life Paths of Young Men of Color (www.jointcenter.org)

During the past twenty-five years, a series of policies enacted have had a negative impact upon young men from communities of color. These policies, which have been enacted and often amended incrementally, range from the abandonment of rehabilitation and treatment for drug users in favor of interdiction and criminal sanctions in the 1980's, to state policies to divert youthful offenders to adult criminal systems and the imposition of zero tolerance policies to exclude youth with problems from public schools in the 1990's. The hardening of these policies has had a cumulative effect of limiting life options for young men of color as indicated by increasing high school drop-out rates and declining enrollment in post-secondary education and by increasing rates of incarceration.

The LITE HOUSE After-school Program works tirelessly to keep young people out of prison. LITE HOUSE provides homework assistance, mentoring, tutoring, and classes and clubs in sports, mathematics, chess, and dozens of other subjects. The After-school Alliance is a nonprofit public awareness and advocacy organization supported by a group of public, private, and nonprofit entities working to ensure that all children have access to after-school programs by the year 2010. Email: mrobinaonlitehouse@comcast.net

Edrea Davis has worked in all areas of communications management. She has coordinated publicity campaigns for a host of high-profile celebrities and dignitaries. Her articles have been published in newspapers across the country; and, she produces dogonvillage.com, one of the oldest black sites on the Internet. Previously, Edrea served as executive producer at a Los Angeles film company where she managed the production of national television commercial campaigns. The New Jersey native was educated at Georgia State University and currently resides in the Atlanta area. She spends her spare time learning new facts from her brilliant grandchildren. SnitchCraft is her debut novel.

Edrea Davis